May the Best Man Die

DEBORAH DONNELLY

A DELL BOOK

MAY THE BEST MAN DIE
A Dell Book / October 2003

Published by
Bantam Dell
A Division of Random House, Inc.
New York, New York

ISBN 0-440-24129-4

Manufactured in the United States of America
Published simultaneously in Canada

OPM   10   9   8   7   6   5   4   3   2   1

For Julia

Acknowledgments

My professional appreciation goes to Anne Bohner, Jaime Jennings, and Kate Miciak at Bantam Dell, and to my agent, Laura Blake Peterson. For this book, Glenna Tooman helped me with brides, Ava Sundstrom with homicides, and the guys at Seattle Coffee Company with an inside look at a roasterie. On the personal side, bouquets to writers Diane Hall-Harris, Libby Hellmann, and Roberta Isleib, who helped me stay sane, and to Bridget Dacres, Susan Hettinger, and Laurel Sercombe, the best Girl Group that ever harmonized. Most of all, and always, love to Steve.

May the Best
Man Die

Chapter One

I DON'T DO BACHELOR PARTIES.

Wait, that sounds like I jump naked out of cakes. And who makes cakes that tall and skinny? What I mean is, I don't *plan* bachelor parties. Weddings, yes. Rehearsal dinners, of course. Bridesmaids' luncheons, engagement cocktail parties, even the occasional charity gala, when business is slow.

The business in question is "Made in Heaven Wedding Design, Carnegie Kincaid, Proprietor." I've got a pretty decent clientele in Seattle by now, and sometimes I accept non-nuptial referrals. But I don't do bachelor parties, for two very good reasons.

First off, I resent the symbolism, the whole bit about the doomed groom's last spasm of freedom before he turns himself in at the matrimonial slammer. I'm in favor of matrimony, after all. I might even try it myself someday. But that's another story.

The second and more compelling reason is that no event planner in her right mind will touch a party where the guests are hell-bent on drinking themselves into oblivion, and behaving as poorly as possible *en route*. The potential for disaster is huge.

So why, at ten P.M. on the twelfth of December, was I

standing out in the freezing night wind, hammering on a locked door behind which lurked a gang of undoubtedly drunken bachelors?

Because of Sally "Bridezilla" Tyler.

I had inherited Sally's New Year's Eve wedding from Dorothy Fenner, my longtime, more-or-less friendly competitor in the Seattle bride biz, when Dorothy's fuddy-duddy husband purchased two tickets on a world cruise and a prescription for Viagra. I appreciated her vote of confidence—let's face it, I desperately needed the revenue—but it was turning out to be hard-earned. This particular bride, besides being lovely and wealthy, was a control freak of the first order.

Most brides are content to let the best man handle the bachelor party, but not Sally Tyler, oohh no. She supposedly wanted me to plan this one so that my valuable services could be her wedding gift to Frank Sanjek, her devoted (not to say besotted) fiancé. But I saw through that little fiction.

What Sally really craved was more scope to contradict, criticize, and generally micromanage Frank's every waking moment. Though why she thought my involvement would prevent Jason Kraye, the know-it-all best man, from pouring too much booze, or showing porno movies, or doing anything else he pleased, was beyond me. I'm a wedding planner, not a governess for overgrown boys.

Anyway, I declined Sally's request, she fumed, and tensions mounted. And then Jason Kraye broke the deadlock by coming up with the perfect party site: the Hot Spot Café on the south side of the Seattle Ship Canal, owned by a buddy of his and closing soon for a major remodel.

Said buddy was offering use of the Café for free. The guests could do their worst, with Jason as master of ceremonies, and I could steer clear. The only catch was that the party had to happen ASAP, on a Sunday night.

But Jason dismissed that little issue with the haughty comment that anyone who couldn't skip work Monday could just sleep it off on company time. He promised Frank a memorable blowout; Frank loved the idea, and that was that.

I even made peace with Sally by arranging for the food: a bachelors' banquet of serve-yourself Greek appetizers, catered by my friend and colleague Joe Solveto. But I stipulated that I personally would *not* be visiting the party premises. Frank thanked his bride for her generous gift, and everybody was happy.

Until now. I'd been working late the night of Frank's bachelor party, at my borrowed desk in Joe's catering office, when my cell phone sounded.

"Carnegie, it's Sally. You've got to go over to the Hot Spot right away."

I could picture Sally in my mind's eye: a mere slip of a girl, with milky skin and white-blonde hair, but possessed of a dark, furious glare that could pierce your vital organs like a stiletto chipped from ice. At this point, my innards were practically perforated.

I sighed. "We've been over this already. Jason's in charge of the party, not me."

"I know that! But he needs you. *Now.*"

"Why didn't he call me himself?" I stalled. "What's wrong?"

But as I spoke, my stomach was clenching at the thought of all the things that might be wrong: property damage, an angry neighbor, an injured guest . . .

"Just *go*, OK?" The stiletto stabbed deeper. "Why are you

always so difficult? You're, what, two minutes away from there?"

Solveto's was in the Fremont neighborhood, on the north side of the Ship Canal. "Not exactly, but—"

But Sally had already hung up, and didn't answer when I called her back. So, roundly cursing Ms. Tyler and the stack of wedding magazines she rode in on, I climbed into my van and drove south.

By the time I reached the Fremont Drawbridge, my gloom had lifted just a bit, and for an unusual reason: the weather. Usually, Christmas in Seattle is gray and drippy; you get used to it. But this year, December had surprised us all with clear skies and genuinely cold temperatures. This evening had a very non-Seattle, winter wonderland feel, with Christmas trees and decorations all aglitter in the crisp darkness. Gradually, in spite of myself, I stopped cursing and starting humming "Good King Wenceslaus."

The so-called Artists' Republic of Fremont has gone pretty mainstream these days, now that a big software firm calls it home and the fancy condos are rising high. But there are still plenty of funky shops and tempting restaurants, both new and old, and plenty of customers for all of them. Everywhere I looked tonight, Yuletide shoppers and late-night diners bustled across the intersections, trailing Christmas cheer and pale plumes of frozen breath.

I wished I could join them. Instead, I crossed the Fremont Drawbridge, with its goofy blue girders and orange trim, to the darker, quieter blocks along Nickerson. The festive lights disappeared behind me, and I dropped down a side street.

I was driving Vanna White Too, the new replacement for my dear departed white van. She rode like a Beemer after the clanking and stalling of the old one, and we pulled up smoothly to the undistinguished brick front of the Hot Spot Café. At least there were no police cars in sight, and no ambulance.

The angry neighbors, if there were any, must be deaf by now anyway, given the rock song now throbbing through the Café's front door. The volume was unbelievable, the lyrics incomprehensible, and the message unmistakable: *Me man, you woman, lie down.*

As I said, the Café's front door was locked, so I hammered on it, then tried to peer through the gaps in the curtained windows. No telling if anyone could hear me. After one last pound, I gave up and went around back, hugging myself against the cold. I was still wearing my one businessy suit from a morning meeting at the bank—as if dove-gray silk tweed could make up for all the glaring red ink on Made in Heaven's books.

Meanwhile, all day long the wind had been rising and the temperature dropping. My stylish blazer was no match for the night air, and my short skirt offered no protection against the icy gusts that kept trying to goose me. So now I was shivering as well as irritated and anxious.

Out back, a wooden dining deck extended over a wedge of patchy grass and clumps of shadowy, wind-ruffled bushes. The ground sloped down to an empty bike path and a wide lane of dark, still water between concrete walls: the Seattle Ship Canal.

The Ship Canal is a major waterway between Puget Sound to the west and big Lake Washington to the east, with little Lake Union in between. On summer afternoons, the Hot Spot's patrons could sit out there on the deck to watch the big luxury sailboats and the even bigger barges passing right by: salt water meets fresh water meets beer. But on this wintry night, the splintered planks held nothing but stacks of plastic chairs and a silver veiling of frost.

The frost flashed and sparkled in the light pouring from the sliding glass doors of the Café—glass that was vibrating to a 4/4 beat. I crossed the deck, mindful of my footing, and tugged at a handle. The door stuck a moment, then slid back, and I plunged into the warm, wild atmosphere of Party Central.

A quick look around revealed a scattered crowd of young men, a fog bank of cigar smoke, a spreading puddle of spilled liquor, and a massive serve-yourself Greek mess. Empty plates and glasses littered all the tables, but the mess went far beyond that: from the demolished dolmathes scattered across the pool table, to the fragments of fried calamari stuck to the ceiling, to the spatter of spanakopita on the big-screen TV, Joe's feast had clearly been enjoyed in ways he never intended.

There was broken glass here and there—apparently juggling retsina bottles is now a recognized indoor sport—but no broken heads that I could see. Also no blood, and no police.

And no best man. As I peered through the fumes for Jason Kraye, I spotted Frank Sanjek, the bridegroom. He sat, alone and apparently stupefied, before an oversized TV screen on which two women of improbable physique were silently cavorting in a hot tub. Frank's handsomely cleft chin had sunk to his chest, and beneath the curly brown hair his equally handsome and amiable eyes were drifting shut.

Aside from his devotion to Sally, Frank was a pretty reasonable fellow, though, to my mind, his looks exceeded his brains by a long shot. Still, if he wasn't too far gone by now, he should be able to explain Jason's alleged emergency.

Averting my gaze from the hot-tub hotties, I headed toward him. But my path was blocked by three men, all of them young and none of them sober.

"Hey, she's here!" shouted one, a beefy fellow whose sweatshirt was anointed with something damp and garlicky. At least he smelled more tasteful than he looked.

Mr. Garlic's face was long and lantern-jawed, with coarse blond hair and small round eyes gone glassy with drink. He swayed a bit on his feet, and gazed at me with the oddest expression, a sort of hopeful leer, as he dropped one moist, meaty hand on my shoulder. "She's finally here."

"Brilliant observation," I said coldly. Someone turned off the music. In the heavy-breathing silence, I removed the offending hand. "Of course I'm here. Now where's Jason?"

No answer, just more heavy breathing. Then another of the threesome, a weaselly sort leaning on a cue stick, demanded, "How come you're wearing, like, a suit?"

"How come she's so *flat*?" muttered the other, and there was sniggering all around.

This drunken discourtesy left me speechless. While I gathered my wits to tell them off, some of the other men— the ones who were still ambulatory—began to congregate around us. Not quite a wolf pack—the eyes were too dull, the movements too clumsy. More like a herd of cows. But still . . .

"It ain't whatcha got, it's whatcha do with it!" yelled someone from the back. "So do it!"

Whistles and more lewd comments followed. Make that a herd of bulls. A sort of testosteronic bellowing arose, and I backed away nervously—right into Mr. Garlic. Perhaps it was unintentional, but he didn't so much fend me off as draw me in, and as I stumbled backward, his meaty hands slid around my ribs and halted conveniently at breast level.

I am not a violent woman, but that tore it. In a single un-thinking movement, I wrenched myself away, leading with my right shoulder, and windmilled around to land a ringing slap upside Mr. Garlic's thick head.

It was a toss-up which of us hurt the most—the blow jolted me to the shoulder—but at least I kept my feet. My assailant staggered into a tangled collision with his weaselly friend, and the two of them made an unintended and horizontal visit to the buffet table, accompanied by a mixed chorus of crashing plates, angry shouts, and drunken guffaws.

A painted ceramic platter teetered dangerously on the edge of the table. *What was Joe thinking, giving this crowd his good serving pieces?* I snatched at the platter and stepped back from the fray, as a new voice—a familiar voice—cut across the others.

"Shut up, you disgusting white boys! Carnegie, what are you doing here?"

The speaker was a young black man, tall, with rock-solid biceps gleaming darkly against a sleeveless white T-shirt. He had large, ardent eyes, and a humorous curl to his wide mouth that I knew very well. Not so much from my ac-quaintance with him, but from all the time I spent hanging out with his big sister.

Darwin James, younger by a decade, but with a close fam-ily resemblance, was the kid brother of my best friend, Lily.

"Darwin, what's going on here?" I demanded. There was a plastic carrying bin from Solveto's on the floor near his feet, half-full of crumpled packing paper. I set the platter gently inside it and brushed off my hands. Now *I* smelled like garlic. "I had a call to come see Jason right away. Is someone hurt?"

"Not that I know of." Darwin shrugged, a bottle of orange juice held lightly in one long, muscular hand. "I think Jase is watching the pool players. Want me to get him?"

"Please." I looked around. The herd was moving off, while surveying me sullenly over their shoulders. "Why's everyone staring?"

From across the room, a sardonic tenor voice said, "Mistaken identity, don't you think?"

From the pool room beyond the bar, a rangy, sharp-featured individual sauntered toward us through the debris-laden tables. Jason Kraye's small, light eyes held disdainful amusement, as they often did, and a spark of malice.

Or is that my imagination? I didn't like Jason Kraye. In our planning talks for the wedding, he'd been cooperative enough, but always with an unctuous manner akin to mockery.

"So you came," he continued, smugly folding his arms. "I didn't expect you so soon. The thing is, we need some more booze around here. Some of these gentlemen brought their friends, and everybody was thirsty; you know how it is. Make it a mixed case, OK? And another rack of beer."

"*What?!* You called me over here to make a liquor run?"

The narrow lips stretched into a slow, arrogant smile. Jason, I realized, was also three sheets to the wind, though he held it better than his pals. "You're in charge of the food and drink, aren't you? That's what Sally said."

"If Sally had told me this on the phone—" But of course, that's why she hadn't told me. Because I wouldn't have come.

"Come on," Jason wheedled, quite sure of getting his

way. "You've got your car here anyway, why not do us a favor? All my plastic is maxed out."

"Listen up, Jason," I said. "If you want more liquor, you can take up a collection and get your ass to a 7-Eleven. I'm off-duty."

Then I picked up the Solveto's bin and turned on my heel. It was heavier than I expected—there must be other dishes underneath—and the dignity of my exit was compromised when I stumbled over a shish kebab. But I kicked it sternly aside and strode to the glass door. The door slid open just as I got there, and in walked—no kidding—Santa Claus.

Salvation Army on overtime? I wondered. *A late guest with a sense of humor?*

Behind me, a howl went up from the men. "*That's* her!"

"She's here!"

"Merry freakin' Christmas!"

Meanwhile, Santa glared at me eye-to-eye—he was exactly my height—and said, "Hey, I work alone."

I took a closer look. Beneath the rippling white beard and padded red suit, this particular Santa Claus wore shiny scarlet lipstick and extravagant false eyelashes. I glanced down, past the big tote bag she carried: several inches of her stature came from wickedly high-heeled black boots.

Enter stripper, exit flat-chested wedding planner. I stood aside to make way for Santa, and walked furiously back to my van. *Ho, ho, ho.*

Chapter Two

UNDER NORMAL CIRCUMSTANCES, I LIVE IN A HOUSEBOAT ON the east shore of Lake Union, with the Made in Heaven offices located conveniently upstairs. At the moment, and hugely inconveniently, I was working at Joe Solveto's catering office in Fremont and sleeping on Lily's foldout couch over in Wallingford.

The culprit in the case was that ancient enemy of damp wood, *Serpula lacrymans*. Dry rot. The fungal fiend had infested the houseboat, and my horrified landlady had launched a barrage of chemical and mechanical assaults to annihilate it. Mrs. Castle barely gave me time to load up my laptop and stuff my suitcase before she had the place cordoned off and swarming with guys in Hazmat suits.

At least I was saving some rent, which I needed for the down payment on Vanna Too. After the original Vanna was totaled, the insurance company's measly payout had simply added insult to my minor injuries. But rental savings aside, the prolonged disruption to both my business and my personal life was stressing me out in a serious way. Even my partner, Eddie Breen, who's a champion grumbler himself, was walking on eggshells around me. And Eddie's one of my favorite people on earth.

At the moment, as I left the Hot Spot and headed back

across the Fremont bridge, the award for my *least* favorite person on earth was a split decision between *Serpula lacrymans* and Jason Kraye. Of all the nerve!

Beyond the effrontery of it, Kraye's outrageous demand for delivery service had pulled me away from an important task: a last-minute search through Made in Heaven's relocated files. I was trying to unearth a particularly nice photograph of one of my brides, to show at a television appearance tomorrow morning.

I'd never been on TV before, so naturally I was nervous. Not that I expected the third degree; this was just a segment about wedding planners on a local early-morning show, with a perky interviewer and some softball questions about my job. But my fellow guest would be Beau Paliere, the very, but *very* hot wedding designer from Paris by way of Hollywood, and I didn't want to come across as a local yokel.

Beautiful Beau, as the celebrity mags called him, was in Seattle to attend a one-day-only trunk show by a prominent wedding gown designer—and to keep the media spotlight blazing away on his business and his charms. Beau Paliere was major league, with movie-star clients and plenty of TV experience.

I had failed to wangle an invitation to Mariella Ponti's trunk show—and the chance to hobnob with the wealthiest brides in the Northwest—but a TV appearance with Beau could be priceless publicity for Made in Heaven. *If* I carried it off well. Local Girl Makes Good was the general idea, not Local Girl Freezes Up With Famous Frenchman.

My performance anxiety had to channel itself somewhere, so earlier this evening I became suddenly and unreasonably convinced that my on-screen success hinged on having the camera pan across this one damn photo. I'd riffled through each of my files at least twice, and now the minutes were counting down to zero hour. I had to be awake, dressed, and mascara'd by five A.M.

How do TV people do it? I wondered as I drove back through Fremont. *They must sleep in their makeup.* As I stopped for a light, another Santa—presumably legitimate—used the crosswalk in front of Vanna, his beard flaring white in the headlights. And I could see yet another Claus clone ringing a Salvation Army bell on the opposite street corner. The neighborhood was thick with Saint Nicks.

Joe Solveto's catering business was in a sleek new building on the north side of the Ship Canal, with kitchen and tasting room on the first floor and offices on the second. I stopped in the kitchen first, scribbling a note—"from Carnegie, other stuff still at Café"—and leaving it, with the ceramic platter in its bin, for the dishwasher to find in the morning.

Then I took the elevator up to Joe's storage room on Four. Eddie hadn't unpacked since our move, and his single file box was stashed up there. Maybe it held the photo I was seeking; I'd looked everywhere else.

The fourth floor was empty and dark, and my footsteps echoed in the corridor like the soundtrack of a bad horror movie. Once inside the storeroom, I locked the door behind me, switched on National Public Radio just for company, and looked around to get my bearings.

I was surrounded by treasure.

Like most caterers, Joe relied on cheap, unbreakable dishes and glassware. But his buffets and serving stations always featured a signature Solveto's flourish from Joe's personal collection: exquisite and eye-catching pieces of hand-painted Italian ceramics, like the piece I'd just rescued, or vintage English silver, or glittering Depression glass. Joe got to write off his exotic vacations as merchandise-buying trips, and his clients loved the results.

As the NPR folks intoned about some weighty topic or other, I marveled at the splendid assortment of platters, pitchers, trays, and tureens, any one of which would grace the most upscale table. Reflections from the overhead lights winked across a massive gilt candelabra, sparked from a scalloped cake stand of cobalt-blue cut glass, and lost themselves in a voluptuous clay urn, probably Turkish and undoubtedly valuable.

Along one wall, under a bank of windows, a sturdy worktable was stacked neatly with bubble wrap and bins for transporting these treasures, like the one I'd just left downstairs. A huge silver punch bowl sat ready for packing, with a pad of inventory forms beside it for recording which items were in use, and where. Joe was brilliantly creative, but strictly organized.

Eddie's file box sat underneath the table. I hauled it on top and lifted out the first layer of hastily-packed items: a squat steel pencil jar, a favorite oversized coffee mug (none too clean), and a framed photograph of the freighter Eddie had sailed on, back when he and my late father were cadets together in the merchant marine.

Tim Kincaid and Eddie Breen, my mother says fondly, were the scourge of the seven seas.

Eddie's seagoing past explained the next item in the box: a pair of small but powerful binoculars. Back on the houseboat, he used them to survey the pleasure boats and sea planes that crisscrossed Lake Union. I set them carefully aside, pulled out the stack of file folders at the bottom of the box, and sat down at the table to search.

No luck. There were checklists for the Tyler/Sanjek events, a detailed timetable for Bonnie Buckmeister's Christmas-themed wedding next week, and notes on all our current marketing efforts, including my TV appearance tomorrow. But no photos.

Sighing, I propped my chin on one fist and stared absently out the window. I'd just have to manage without the picture. I had others I could use: a wedding cake, a clever arrangement of place cards, one of our bridal couples dancing. And, of course, the Made in Heaven logo, in its curly copper lettering, which I would try my hardest to get on camera.

But first I had to get some sleep.

As I stood up to repack Eddie's box, something across the Ship Canal caught my eye: a brightly lit window, with a small figure in scarlet clothing moving back and forth across it, an erratic actor on a garish stage. I hadn't realized it before, but Joe's building was directly across the Ship Canal from the Hot Spot Café.

From my upper-story vantage point, I could see right into the Café, where Santa was strutting her stuff. Not that I wanted to see, of course. I swept up all the files I'd opened, tucked them back into the box, and set the mug and the pencil jar on top of them.

Then I picked up the binoculars.

Hmmm... It occurred to me that maybe I had knocked the glasses out of focus, or out of alignment, or whatever it is you knock binoculars out of. And how else could I check except by aiming them at something? That brightly lit window, for example, would be a perfect way to test out...

Whoa. Nothing wrong with the focus. With the lenses at my eyes, the Hot Spot's rear window leapt into brilliant clarity, as did the Saint Nick chick. She had shed the padded red trousers and the beard, and while I watched, fascinated, she strutted back and forth, moving to music I couldn't hear, in just her fur-trimmed jacket, tasseled red hat, and sky-high heeled boots. If I were a young man—or an old one, or one in between—I would have said she had thighs to die for.

Santa's audience, mostly cut off from my downward view by the edge of the Café's roof, seemed not to realize that they were sharing the show with any passing sailboat—or any hidden observer. But in fact, you'd have to be up in a crow's nest, or up where I was, to get just the right angle.

If the bachelors had thought of that, they sure didn't care. As I watched, Frank Sanjek sat heavily on the floor at his comrades' feet. One of his friends, invisible to me from the waist up, poured a stream of beer on Frank's head. He didn't appear to notice.

I could understand why. Dipping and swaying, always in motion, Santa dropped her jacket down from one smooth bare shoulder, then the other, each time letting the white fur border inch lower and lower down the curves of her breasts.

Then, perhaps responding to some climax in the music, she suddenly turned her back to the boys and her front to me, bent forward, and flipped the jacket up behind. If Ms. Claus was wearing much of anything under the jacket, it was too small for the binoculars to pick up. Frank fell over sideways.

I was hastily putting the binoculars down—honest, I was—when my phone rang again.

Chapter Three

THE CALLER WASN'T SALLY THIS TIME, BUT MY ERSTWHILE innkeeper, wondering when I'd be home for the night.

"Oh, jeez, Lily, have you been waiting up for me?"

"No, but Mike just left and I'm going to bed soon. I just wanted to make sure you have your key."

"Mike" was Detective Lieutenant Michael Graham, Homicide, currently courting Lily with an offhanded gallantry that was charming the socks off her—along with everything else—and making me more than a little envious. My dance card, at the moment, could not have been emptier.

"I've got the key," I told her. "I'll try not to wake the boys when I came in."

"Did you find your photo?"

"No, and I should have given up hours ago. Then I wouldn't have been dragged over to the bachelor party." I told her about Jason's summons, and the arrival of Santa.

"So did you stay to watch?" Lily inquired archly.

"Of course not!" I glanced over at the binoculars. The back of my neck was damp. "Why would I do that?"

"Just kidding. Seriously, though, you didn't happen to see Darwin, did you? I shouldn't worry, but I can't help it, I still feel like he's my baby brother. And he was living so wild before he got this MFC job—"

Like most of the party guests, Darwin was a coworker of Frank Sanjek's at the corporate headquarters of Meet for Coffee. The MFC chain of espresso shops had been giving Starbucks a run for its considerable money lately, and they were paying top dollar for young talent.

Frank was a product manager, whatever that meant, and Darwin, until recently an underground comics artist, was now on staff as a graphic designer, juicing up MFC's packaging. Sally Tyler had once dabbled in market research for MFC—that was how she met Frank—but she was now fully employed in being a bitch.

"Actually, I talked to Darwin," I told Lily. "He seemed OK. Come to think of it, he was the only one there who seemed sober. Doesn't he drink?"

"Not anymore. He's been doing AA for almost a year now."

This was news to me, and I wasn't sure how to reply. "Oh . . . well, I wasn't at the party for long, but honestly, he was fine."

"Forget I asked, OK?" Lily hastened to change the subject. "Did you see Aaron there?"

"Aaron *Gold*?" I almost dropped the phone.

"Is there some other Aaron you're smitten with?" I could hear the grin in her voice. "Darwin said he was invited tonight."

"You know perfectly well I'm not smitten with him. I'm not sure I ever was." Just to prove it, I should have changed the subject myself. But I didn't. "I thought Aaron was still in Boston, anyway. How on earth does he know Frank Sanjek?"

"I don't think he does, really," said Lily. "Dar told me that Aaron's on a leave of absence from the *Sentinel*, to write some kind of book about Meet for Coffee."

"But Ivy's *my* client!" It was an irrational reaction, but I couldn't help it. "I don't want him barging in!"

Lily wasn't grinning now, she was laughing out loud. "What's it to you, if you really don't care about the man anymore? Besides, maybe he got there first. Maybe he recommended you to Ivy Tyler for her daughter's wedding."

"What? Did Darwin tell you that, too? How does he know?"

"Calm down," she said, relenting. "Darwin doesn't know anything except that Aaron's working on a book and he's gotten friendly with the guys in MFC's marketing department, so they invited him along to the bachelor party. I guess he didn't go, though."

"I guess not." *Unless he was in the back room shooting pool with Jason. I wonder...* "Um, Lily, I'd better finish up what I'm doing here. This TV thing has really thrown me off-balance."

"OK. Good luck tomorrow. I'm not getting up that early, even for you, but I set the VCR."

"Thanks, Lily. Sleep tight."

The minute I put down the phone, I grabbed the binoculars and focused on the Hot Spot for a second look. Not that I cared whether Aaron was inside. Not that I cared about Aaron at all.

Not that I could see him, either. Santa had left the lighted window, and the revelers milled aimlessly inside, as if the party were winding down. I spotted Mr. Garlic, but no one else familiar—until a flurry of movement drew my attention to the grassy slope below the deck.

There in the silvery frost and the tilted shadows, two long-limbed figures were struggling together, dodging and flailing in clumsy counterpoint. I had no trouble recognizing them as the best man and Lily's baby brother. Jason Kraye was obviously drunk; maybe Darwin was the designated driver, trying to take his car keys away?

But you don't punch people to get their car keys, I thought. And then, *Maybe you do, if you're young and male.* It was hard to tell if this was a ritual scuffle—elk clashing their antlers—or a serious fight. Either way, I can't say it bothered me to see the supercilious Jason getting knocked around a little.

The third figure was less ambiguous: Frank Sanjek, the bridegroom, was kneeling on the grass near the two combatants and vomiting hideously, his head jerking and lolling. *Another male ritual.* I smiled ruefully. Time for me to go home.

But once I went downstairs and gathered up my things, a nagging doubt stopped me from walking out the door. I had assured Lily that her brother was fine, and now he was apparently in the middle of a fistfight. Shouldn't I check on the outcome?

For that matter, shouldn't I make sure that the amiable, sensible bridegroom wasn't unconscious and abandoned by his drunken friends, out in the freezing night? Eddie tells me I fuss too much about our clients, and maybe it's true. But I was eager to see Sally Tyler walk down the aisle and out of my life on New Year's Eve, and to that end, I needed Frank Sanjek safe and sound.

So I dashed up to the storeroom, hurried over to the worktable, and raised the binoculars to my eyes for the third and last time.

There was even less to see than before. Some of the Café's windows had gone dark, making it hard to get a clear view into the shrubbery. But at least Frank was on his feet; I watched him stagger to the sliding door and wrench it open.

I didn't spot Darwin, or Jason either, but they might have already left.

The stripper was just leaving, striding briskly up the sidewalk, head up and shoulders back after a job well done. And someone else was working his way down through the bushes toward the bike path, but I couldn't make out his face, or whether he had a bicycle waiting for him. The guys were supposed to take cabs or buses home instead of driving, but even a bike could be dangerous—

"Bird-watching?"

I jumped, and Eddie's binoculars slipped from my suddenly clumsy fingers, to land in the silver punch bowl with a enormous and resounding *gonnng*.

I was shocked, and not just because a man had suddenly materialized in the doorway. I was shocked by who it was. Aaron Gold. The man I'd been dating; the man I'd been falling for. The man who only recently mentioned—on the very same night that I decided to give way to passion and invite him into my bed—that he had a wife back in Boston.

I hadn't spoken to him since.

Unlike the younger party guests, Aaron wore a tie. But it hung loose from his collar and his crow-black hair was mussed. My former suitor's deep-set brown eyes gleamed glassily, and when he smiled, the familiar swift white grin came out lopsided. Even from where I stood, halfway across the room, I could smell the combination of cigar smoke and retsina.

So he was shooting pool in the other room. And then afterward, he must have been watching Santa . . .

"No birds at night," said Aaron, shaking his head sagely. A lock of hair flopped down into his eyes. "I know! S' Christmas. You're gonna find out who's naughty or nice. Merry Christmas, Stretch."

I stood with my back to the reverberating punch bowl and took a deep, shaky breath. I didn't know how long Aaron had been watching me, or whether he guessed that I'd been spying on Santa's striptease earlier. I also didn't know how I felt about him, after the last few weeks of angry silence and unwilling tears.

And what neither of us knew, and wouldn't learn until the next day, was this: of the three young men I had observed on the grass behind the Hot Spot Café, only two were still alive.

Chapter Four

AARON COCKED HIS HEAD. "AREN'T YOU GOING TO SAY MERRY Christmas back? Isn't that what you Christians do?"

"Merry Christmas," I said softly.

It hurt, it actually physically caused me pain, to see him. We'd known each other less than six months, and been parted for less than one. *Did I really care for him that much? Do I still? And how the hell did I forget to lock that door?*

I tried for a sterner tone. "How did you know I was here?"

Aaron hesitated, considering. Not falling-down drunk, but with a certain satellite delay between brain and voice. The fluorescent light cast shadows beneath his high cheekbones, and gave a sickly tinge to his smooth olive skin. Or maybe that was just the retsina.

"I, ah, took a walk, to clear my head, you know? Your van's out front, and I saw the lights on. I'm a reporter, Slim, I figure things out." He squinted peevishly at the shelves around us and kept talking. Or buying time. "Looks like a goddamn store. More Christmas shopping! If I see one more how-many-shopping-days-till-Christmas commercial, I'm gonna murder my television. What is all this stuff, anyway?"

"It's part of Joe Solveto's catering business," I said mechanically. "He uses—oh, for heaven's sake, what does it matter? Why are you here?"

But I knew why, and Aaron confirmed it. He drew a heavy oak banker's chair from its place at the worktable and straddled it, folding his arms across the chair back and dropping his chin onto them as if his head was too much trouble to carry.

He sighed. "Carnegie, why won't you talk to me? I keep calling—"

"And I wish you'd stop!" I said, louder than I meant to. I felt awkward and off-balance, under siege here in this building that wasn't even my own territory.

"Did you read my E-mail?"

"No, I didn't. I just want you to leave me alone."

"But I can't. I *won't*." He lifted his head. "You have to listen to me, Slim."

"I don't have to do anything. And quit calling me those stupid names!" I turned away to finish repacking Eddie's box and set it back beneath the table. I was trying not to cry. Redheads look hideous when they cry. "I did listen to you, and you lied to me. End of story."

"It doesn't have to be the end of anything," he said stubbornly. "Don't you see, I was trying to give you some time to get over that son of a bitch, what's his name—Walters."

"Walker."

Over the summer I had fallen hard for Holt Walker, a good-looking attorney whose every word, every action, was false from the very beginning. After that fiasco, Aaron had been a breath of fresh air.

Scratch that. Aaron had *pretended* to be. He wasn't a criminal like Holt, but something much more hackneyed: the married man from out of town, with no one to give him away. The brash, fast-talking operator. The manipulator. And

I was the patsy. I wasn't sure which was worse, the broken heart or the wounded pride.

"Right—Walker," he was saying now, trying to enunciate, but slurring a little. "You were upset about him, underrstambably upset."

I retreated farther, to lean against one of the windows overlooking the Ship Canal. We both fell silent for a long moment. The canal water looked icy cold. Beyond the bare trees lining the bicycle path, the windows of the Hot Spot were dark, the deck and shrubbery deserted. *The party's over.*

I raised my gaze to my own reflection, and to Aaron's. Our eyes met in the glass, and he tried again. "I was just giving you some time to get your balance back, you know? Before I told you about this situation I'm in."

"That's all marriage is to you? A situation?"

"Aw, Carnegie, don't be this way."

I closed my eyes. I wanted to retreat from the building altogether, but I couldn't very well leave an intruder here, late at night in Joe's sanctum. What if he fell over in a stupor and broke something? I had a confused vision of splintered crystal and shards of pottery—anything to distract me from the plain fact that I'd made a fool of myself over Aaron Gold.

"What a sensitive guy you turned out to be," I said at last, keeping my back turned. "Lying to me for my own good, that was big of you."

"Would you stop talking about lying?" he protested. "I didn't lie to you, not really—"

"Not *really*?!"

This was more like it. Righteous anger felt so much better than humiliation and regret. I whirled to confront him and raised my voice, letting the anger flare up, goading myself into fury.

"You spent weeks sweet-talking me, acting like a light-hearted bachelor, trying to persuade me to sleep with you, and all the time you were married! That's not *lying*?"

"OK, technically, yes, I was married, I mean, I am married, but there's going to be a divorce. I just don't know when—"

"Oh, spare me!" I snapped. "What kind of naïve idiot do you think I am?"

Aaron rubbed his eyes with both hands, and blew out an exasperated breath. "This is all my fault."

"You're damn right it is!"

"I should never have said anything on Thanksgiving," he continued, as if to himself. "I should have waited, I shouldn't have blurted it out like that."

"So, it's just that your timing is off, is that what you're saying? Cheating's only a problem when you confess on the wrong schedule?"

"Would you please calm down? You're making this sound like a soap opera."

"It's worse than that! It's disgusting and m-mortifying." Hot tears brimmed in my eyes, ready to spill over, but I refused to let them. I had my pride. Maybe too much of it, but Aaron had hurt me badly. "I trusted you! All through Thanksgiving dinner at Lily's, I couldn't wait to get home and make love to you. And then you told me...you told me...Just go away."

"But, sweetheart—"

"Don't call me that! Don't say another word. I'm busy, I've got to be on TV in the morning."

He looked dazed. "TV?"

"Never mind, just go."

Aaron scowled at me, silent at last. Then he set his jaw and walked out the storeroom doorway with the too-careful gait of a man trying to act sober. I waited till I heard the elevator descend, then I found the staff rest room and threw cold water on my cheeks until the bones ached.

As I drove through the frosty, empty streets to Lily's house, I stared out dully at the Christmas lights floating by. On almost every block, chimneys and porches were outlined in twinkling stars of white and red and green, with the occasional illuminated sleigh or Mickey Mouse in a Santa hat, standing guard on a lawn. In some windows Christmas trees stood dark, their bulbs unplugged for the night, their glitter and garlands catching stray gleams from the streetlamps.

I like Christmas. It's a little hard sometimes, being single at the holidays, but I like the decorations and the special recipes and hunting out just the right gifts for my family and friends. Last year I had woven strings of tiny blue lights through the railings around my houseboat, charmed by their firefly reflections in the water. This year, I helped Lily's boys decorate their tree, which was fun but not the same.

I'm homesick, that's all, I told myself as I drove. *Sleazy men are a dime a dozen; you have to shrug them off and keep going. I'm just homesick. And besides, Aaron hates Christmas. Why would I want a man who hates Christmas?*

At Lily's boxy little bungalow near Woodland Park, I climbed the steep concrete steps, slick with rime, and let myself stealthily through the front door. Ethan and Marcus loved having Aunt Carrie come over to play, but right now they needed their deep, innocent sleep.

I dropped my tote bag on the easy chair by the Christmas tree, smiling a little to see that Lily had unfolded the couch and made up my bed for me. She'd put out an extra quilt against the chill, and perched one of Ethan's innumerable plastic dinosaurs on the pillow, to make me laugh.

What a peach. Thank God for the people you can actually depend on.

Yawning, I grimaced at my watch. No deep sleep for me, not tonight. I patted the stegosaurus on the tail and tiptoed down the hallway past the boys' room, to brush my teeth. But a narrow band of light slipped out beneath Lily's door, accompanied by a throaty whisper.

"Hey, girl!"

I pushed the door open. My hostess lay propped against her pillows in a long-sleeved, low-cut velour gown of royal purple, her favorite shade. The glow of the bedside lamp illuminated her large, lively eyes, so much like her brother's, and gilded her coffee-colored skin. Lily was, as Eddie put it, "quite a tomato."

Just now, the tomato was hanging up the phone, and looking as high up as I felt low down.

"He called me to say good night, *again*!"

Lily giggled like a girl, a girl in love. She hadn't been clobbered by romantic calamities recently, as I had, but she'd been deeply lonely ever since her divorce.

"I *knew* it was him," she went on. "I just picked up the phone and started laughing! I swear, we were laughing all evening."

No need to ask who "he" was. I sat on the edge of the bed and folded my arms, still cold from the drive. Though I half-expected Lily to ask why I'd been crying—we can read each other like books, favorite old books—she was too busy singing the praises of the wise, the witty, the altogether wonderful Michael Graham.

I wasn't all that much in the mood to listen, but she is my best friend.

"Fran Lewis took my kids along with hers to that new Disney thing, bless her heart, so I made dinner here—Cornish game hens with a chestnut stuffing—and it all got *very* sexy, gnawing on the bones. What was that movie with the great eating scene?"

"*Tom Jones.*"

"That was it." She grinned. "We got *très* Tom Jones. Finally Mike swept me off to bed and the chocolate soufflé burned to a crisp before we smelled the smoke! Can you imagine?"

"I sure can."

"So we opened all the windows, and then we were *freezing,* so we climbed in bed again and just talked and laughed. We had to watch the time, of course, because of the boys, but when they got home, Mike tucked them in and read them a story..." She drifted to a dreamy pause, then shook her head. "Am I crazy, Carnegie? Is this really going to work?"

I thought about it: a mixed-race marriage, a hard-pressed detective taking on stepchildren, a strong-minded woman taking a new path in life. But I only thought for a moment.

"He's a wonderful man, Lily."

"He is, isn't he?" She leaned back into the pillows. "He said the cleverest thing—"

"Look, I'm sorry, but I'd better get to bed."

"Oh, right! You need your beauty sleep for the camera. Just tell me, before you go—"

I rose, bracing myself for a question about Aaron. But of course Lily didn't know that he had appeared at Joe's. And I didn't plan to tell her.

"Tell me," said Lily. "Did Darwin honestly look sober? I don't mean to spy on him, but a bachelor party! It's such a temptation. And Dar said Jason Kraye has been kidding him at work about not drinking."

Impulsively, I leaned down to give her a hug. No need to mention the scuffle I'd seen.

"Cross my heart, big sister. He was sipping orange juice and looking tall, dark, and handsome like he always does. Sweet dreams, now."

"You, too, Carnegie. You're going to knock 'em dead tomorrow, I just know it."

Chapter Five

I DROPPED A SOUP TUREEN AND SCREAMED. NO, SOMEONE ELSE was screaming, a high stuttering scream...

The alarm clock. It wasn't screaming, just sounding its tiny metallic stutter on the arm of Lily's couch where I'd put it a few—painfully few—hours ago. I fumbled a hand from under the afghan to silence it and hauled myself upright, feeling sick and hollow with fatigue. And nerves: *live* television! What was I thinking?

I should have said no, I thought now. *Or else given up on that photo and gone to sleep right after dinner. I could still call it off, call the station and say...what? That I have the flu? Would they believe that?*

Throughout this cowardly monologue, I was showering, dressing, and painting my face. Then, in my grim determination not to think about Aaron, I began to review all the on-camera advice I'd gotten from Sally Tyler's mother. I liked her vastly more than the bride herself, and she had drawn on her own experience to coach me for this morning.

"Wear something simple, in a soft color. No crooked collar points or busy stripes. You want them to look at your eyes. If your mouth goes dry, bite the tip of your tongue to get the saliva flowing. And remember, the interviewer's job is to make you look good. Trust her."

One hour to the minute after the alarm had sounded, I was tapping on the intercom doorbell at the side entrance of KCBR. The air was still cold, but damper than last night, under a low and starless predawn sky. I wondered briefly if it would snow. Between the steep hills and the inexperienced drivers, Seattle's rare snowstorms always bring the city to a halt. Too bad it hadn't dumped a couple of feet while I was asleep.

A frazzled young man with a clipboard opened the door, checked off my name, and hustled me down a narrow hallway taped with Christmas cards, nodding like a bobble-head doll and talking nonstop all the way. I trotted along, trying to answer his questions and wondering if my lipstick was smeared.

"Hi, I'm Doug, you want coffee? I'll get you some. Is it *Car*-negie or Car-*nay*-gie? *Car*-negie, great, I'll tell Mandy. You brought some photos? Great, give 'em here and I'll get them propped up to scan. Great. I'll have you wait just a minute while we set up, then I'll get you miked. OK, great, the rest room's right there, I'll be back in a sec."

We had arrived at the end of the hallway, near a maze of empty cubicles. A tall pegboard held tight, tidy loops of variously-sized computer cords and cables, along with a ferocious notice that read: "We use the over-under method of winding. If you don't know it, ASK SOMEONE WHO DOES; don't just dump cords here!!!"

Past the pegboard I could see a large open area, ringed with equipment, where preoccupied individuals moved busily under the glaring lights. Doug dashed off like the White Rabbit, muttering my oddball first name under his breath.

I was used to the pronunciation question. My late father

was a self-educated man, schooled in the legion of small libraries that Andrew Carnegie endowed across the country. So Dad named me after the dear old robber baron, conveniently forgetting his less noble acts—and also how he pronounced his name. My mother still called me Carrie, but I liked it unabridged.

Abandoned by Doug and feeling rattled, I took shelter in the ladies' room, to fool with my makeup. A motley collection of hairsprays and gels was ranged along the countertop, but my long hair is stubbornly curly by nature, so I don't do much with it. I just fixed my lipstick and stared morosely into the mirror, wishing I was elsewhere. Then I took a deep breath, did a couple of shoulder rolls, to loosen up, and went out to meet Beautiful Beau Paliere.

And *boy,* was he beautiful. I beheld him in the cubicle area, lounging elegantly against a desk: an exquisite man in his late thirties, with a body like a gymnast and a face like a dangerous angel.

Like many men, Beau was a touch shorter than me. But unlike most of them, he was dressed entirely in snug, stylish black. His hair was black as well, almost blue-black, like a comic-strip Superman, and rising in thick, glossy waves from a tanned forehead. Together, dark hair and dark clothes made a wonderful foil for his eyes, which were long, lazy, and intensely blue, fringed with lush black lashes. Bedroom eyes.

"Ah, you're the local person," he said, with just a shade of a French accent. He shook my hand and favored me with the smile that had graced so many magazine covers.

How do you get tan fingers? I thought inanely, as he held my hand just a moment too long. That was all the thinking I could manage, because the butterflies in my stomach were drowning in a tidal surge of lust. The man was one big magnet. I could feel myself being sucked into his orbit like a wandering asteroid trying to edge past Jupiter.

Within minutes, Beautiful Beau and I were seated up on a platform, being fussed over by young Doug. The furnishings were faux living room, with an empty chair between us. A low coffee table held a water pitcher, glasses, and a bowl of red carnations mixed with holly—all very cozy and seasonal.

Beau and I kept mum, because the guy-and-gal morning team was just a few yards away, wrapping up a segment at the long, logo'd news desk. They spoke smoothly and warmly to their invisible audience as the cameras wheeled before them.

"And I'll be back in just a moment," said the gal, "to talk with the gentleman from Paris who you've all been waiting for, Beau Paliere!"

No mention of me, but I was too busy to notice, because Doug had his hand down my cleavage—what there was of it. My simple, soft-colored knit top was apparently too simple; there was nowhere to clip the tiny black microphone. It ended up dangling near my collarbone like a big black insect, while Beau's simply disappeared against his silky shirt. Then Mandy took the chair between us, and we were on the air, up close and personal.

Mandy was a wire-thin blonde with the kind of exaggerated features that work so well on television: super-sized brown eyes, cheekbones sharp as my shoulder blades, and a dentist's dream of wide white teeth. Her nose was an adorable little button, though, and her chin was small and pointed, giving her an altogether kittenish look.

A perky kitten, with a silvery laugh and a high-pitched voice full of exclamation points.

"Weddings!" she perked at the camera. "What a fun, crazy time for brides! And who better to tell us how to handle the craziness than today's guests: Beau Paliere and Car-nay-gie Kincaid!"

She gave Beau a long, glowing introduction, and as he responded to her compliments, you could see his charm ratcheting up a notch, from Delicious to Devastating. The two of them leaned closer and closer together, and the silvery laugh got a little giddy, until finally Mandy tore her gaze away, to glance at me.

"Car-nay-gie, you're based right here in Seattle, aren't you?"

"It's *Car*-negie," I said with what I hoped was a friendly smile. "I know Andrew Carnegie is pronounced the other way, but my father—"

"Whatever!" Mandy ground her glorious teeth a little at the wasted airtime. "Have you ever planned a really big wedding, like the ones Beau is famous for?"

"Nothing quite on that scale," I admitted. Beau's scale included fleets of limos, acres of flowers, and guest lists full of pop stars, European royalty, and the occasional president of the United States. "But I have put together some unique events here in town. For example—"

"Tell us, Beau, are you going to do a wedding while you're here in Seattle?"

"Alas, *non*," he said, the bedroom eyes working overtime and the accent deepening, "but if I were invited to a wedding here, I would, of course, attend. Or if I meet someone *magnifique*, who knows? I might end up planning my own!"

Mandy squealed, in a silvery way, and conducted the rest of the segment almost in Beau's lap. She tossed me the odd question over her shoulder, but mostly she was intent on asking about "Beau's Girls," the bright and beautiful young women who conducted Paliere events in L.A., New York, and points in between. Beau's Girls were all slim and blonde, and I swear Mandy was considering a career change.

"They say you have a Girl in every major city," she said slyly, loving the innuendo. "Is that true?"

"Not quite." His deep blue gaze flickered toward me, then focused burningly on Mandy again. I expected to see a smoky little spot appear between her eyes, like a dry leaf under a magnifying glass. "There is no Beau's Girl in Seattle. Not yet. But I think your city is ready for the Paliere touch!"

Mandy, what a surprise, wanted to hear all about "the Touch," and Beau went on to extol his particular kind of wedding—the ones I call, in private, Best Performance in a Nuptial Drama. The magazines were full of them these days: the vast budget, the extravagant stage set, and the bride jeweled and gowned as if to accept an Oscar.

"It's her big moment," said Beau, gazing into Mandy's big brown eyes, and then into the camera's small red one. "Her one chance to be a superstar. Everything must be *perfect*."

"But perfection isn't really the point, is it?" I interrupted, thoroughly exasperated by now. I was rapidly departing from Monsieur Paliere's magnetic field.

"But of course it is the point!" he said winningly. " 'Beauty and perfection in every detail.' It is my personal mantra."

I remained un-won. "I have to disagree. Surely the point is to have a meaningful ceremony, and then a fun reception that matches your own personal style. If you bankrupt yourself just to imitate the celebrities, and treat your guests like a studio audience—"

"Of course," said Beau, in a tone of deep Gallic condolence. "If you are doing budget weddings, Car-nay-gie, then you cannot attempt the glorious gesture, the really magnificent *mise-en-scène*. But what a shame for the bride to lose her one opportunity to shine, merely to save a few dollaars."

"That's not what I meant!" I protested, leaning forward, quite sure by now that my face was flaming scarlet.

That was when the damn microphone dropped in the damn carnations, and things went downhill—steeply—after that. The camera cut to a video of Beau's recent triumphs while Doug rewired me, but he might have saved himself the trouble. I spent the rest of the segment failing to get a coherent word in edgewise. They say there's no such thing as bad publicity, but this was an utter fiasco.

At least the fiasco kept me from brooding about Aaron for a little while—though I managed to do a certain amount of that anyway as I drove back to Lily's.

I could have gone straight to work, but I wanted to scrub off all the makeup and change into something that felt more like me, or at least something loud and complicated and unphotogenic. And maybe look at Lily's videotape in private, with the faint hope that what felt like an endless, humiliating ordeal was merely an awkward, forgettable few minutes. *Not much chance of that,* I thought darkly as I parked the van.

Not much privacy, either: Lily's Volvo was still at the house, wedged into the narrow little driveway between its concrete retaining walls—a paint-scraping specialty of old Seattle neighborhoods. Oddly, the front door was ajar. I ran up the steps and pushed it open.

"Hello? I thought you'd be at work by now. Did I look as bad as I—Lily, what's wrong?"

She was sitting at her kitchen table, by the window

overlooking her tiny backyard, with a cup of untouched coffee and an open phone book in front of her. She looked up eagerly when I entered, but when she saw it was me, the disappointment on her face was almost comical.

Almost. I know Lily's expressions like my own, and I could tell this was bad. Maybe the worst.

"Oh, God, is it one of the boys? Or Mike? What happened?"

"The boys are fine," she said, and forced a teary smile. "Mike, too. He took them to day care and school for me. He's wonderful, isn't he?"

"He's the best." I sat across from her. "Now, what happened?"

"It's Dar," she said, and her voice broke on the name. "He left a message during the night. I could hardly understand it. He was, he was . . ."

"He'd been drinking," I said gently, and put a handkerchief into her hand.

"He was drunk!" Lily wiped her bloodshot eyes and took a long, determined breath, taking up a burden she thought was off her shoulders for good. "Carnegie, it was just like before. He was high and excited, talking about the bachelor party, and then he crashed and said how sorry he was to disappoint me again, and then he got angry at himself and started shouting. He just went on and *on* till the tape ran out. I was so angry, I erased it! But what if he's in trouble? What if he crashes his car? That could be the last time I ever hear his voice, and I *erased* it . . ."

She dropped her head and sobbed like a child, and I knelt on the floor by her chair, to hold her.

"I raised that boy," she said against my shoulder. "My parents worked so hard and so long, and I raised Dar like he was my son instead of my brother. If that was the last time—"

"It won't be the last time, Lily, I'm sure it won't. Darwin's probably home asleep."

"No, he's not! I talked to his roommate, he hasn't been home! I called his office and his friends—the ones I know about—and now Mike's checking on accidents."

On the mention of his name, Lieutenant Michael Graham let himself in at the front door. This time Lily and I both looked up eagerly, but Mike shook his head. He had crinkly dark brown hair and a gently somber expression, which had deepened now to pained sympathy.

"No word."

Lily fled to the bathroom, to pull herself together, and Mike joined me in the kitchen.

"She told you?"

"Yes. Listen, I have a meeting in a few minutes, but I could cancel—"

"Thanks, Carnegie, but for once, it's my day off." He poured Lily's cold coffee down the drain, and began to make a fresh pot, moving about the kitchen with quiet competence.

He knows the place as well as I do, I found myself thinking, and was somehow disconcerted by the thought. Disconcerted, too, by how natural it seemed to take my cue from Mike, instead of vice versa. "Should I wait here till she's dressed?"

"No, go ahead to your meeting. I'll let you know what happens, I promise."

Then he patted my shoulder—in lieu of a hug, I think, since we weren't quite on hugging terms yet—and walked me to the door. I was halfway to Fremont before I remembered about my videotape.

Well, better to forget the TV debacle and Aaron both, I decided, and even Darwin's troubles. I had to concentrate instead on my breakfast date with the mother of the bride. Thank heaven she was one of the good ones. In fact, the only thing making the insufferable Sally's wedding at all sufferable was the chance to work with her mother, the one and only Ivy Tyler.

Chapter Six

YES, I MEAN *THAT* IVY TYLER, THE VISIONARY CEO, THE woman who got rich and famous by staking out the corner of Espresso and Motherhood. Meet for Coffee, Inc., also known as MFC, was her brainchild: a totally kid-friendly company, with baskets of toys, easy-listening music, and child-safe furniture in every café. And there were more MFC cafés springing up by the week.

I'd read the rags-to-riches story a couple of times: young Ivy, abandoned by the teenaged father of her baby, started out in the ranks of the working poor. She had struggled to pay the bills and tend her pretty little daughter, and vowed that one day she'd change things for women in the same harsh and lonely straits.

Change things she had, in her own unique way. Today, MFC boasted a loyal workforce of part-timer parents who got a day-care benefit along with their health and dental. Turnover was low and morale was high, and many of those moms and dads brought their offspring to work, giving each café a homey atmosphere, like one big community kitchen table.

And thousands of customers were happy to pull up a chair. For adults-only business meetings, you went to Starbucks, or one of the many independent coffeehouses. To

chat with your neighbor—or your work-from-home bro-
ker—without the use of baby-sitters, you packed up the kids
and went to MFC.

Ivy turned out to have a knack for picking the right man
for the right job; her brilliant chief of operations, Simon
Weeks, was a case in point. In a few short years, Meet for
Coffee had become one of those "why didn't somebody
think of it sooner?" business triumphs. Ivy and Simon
showed up together on the covers of *Forbes* and *Fortune;* by
herself, Ivy was featured in *Oprah Magazine* and *Family Circle*. And along the way, the company's stock price climbed
like a rocket, showering sparks of wealth on all concerned,
with no descent in sight.

Happily for me, Ivy was lavishing some of her well-gotten
gains on her daughter's wedding. She had married a second
time, to an eminent conductor, but he was retired and reclu-
sive. Ivy was the one writing the checks. Although mother
and daughter were prickly with each other, those early years
of deprivation had left their residue of guilt, and now whatever Sally wanted, Sally got. This indulgence might be spoil-
ing the girl's character, but it was helping my bank balance
no end.

This morning, Ivy and her checkbook were meeting me in
Fremont, to talk menus with Joe. The early-morning quiet
was beginning to buzz with rush hour, but I found a spot not
too far from Solveto's. Looking around, I saw the mother of
the bride right across the street, climbing out of a nifty scarlet gas-electric hybrid with a license plate that read MFC
ONE.

Ivy was a middle-aged, dark-eyed blonde like her daughter, not slim, but reasonably trim, and beautifully groomed
in a no-nonsense way. This morning her cropped silver-

blonde hair was set off by a severely elegant black wool coat and a scarf, scarlet as well, whose fringes fluttered as she strode briskly toward me. Ivy did everything briskly.

"Carnegie!" she called through the clear, chilly air. The cloud cover had dissolved; no snow today. Ivy jaywalked toward me, smiling and then making a face. "I saw the interview!"

I groaned as she reached me. "You were up that early?"

"No choice." She yawned, showing nicely capped teeth in front and a mouthful of silver fillings in back. "I took the red-eye up from San Francisco. Those people really know how to brew coffee! I recognized you on the TV at the gate, and stayed to watch."

"So tell me, how bad was it?"

"Honey, you got screwed in public."

"That's what I thought." I pointed up the block at Fremont's MFC. "Shall we go drown my sorrows in some coffee? We've got time before we see Joe."

She gave a quick bark of laughter. "Are you joking, with all those rugrats underfoot? Come on, there's a Starbucks around the corner. I'll pretend it's market research."

Soon we had a table for two, and I was telling Ivy my troubles—the professional ones, not the personal. If Aaron Gold was writing a book about her company, I might run into him in Ivy's presence, and I wanted our unfortunate history strictly out of the picture. I just wished I could discipline my emotions as easily as I curbed my tongue.

"What did I ever do to Beau Paliere?" I whined. "I was just trying to be sensible about real-world weddings, but he made me sound like some cut-rate Las Vegas Wedding-O-Rama."

Ivy looked at me narrowly over the rim of her quad

Americano, no room for cream. If I absorbed that much caffeine all at once, I'd be vibrating for weeks.

"Don't you see his strategy?" she asked. "It wasn't you personally. He just needed a Brand X."

"Huh?"

"Obviously, Paliere is planning to expand into the Pacific Northwest market. It's less sophisticated than New York or L.A., so he knows there's going to be price resistance, and he knows there's going to be customer loyalty to the local vendors like yourself. With Dorothy Fenner out of the picture, you could become a major competitor. So he positions you as a penny-pincher, and he plants the idea that less-expensive weddings are second-rate and unromantic. One stone, two dead birds."

Ivy went back to sipping her jet fuel, and I sat back and sighed. "So what can I do about it?"

"You've got three options," she said, counting them out on the palm of one hand with the neatly-manicured fingers of the other. Ivy had large hands for a woman, and wore no jewelry save for a narrow wedding band in white gold. "Number one is to ignore him, which believe me, you don't want to do. You'd be playing catch-up for the rest of your career."

"And the other two?" This woman was leagues beyond me in the business world, but she treated me like a fellow entrepreneur. It was flattering, and even better, energizing.

"Simple," she said. "Either you fight him on his own ground, and probably lose, or you position *yourself* as an appealing alternative to his shallow, flashy, spendthrift approach. Tell me, what's your mission statement?"

"Well . . ." *Keeping my head above water* sounded so lame. "Well, my business card says I do elegant weddings with an original flair."

"Not bad. But elegant in what way? Original on a budget, or original expensive? How do you distinguish yourself from the competition? If you really want to succeed, you need a brand."

"Like MFC?"

"Exactly." Ivy smiled, a genuine smile that was worlds away from the well-rehearsed verve of TV personalities. Here were crow's-feet not yet Botoxed into blankness, and eyes that looked deep into yours. "You might think they're apples and oranges, MFC and Made in Heaven, but no matter what your product, brand identity is crucial."

She pulled out a sleek little PDA—I still use a notebook myself—and stabbed at it with a stylus. A platinum stylus, I might add, with a tiny diamond set into the top.

"Let me have you meet with someone on my staff, Madison Jaffee. Is Wednesday morning OK?" Stab, stab. "Maddie's a whiz kid, she can walk you through the whole branding process." A final stab, then she put the gadget away. "Meanwhile, I need your help with something."

"The rehearsal dinner—?"

"No, it's not about the wedding." She reached for her coat. "But let's not talk about it here, of all places."

She hurried me back toward Solveto's, only to halt in the entranceway of the building. I was eager to get inside, out of the cold, but a major client is a major client.

"This is strictly confidential, Carnegie. Understood?" Ivy waited for my nod, then continued. "You've heard of Habitat Coffee?"

"Sure." Habitat was a small roaster just north of Seattle, which specialized in shade-grown coffee from Mexico.

The idea, as I understood it, was that clear-cutting forest to make way for coffee was taking a toll on bird populations.

Shade-grown equals bird-friendly. As more people got the idea, Habitat's red-feather logo was showing up in independent cafés around Seattle and beyond. I'd even seen displays of Habitat coffee beans on my last visit to my mother in Boise. And that's Boise, *Idaho*.

"You don't hold stock, do you?" I shook my head, and Ivy lowered her voice even further. "Good. I don't want any nonsense about insider trading. You see, we're working on an acquisition of Habitat. We plan to announce it after the first of the year, and I want to do a big reception and press conference about it. Welcome the new employees to the MFC fold, celebrate our dynamic partnership, yadda yadda yadda. Basically a good, upbeat photo op for next year's annual report, and a couple of inches in the *Wall Street Journal*."

"And you want me to coordinate the event?"

"Exactly."

"I'd be delighted." It wasn't a wedding, but my calendar for the new year was disturbingly empty. And I was more than happy to go the extra mile for Ivy Tyler. "Where shall we start?"

"First off," she said, nodding her approval and cutting to the chase, "I need you to go up to the Habitat facility in Snohomish, ASAP, and tell me if the roasting plant itself will work as a venue or if we have to find someplace else. Simon will be upgrading the whole operation soon, he says their fire protection's bad and their security is worse."

"That's Simon Weeks?"

She smiled warmly. "Yeah. Simon's my go-to guy. If he says tear the place up, we tear it up. But I don't want to start yet, if we can use the plant for a reception first. So, can you fit in a scouting trip?"

"I think so," I said. "Snohomish is what, an hour's drive north? That shouldn't be a problem. Let's go upstairs and check my calendar."

On the way up, I began to comment on last night's bachelor party, but Ivy frowned and shifted her stance at the mention of Jason Kraye. *Aha,* I thought, preening a little at my skill with body language. *She doesn't like him, either. I wonder what she really thinks. of Frank Sanjek? Frank must seem a little watered-down for a quadruple-shotter like Ivy.*

"Say, I've been meaning to ask the party expert," she said now, rather awkwardly changing the subject. "Why do my guests always congregate in the kitchen? At my Christmas cocktail party for the managers, I put the food in another room, I even put the *booze* in another room, along with a neighbor dressed as Santa, but still, everyone jammed in by the sink and the stove."

I laughed. "I've got a theory about that. Kincaid's Law of Leaning."

"Leaning?"

"Yes. Have you ever sat down at a party, and then some tedious bore sits next to you and you're trapped on the couch for hours?"

"Have I ever!"

"We all have," I said, as we entered my little office on the second floor. I waved at Kelli, the pink and plump receptionist, on the way. Joe had a nice staff. "Most people stay on their feet at parties, so they can circulate. But standing gets uncomfortable after a while, so they gravitate toward something to lean on. And kitchen counters are exactly the right height for leaning. That's my theory, anyway."

Ivy raised her eyebrows. "Good theory. You know, I could use someone like you as an undercover shopper, to scope out customer behavior and report back. If you ever get tired of brides, you let me know."

I didn't mention how tired I was of Ivy's daughter. Instead, I cleared some time to visit Habitat the next day, and asked for contact information.

"Talk to Kevin Bauer," said Ivy, jotting down a number. "He founded the company, and he's still pretty hands-on, so he can show you around personally. If you talk with anyone besides Kevin, it's strictly a casual visit. No mention of MFC. Right?"

"Right."

"Good. Now point me to the ladies' room before we get to work with Joe."

"It's right down there, past the elevators—oh, good morning!"

As I opened the office door for Ivy, I nearly collided with Eddie Breen, my not-very-silent partner. His slight frame was swathed in an ancient but dignified black topcoat, his jug ears glowed rosily against his sparse white hair, and his teeth were clenched on the inevitable unlit cigar.

"Morning, Carnegie. Jesus H. Christ, it's colder than Christian forgiveness out there." Then he spotted Ivy, and the steel-gray eyes brightened. "Ms. Tyler! Pleasure to see you."

Eddie was normally gruff with our clients, believing as he did that enthusiasm for matrimony was possible evidence of an unsound mind. His own interest was all in numbers: taxes, timetables, discounts with vendors, and response rates from direct-mail advertising. We made a perfect team: the young front woman and the veteran back room guy. I even let him boss me around a bit—as long as he doesn't smoke in the office.

But Eddie had been mellowing lately, to the point of actually smiling at certain clients. Most mothers of the bride bored him to tears, but not Ivy Tyler. Eddie wouldn't set foot in an MFC—he was a Nescafé man, and proud of it—but he admired business savvy wherever he saw it.

Apparently that wasn't all Eddie admired. He stepped aside for Ivy to pass, returning her friendly nod, and as she disappeared around the hallway corner, he shook his head and said, "Now that's a fine-looking woman."

"Eddie, you rogue!"

Unseen by either of us, Joe Solveto had emerged from his office. Joe was quite the character: fiendishly shrewd about his business, theatrically debonair about his wardrobe, and wickedly willing to play up his sexual orientation just enough to make Eddie uncomfortable.

"Better keep this man away from the brides, Carnegie. You know how girls love a sailor. Of course, so do I."

Eddie's cigar swiveled irritably. "That's enough of that. Where's the file box I sent over?"

"Fourth floor storeroom." Joe ran a hand through his stylishly mussed fair hair. "Shall I come help you find it?"

My partner refused, of course, and stomped off to the elevator, still in his coat. Joe laughed and turned to me.

"And how was Beautiful Beau?"

I was starting to tell him when my cell phone sounded. Thinking it might be Mike, I gestured an apology at Joe and took the call.

"Carrie, how was your television show? I'm sure you were wonderful!" Mom is the only person who calls me Carrie, and surely the only one capable of such a dubious opinion.

I mouthed the words "my mother" at Joe, who grinned and signaled that he'd be in his office when Ivy returned.

"Hi, Mom."

"Was Beau Paliere just as handsome in person? Did you talk to him after the show?"

"Not really—"

"Because it seems to me that you two would have a lot in common. A lot of shared interests. How long will he be in Seattle?"

"I have no idea, Mom. This isn't a good time—"

But she had rushed to another topic, sounding rather embarrassed—not a typical state for my mother.

"Carrie, about Christmas. I've been meaning to tell you, but I didn't know how to say it."

"Say what?"

"Well, dear, I'm thinking of doing Christmas differently this year. Would you mind terribly if I went on a little trip instead of having you come home? Timmy can't make it anyway, you know . . ."

This was disappointing—even without my brother's company, a few days of visiting with my mother and seeing old friends would have provided some much-needed Christmas cheer. But I didn't mind *terribly,* and wouldn't have said so if I had.

"That's fine, Mom. I want you to suit yourself, you should know that. Where are you going?"

"The Oregon coast. Just a trip with friends, you know, to a little cottage in Cannon Beach. I miss the ocean." Mom had lived in harbor cities for much of her life, and only moved inland to Idaho when a teaching job took her there. "Are you sure it's all right?"

"Of course! In fact, this will work better. I'll spend Christmas with Lily and the boys, and I'll get over to Boise later this winter, when I'm not quite so busy. I could take some extra days at Sun Valley, I hear they do fabulous weddings at the lodge there. But I've got to go now, Mom, I've got a client. Love you, bye!"

All through the menu meeting with Joe and Ivy, my attention was split between assessing various foodstuffs and pondering various questions, like how much Made in Heaven would suffer from my appalling TV debut, and how long it would be before Darwin James would turn up. And how bad Aaron's hangover would be; served him right.

I also recalled Lily's remark that Jason Kraye had teased her brother about not drinking. Perhaps Darwin hadn't fallen off the wagon; perhaps he'd been pushed. *Damn that Jason, anyway.*

"Carnegie?"

"Hmm?"

Ivy sounded peeved. "I said, do you think we've ordered enough foie gras and figs?"

"Sure," I said, covering. Sally must have gotten her genes from somewhere, after all. "Joe's a past master at calculating these things."

"Fine, then, we're done." As we rose, she said pointedly, "You'll let me know how tomorrow goes?"

"Absolutely."

Once she had left, a thought struck me. "Joe, what do you know about Ivy's husband?"

"The notorious Charles?"

"Notorious for what?"

"My dear, you are such a philistine." Joe perched on his desk and crossed one exquisitely tailored leg over the other. "No wonder you get along so well with Eddie. Does he take you to monster-truck rallies?"

"If you're not going to tell me—"

"All right, just to save you from embarrassing yourself with our client. Charles Tyler was a conductor, not a celebrity exactly, but fairly well-known."

"I knew that."

"Did you know he was a composer, too? Modern stuff, the kind that the harder it is to listen to, the better it's supposed to be."

I nodded. "OK, I'm remembering now. British, but he lived here?"

"Exactly. And he still lives here."

Joe himself was an aficionado of early music—recorders and lutes and such. But even as he rejected modern music, he devoured musical gossip. He went on to inform me that everyone in the know was amazed when Tyler, instead of snapping up some soprano, fell for a Seattle cocktail waitress named Ivy, with a little kid in tow. He even bought her a coffee shop to keep her occupied while he toured.

"He was sort of a nineteenth-century gentleman, you know? Edgy modern music, but no taste for technology, and a kind of *noblesse oblige* about lifting Ivy up from the working people. But things went wrong."

Some years after the unexpected marriage, Tyler had suffered a nervous breakdown, and soon after that it came to light that his agent had embezzled most of his money. The great conductor declared bankruptcy and went into seclusion, and his blue-collar wife gradually emerged as a captain of industry.

"The rumor is that Tyler has a degenerative disease," said Joe. "Nerves or brain or something. It's the kind of thing they don't delve into when they profile Ivy in the women's magazines. She protects his privacy at all costs."

I wondered how deep Aaron was going to delve, in the

book he was writing. But then I wondered a lot of things about Aaron—like whether I was being too hard-nosed about him—and I was determined to stop. I thanked Joe and returned to my office.

I meant to put in a full day, what with the arrangements for Tyler/Sanjek and the last-minute details of Buckmeister/Frost, the extremely Christmassy wedding I had coming up on the twenty-third—"Christmas Eve Eve," as Bonnie Buckmeister called it.

But by lunchtime I was yawning, and yearning to burrow deep under Lily's quilts and stay there. Mike still hadn't called me though, which meant that Darwin was still missing. Would I be intruding if I came home early, or would Lily have gone to work after all, just to get away from the silent telephone? *If only I had the houseboat back*—

Then Kelli appeared at my desk, owl-eyed, and banished all thoughts of sleep.

"There's a policeman asking for you!" she whispered, pleased with this melodramatic break in the routine. Kelli dotted the "i" in her name with a little heart. "But he's not wearing a uniform. He called you Car-*nay*-gie. That's not right, is it? I didn't think that was right. Oops, here he comes."

Chapter Seven

DETECTIVE BATES WAS A LARGE, FLORID MAN WITH DULL BLACK hair and a wheezing voice.

"I went to your office," he said with a slight air of grievance, "and your neighbor told me you were working at this address."

I nodded uneasily. "What can I do for you? Is there something wrong?"

He heaved a large, wheezy sigh, sounding even more tired than I felt. "Ms. Kincaid, a man's body was retrieved from the Ship Canal this morning. His wallet was gone, and we need to ID him as soon as possible."

"But why are you telling me?" My own voice sounded faint and faraway.

Bates was watching me closely. Not until later did I realize that he had come in person, instead of telephoning, just so he could observe my expression as I heard the next words.

"Your business card was found in his pants pocket. Would you be willing to take a look at the body?"

Not Aaron. I don't know how my expression looked to Bates, but that was all I could think of, at least at first. *Surely not Aaron. He wasn't drunk enough to fall in the canal.* And then, remembering Lily's tearful face, *Oh, my God, not Darwin...*

Things got a bit hazy after that. My throat closed up and my brain went on automatic pilot, and I didn't even ask whether the drowned man was black or white. I didn't ask anything at all.

Detective Bates talked some more, then he drove me somewhere downtown, and then I was standing in a bright, chilly room, looking through a parted curtain. Behind the curtain was a sheet of glass through which I saw a woman in blue hospital scrubs. She reached down with gloved hands to the draped figure lying before her, and pulled back the cloth to reveal a face.

But not the face I feared to see. The dead man wasn't Aaron, or Lily's brother, either. The pale features, puffy and slack from soaking all night in the cold, dark water, belonged to Jason Kraye. I made the official identification statement, the curtain closed, and I turned away.

It took a moment to find my voice. "He must have fallen in after the party. I guess he couldn't swim. Or maybe he was too drunk to."

"Or maybe he was dead before he hit the water."

"What!"

"I never said he drowned." Once again, Bates was watching me intently. "Someone slashed him across the upper left thigh and severed the femoral artery. This man bled to death."

There was a plastic chair near the door of the horrible room, and I dropped into it, hugging my arms to myself as if to reaffirm the reality of my own warm flesh. Alarmed, Bates softened his manner.

"Can I get you some water? No? Just take deep breaths." He waited a moment, then got back to business. "Ms. Kincaid, I need to ask you some questions about your whereabouts last night. Could you come with me, please?"

Two hours later—two long, repetitive hours—I was back at Joe's with a grinding headache and the mother of all guilty consciences. Not about Jason Kraye's murder, of course. By the time I explained my movements, and provided phone numbers for Frank Sanjek and Lily James and Aaron Gold so they could back me up, Detective Bates seemed satisfied that I was a witness, not a suspect.

At least I think he was.

In any case, with the victim identified and a team dispatched to search the Hot Spot Café, the detective proceeded to grill me about the bachelor party, down to the tiniest detail: who was there, what they said, how they behaved. And, like the dutiful citizen I am, I obliged.

But. Bates didn't ask me whether I'd seen Jason Kraye *after* the party—through binoculars, say—and somehow I hadn't volunteered that information. Why not? Surely what I'd witnessed from the storeroom of Solveto's Catering last night was just drunken horseplay between the best man and Lily's brother. Just high spirits and retsina. Surely Darwin had nothing to do with Kraye's death.

But if I really believed that, why wasn't I speaking up? I sat, pondering this question, while Eddie and Joe left me tactfully alone, and Kelli peeked in at me from time to time, all aquiver with curiosity.

I pondered something else, as well. If I was really, completely over Aaron Gold, why had I immediately feared for his safety when Bates told me that a man had drowned? Why was the thought of Aaron's death such an utter nightmare?

Then a phone call summoned me back into my workday.

"Hey, Kincaid, you standing me up or what? I already ordered my gumbo, and once I eat it, I'm going home to crash. I been up since three."

"Oh, Juice, I'm sorry! I completely forgot."

"That's not like you, Kincaid. But no prob." Juice Nugent was a green-haired, tongue-studded, supernaturally talented young baker. She had once lived on the streets, but now she worked a day job at a bakery downtown and did wedding cakes—her true love—on the side. "So, you want to reschedule?"

With baker's hours, mid-afternoon is dinnertime; our final meeting on Buckmeister/Frost was supposed to be at the Blue Bayou, a Cajun restaurant near Juice's apartment in Ballard. I could hear her slurping a spoonful of gumbo, and suddenly I could smell it, too. The Bayou served up divinely incendiary food all day long, eat in or take out. If angels could eat, they'd get takeout from the Bayou.

Viewing a corpse should have quashed my appetite, I know, but I hadn't had a thing since breakfast, and not much then. And I really love gumbo. And I really hate feeling guilty.

"I'll be there in fifteen minutes. Then I'm going home myself. It's been a long day."

The Bayou's dim little foyer was crowded with regulars, all waiting for their cartons of crab cakes and dirty rice, but the table area was half-empty. Not that Juice is hard to spot anyway, between her chartreuse buzz cut and her Gay Pride buttons. She sat in a booth bedecked with Mardi Gras posters, chowing down and drinking Anchor Steam out of the bottle.

In rare deference to the weather, black leather pants had replaced Juice's customary short shorts, but her customary cowboy boots were very much in evidence. They were alligator today, in a shade of pink that no gator has ever aspired to. Still, the Buckmeister family had bonded with Juice over cowboy boots, so who was I to quibble? I ordered, and we hunkered down to talk serious Christmas cake.

Bonnie Buckmeister and her parents, Buck and Betty—Eddie called them the Killer B's—were thorough-going Yuletide nuts. The groom, Brian Frost, was still out of the country on business; Bonnie had assured me that her Brian adored Christmas just as much as she did.

So Buckmeister/Frost was going to out-Christmas Dickens: a full choir caroling at St. Mark's Cathedral, bridesmaids in holly-green gowns with glowing bouquets of red amaryllis, and a wedding feast served up in the beautiful old domed ballroom of the aptly named Arctic Building on Third Avenue. Joe Solveto had dreamed up a hot chocolate bar, with colorful mugs and candy-cane stir sticks and generous shots of Kahlua. The party favors would be snow globes with Santa Claus inside, and instead of numbering the guest tables, I was naming them after reindeer.

As the bachelor said to the stripper, Merry freakin' Christmas.

But the cake—or rather cakes—would be the showstopper. Juice, an absolute wizard with blown sugar, was creating a series of gift-shaped confections, one minicake per table, each one unique and each exquisitely adorned with sweet, glistening ribbons and edible tree ornaments. The bride and groom would cut into a special, larger cake, with a fudge-frosted Yule log on top to freeze for their first anniversary. All we needed to settle now was the total number of cakes and the delivery arrangements.

This was the kind of work I loved: being creative and yet efficient, enjoying the enthusiasm of other entrepreneurs, getting paid, in effect, to throw a fabulous party. But this afternoon I was depressed and inattentive, and my efforts to hide the fact were futile.

"What's with you today, Kincaid?" Juice finished her beer and belched in contentment.

"Oh, it's nothing. Actually, it's not nothing..."

I floundered to a halt. If I wasn't asking Eddie's or Joe's opinion on this—or, heaven forbid, my mother's—then why ask a former runaway with a punctured tongue? *Because that's the only way to get the answer you want to hear,* said my conscience. I told it to shut up.

"You see, Juice, there's this decision I made..."

Chapter Eight

MY CONSCIENCE IS NO FOOL, EVEN IF I SOMETIMES AM. ONCE I explained my dilemma, carefully substituting "a friend of a friend" for Darwin's name, and "possibly involved in something illegal" for Jason's murder, Juice came down hard on the side of silence, just like I needed her to.

"Man, don't *ever* finger somebody you care about, not even for jaywalking! I mean, don't out-and-out lie to the cops, 'cause they'll nail you, but if they don't ask all the questions, you don't have to give 'em all the answers. And if this friend's friend is innocent like you think, you'll land him in a world of hurt for nothing. Life's enough trouble without making more. You did the right thing."

"That's what I thought," I said, taking heart. "It was only by accident that I saw . . . what I saw, and I'm sure it was completely unrelated to . . . to what happened later. Listen, I'm not quite finished here, so if you want to take off, go ahead. And thanks a lot."

Juice slapped me on the shoulder and left, the fishing lures and other trinkets sewn to her motorcycle jacket jingling as she went. I sat brooding, crumbling a sourdough roll and watching the fragments drift into the remains of my gumbo. If I'd done the right thing, why did I feel so wrong?

"Carnegie?" said a man's voice, and I could tell by the

tone it wasn't the first time he had said it. "Carnegie, are you OK?"

"Mike! What are you doing here?" An inane question—detectives have to eat, too—but his sudden appearance in Juice's seat had startled me unduly. I really, really needed to be asleep. "Is Lily with you?"

"She's at work, and so am I, now." Mike gestured toward the Bayou's foyer. "I'm getting takeout for the troops in the Homicide Van, eight jambalayas and ten bread puddings. We're set up at the Hot Spot. Carnegie, they told me you ID'd the body. Are you sure you're all right? I hope they didn't show you—"

"The wound? No, just his face." I shuddered. "That was enough. It must have been a mugging, don't you think, if someone took his wallet?"

He shook his head. "Unlikely. Why would a mugger be back there behind the Café? Besides, we think Kraye passed out before he was knifed. Damn near half his blood was pooled in the grass. Pardon my French."

"Behind the Café?" I said weakly. "I assumed he was killed on his way home . . ."

"No, it happened right below the deck of the Hot Spot." Mike was distant and preoccupied, almost talking to himself. "A mugger might have dragged the body into the Ship Canal, but from the look of the site, Kraye somehow got up after the attack, staggered down to the water's edge, and fell in. We're searching for the wallet, but I'm betting it just came out of his jacket in the water. Probably out in the Sound by now. I don't believe this killer was looking for money."

"How could anyone *do* such a horrible thing?" It sounded trite as I said it. Mike had surely seen worse. "Of course,

Jason could be a pretty disagreeable person, I know that my-self—"

"He was a person," said Mike. "That's all that matters. There's somebody walking around today, in Seattle or some-where else, who took a life. And I'm going to find him."

"No matter who it is?"

Mike looked at me, and his hazel eyes went cold. It was eerie; I could feel myself transforming from his lover's best friend into Joan Q. Public, potential source of evidence.

"Carnegie, you know something."

"I don't know anything! It's just a little detail—"

"There aren't any 'little' details, not at this stage of an in-vestigation." He leaned eagerly across the table. "At this stage, the odds of solving a murder get worse by the hour. We get lies, we get misinformation, we get people holding back the one piece of the puzzle that could break the case open. If you know, saw, heard, or even *guessed* anything that might be relevant, you need to tell me. Now."

So I told him. About the binoculars, the stripper, Darwin's scuffle in the frozen grass. Everything. Mike pulled out his phone while I was still speaking, and when I finished he strode to the counter, grabbed his order, and left the Bayou at a run. Man on a mission.

My own mission was just as urgent: to let Lily know what I'd done. But she didn't answer her phone at work, and I was reluctant to leave too specific a message on her voice mail, for fear of someone else hearing it. So I settled for ask-ing her to call me as soon as she could, and made my de-jected, slow-motion way back to Vanna.

I drove through the early December darkness to Lily's empty house, and within minutes of opening the door, still fully dressed, I was deep asleep under the fragile shelter of my best friend's quilts . . .

"How *could* you?"

I came to with a heart-thudding lurch and no idea how long I'd been sleeping. My best friend loomed above me like an avenging angel.

"How could you tell them Dar's a murderer? He'd never hurt anybody!"

"Lily, I didn't tell them that. I just told the truth, about what I saw—"

"About your spying, you mean."

"I wasn't spying! Look, I'm sure the police just want to talk with Darwin, like they talked to me. I mean, they even suspected *me* for a little while, but—"

"So that was it! They suspected you, so you accused Darwin instead. That's why you didn't even warn me what was going on. I had to hear it on the phone from some desk sergeant!" Lily raged up and down the living room, between my temporary bed and the boys' Christmas tree. Her coat was still on, her hair disheveled, and she'd left the front door open to the cold. "They called me at work. They're searching for him, and they wanted me to describe his car. Me! As if I'd help them harass my baby brother. And then I called Mike and he said it was you . . . you *bitch*!"

I had never, *never* seen Lily so shockingly out of control. I sat up in bed—my little island refuge in this sea of turmoil—and tried to frame a rational reply.

"Lily, listen to me, please. I tried to call you. And besides, I'm sure the police are talking to everyone from the party, not just Darwin. He's not the only one who was drunk last night."

She stopped pacing to glare at me, her eyes wild. "He's the only one who's black."

"Surely you don't think that here in Seattle—"

"You know all about it, do you, Carnegie? You know all about racial profiling, and what it's like to be a young black man in a white-bread city?"

"Of course I don't. But I know Mike is an honest man! He's going to check for blood on Darwin's clothes, and there won't be any. Then he'll do everything he has to, to prove what really happened. And he'll make sure that Darwin is treated fairly. You trust Mike, don't you?"

Lily, exhausted now, sank down on the foot of the bed and nodded silently. My heart ached for her.

"Come on, Lily, let's get a grip here. Don't you need to pick up Marcus and Ethan?"

She shook her head. "Fran took them home for dinner."

"All right, then. What can we—"

"Lily?" Across the room, Darwin himself was standing in the open doorway.

"Dar!" Lily flew to her brother and wrapped her arms around him. His handsome young face was haggard and grave, and he wore new-looking khakis and a pristine red sweater. Where were last night's jeans and T-shirt? My stomach turned over.

"I'm sorry," he murmured, patting the back of Lily's head as she poured out all her anxiety and love. "I'm so *sorry*, Lil. I thought I'd be OK, just one drink, you know? Just one." He breathed a sigh that came up from deep inside, and held her away from him by the shoulders. "I won't do it again, big sister, I promise. You believe me?"

"Never mind that now, baby. The police are looking for you—"

"They already found me." Darwin smiled, painfully, and jerked a thumb over his shoulder. "Mike said he'd give me five minutes, just to show you in person that I'm OK. I'm going to the station with him, voluntarily and all, and get it down in writing that I'm innocent. But I don't want you coming. I want you to stay home with my nephews."

I joined them at the door and saw Mike standing at the bottom of the steps, his breath visible in the yellow glow of the streetlight.

"Darwin," I said hesitantly, "did Mike tell you that I saw you fighting with Jason?"

"He told me."

Lily folded her arms and turned her back, staying close to her brother.

"Do you understand that I had to tell the truth?"

"Oh, yes," said the young man softly, sounding anything but young. "That's the first thing you learn in recovery, Carnegie. To stop lying, to yourself or anybody else. I understand, and I forgive you."

Then Darwin James kissed his sister, and descended the steps, to face whatever was coming next.

Lily watched them drive away, and stared down the empty street for a few minutes more. When she looked at me, her familiar face was a stranger's.

"He may forgive you," she whispered through her tears, "but I don't think I can."

Chapter Nine

AURORA AVENUE NORTH, ONCE IT CURVES PAST THE LOVELY city park at Green Lake, becomes an unlovely strip of low-end retail. The strip offers, among other delights, an abundance of fast food, used cars, and cheap motel rooms. On the night of that dreary Monday, I sat in one of those rooms and had myself a good cry. Then, double-teamed by a marshmallow mattress and a troubled mind, I had myself some bad sleep.

On Tuesday morning, I sat on the marshmallow's slick polyester bedspread—the orange paisley swirls stayed imprinted on your retina when you closed your eyes—and vowed to find better quarters by nightfall. I could always check into a real hotel, and charge it, but my credit card balances were astronomical already. Along with my father's red hair, I've inherited his horror of debt; surely I could find someone else to crash with.

Lily hadn't kicked me out, exactly. After Darwin left, she just stalked into her bedroom and shut the door. But I got the message. We would sort this out eventually, once Lily was ready, but she was a long way from being ready. *Maybe when Darwin is cleared. If he's cleared.*

I set aside that grim idea and tried to think about my

workday. Top of the list, even before I drove down to Fremont, was to call Ivy Tyler's office.

"I heard all about Jason Kraye," said Ivy, her voice flat with strain. "Horrible. Just horrible."

"Shall we postpone the wedding?"

"I . . . I'm not sure." Even the redoubtable Ivy, it seemed, could be knocked off-balance by murder. "I suppose that's up to Sally."

"And Frank," I pointed out, observing the forms, but knowing full well who would actually make the call.

"Yes, Frank, of course. The police are interviewing him right now in our conference room."

Of course, I thought. *Frank must be a suspect, too.* But the thought of Sally's pushover bridegroom slashing someone to death was absolutely ludicrous. *Still, somebody did it, and if it wasn't Darwin . . .*

"—rumors everywhere, and no one's getting any work done." Ivy heard herself sounding callous. "I mean, it's only natural that a tragedy like this is disruptive to . . . Dammit, Carnegie, I sound like one of my own PR people. It's a mess, that's all. It's horrible and it's a mess."

I couldn't have agreed more. "Ivy, we can talk about the wedding later—"

"No," said the woman who was holding her own against Starbucks. "No, when decisions have to be made, you make them. Can you come downtown to my apartment, before you go see Kevin Bauer? Sally and Frank can meet us there."

"Before? . . . Oh, right. Sure, give me about an hour." I had forgotten all about my afternoon field trip to Habitat. *And who knows how long that's going to take,* I fretted. *Maybe I should just live in Vanna.*

On that note, my next call should have been a bitter complaint to my landlady. But I ran out of steam when I heard the recording of her cultured, quavering voice.

"This is Mrs. Frederick Castle, and I am not here to speak with you. You may leave a message if you wish, but please speak slowly and distinctly..."

Mr. Frederick Castle had been dead for decades; his widow was an old lady of the old school. And it wasn't her fault about the dry rot, after all.

Sighing, I settled for leaving a ladylike request that she call me back at her convenience. Then I phoned Joe's office, to check in with Eddie. I didn't tell him about the motel, just that I'd overslept and had a meeting downtown.

"Long as you're down there, Carnegie, why don't you go see Boris and have him check over those estimates for Buckmeister/Frost? Get 'em signed in blood this time. He keeps changing the numbers for the pewbacks and the table-tops. Last time I called him, he hung up on me!"

Boris Nevsky, known more or less affectionately as Boris the Mad Russian Florist, was a genius with flowers but a dunce with customer relations, and sometimes I had to run interference for him.

"Eddie, you know perfectly well that Boris can't guarantee the price of fresh flowers down to the penny. He's always close, though."

"Hmph. He's always a pain in the behind. Just because you used to go out with him, doesn't mean he can—"

"Eddie, don't start."

"Sorry, sorry. I forgot you had a nasty shock yesterday. You need some Christmas cheer, sister. How about stopping in at the library, maybe take Lily out for a nice lunch? She always perks you up."

I flinched, glad he couldn't see my expression. "Lily's awfully busy lately. Maybe another day."

Eddie was right; my seasonal spirit was wearing thin this morning. And it wore even thinner when I arrived downtown to find the Bon Marche parking garage already jammed with early-rising Christmas shoppers. I wound my way to a spot at the very top level, open to the icy wind off the Sound, and trotted down the hill on Stewart Street to the Pike Place Market, past the ubiquitous Salvation Army Santas and the inescapable Yuletide Muzak. *Comfort and joy, my foot.*

Ivy Tyler had a large and secluded house in the country somewhere, but for business entertaining or late nights at the office, she kept an apartment in one of the Pike Place Market buildings. She was one flight up from all the produce stalls and the fishmongers and the multitude of shops, and right behind the big neon clock that's been glowing next to the big neon "Public Market" sign since the 1920's. It was typical Ivy, to locate her *pied-à-terre* right in the hectic heart of the city.

I'd been there once before, when Dorothy Fenner first introduced me to Ivy, and had time during that visit to admire the building's amenities—even the hallways had classy side tables and lamps, like a gracious old hotel—and the apartment's view of Puget Sound, where the squat white Washington State ferries moved among the mounded green of the islands. Time, too, to appreciate Ivy's taste, which ran to postmodern furniture and exquisite little oil paintings and bits of statuary.

Today, though, there was no time to do anything but duck and cover. The bride was going ballistic.

"Postpone?" I could hear Sally's near-shriek even before

Ivy opened the apartment door to me. "Postpone *my* wedding because of a drunken brawl at *your* stupid bachelor party?"

"It wasn't a brawl." Frank's voice was subdued but sullen, a heels-dug-in voice. "Jase was murdered. Don't you think, just out of respect—"

"Oh, please! When did Jason Kraye ever respect anybody else?" Sally, in a pale jacket trimmed with paler fur, stood defiantly in the living room, tossing her silky blonde hair and looking daggers at her beloved. When she saw me, and noticed Ivy's frown, she tempered her manner—but only a little.

"All *right,* Mother, I'm sorry he's dead, but I've been planning this for a year and a half, for God's sake. How do you reschedule a New Year's Eve wedding? Put it off till next December? Postponing would ruin *everything.* Besides, I've been lifting weights for months to get buff for my dress. I can't keep this up forever."

Ivy forbore to comment on her daughter's travails. "Let's just sit down and discuss this, shall we? Tell me, Frank, would it be important to you to delay the wedding? And for how long?"

"I...I don't really know." The groom's mild, good-natured features had tightened into a perplexed frown, and his voice, dull with shock, kept trailing off into silence. "Jason kind of volunteered himself to be best man...He was my roommate at the frat, and we went snowboarding together and all, but we weren't really that close...I still can't believe...I mean, jeez, *murder?*"

Scratch Frank off the list, I thought. *No way did this guy kill anyone.*

He looked at me in appeal. "Carnegie, is there some kind of etiquette rule about this? What do you think we should do?"

"It's not my decision, and there's no rule," I told him. "It's just a question of how you and Sally feel about proceeding. Maybe you should take some time to think it over."

"I don't need any more time!" said Sally. She flopped down into the postmodern curves of Ivy's purple sofa—in that price range, it's probably called eggplant—and folded her arms like a nine-year-old facing a plate of, well, eggplant. "I want to go ahead, and that's all there is to it."

The phone rang then, and Ivy surprised me by rushing to pick it up, apparently forgetting her daughter for some other, more urgent concern. I assumed it was MFC business until I heard her first words.

"Charles! Did you sleep at all? I hated to leave you this morning, but Dr. Lawrence said . . . yes, she's here, they both are. Of course." She offered the phone to Sally, with a murmured, "He says he finally got some rest."

Sally also surprised me. She sat up straight to take the call from her stepfather, and spoke with a deferential solicitude quite unlike her usual snap and snarl.

"Here I am, Charles. Yes, it's dreadful about Jason. Frank and I feel just terrible. In fact, Frank thinks we should delay the wedding . . . really? Could you tell him that? I'm sure you're right, thank you!"

Triumphantly, the bride presented the phone to her groom, and I watched, fascinated, as Frank in his turn grew solemn and respectful. Even in retirement, Ivy's husband must be quite a formidable personage. After a few "yes, sirs" and "I understand, sirs," Frank ended the call and looked at the three of us, all watching him expectantly.

"Charles says he feels pretty strongly that we shouldn't delay. He says it won't help Jason any. I suppose he's right, isn't he? So I guess we're good to go."

Chapter Ten

SALLY SQUEALED AND HUGGED FRANK, NINE YEARS OLD AGAIN for a moment, and then slithered into a full-body embrace that was anything but PG-13. *So that's why he puts up with all the tantrums.* Ivy smiled at them indulgently, and not for the first time I marveled at how a brass-tacks businesswoman could turn so quickly to mush. I would have slapped the girl silly by now.

"When you have the time," I pointed out dryly, "you'll need to think about a new best man."

"Oh, yeah," said Frank, over Sally's shoulder. "I could ask Craig Clark, I guess, or Lou Schulman . . ."

As if being best man were some minor favor: lend me ten bucks, be my best man. *Well, not everyone cares about tradition* . . . My own phone chirped, and the display showed Mrs. Castle's number.

Eager for good news, and irritated with Frank, I excused myself to take the call in Ivy's sleek little kitchen. But the news wasn't good.

"Another *week?*" I sagged against the stainless-steel fridge in dismay. "Can't they do the new plumbing any quicker? . . . Oh. I understand, Mrs. Castle. No, I'm not at my friend's place anymore, that didn't work out. Well, don't worry about it. I'll find a motel. Bye."

"Motel?" Ivy was standing in the kitchen doorway. "Carnegie, what's going on?"

I explained the situation, and she responded in high executive gear. "You'll stay here, of course. The guest room is always made up, and I don't stay over all that often anyway, especially when Charles isn't well. Is your luggage at Solveto's?"

"Actually, it's in my van. But are you sure—"

"Frank can bring it up for you." She strode back into the living room. "Frank, take your hands off my daughter for a minute and run down to Carnegie's van with her."

So that was that. Within the hour I was unloaded, unpacked, and walking down Post Alley toward Boris Nevsky's studio in Pioneer Square, enjoying the remarkably blue December sky and feeling ridiculously cheered to be Ivy Tyler's houseguest. *I'm not just a consultant; I'm a friend.* That felt good.

I was even pleased that Sally's wedding was still on, and not just because of the money. Everybody's got their own ideal New Year's Eve, and mine involves music and dancing, not video rentals or a good book. I wouldn't have a date for the Tyler/Sanjek bash, but at least I'd be at a party at midnight. *Maybe I'll kiss a waiter, or one of the drummers. Or all of the drummers . . .*

I stopped at an MFC, where a table full of preschoolers was crayoning Christmas cards, and treated myself to a piping hot latte with a shot of chocolate syrup. Sipping as I walked, I positively beamed good will at the passersby. *Lily and I will make up soon; I'm sure we will. And when I do move back home, I'll have actual water pressure in the bathroom; imagine that.*

The sky was blue but the air was biting, and I was grateful to step inside the fragrant warmth of Nevsky Brothers Flowers. There weren't actually any brothers, just Boris and his Aunt Irina, the shy and tiny crone who tended the bucket shop up front. Today Irina was surrounded by her usual tubs of single irises and ready-to-go roses, but also by gift-wrapped pots of scarlet poinsettia and gaily beribboned mistletoe balls.

I was admiring them when her nephew blew into the room like a gust of wind off the steppes of Mother Russia.

"Kharrnegie!" Boris pulverized my rib cage with a grizzly bear hug. The Mad Russian did nothing by halves. "You come to luke at Tyler flowers! I have outdone even myself. Which only I could be the one to do, no?"

"Only you, Boris. But let's get Bonnie Buckmeister's numbers nailed down first, OK? Do you really need six dozen amaryllis?"

We settled on five dozen, with corresponding quantities of ruby-red hypericum berries, bright-leafed English holly, and crimson roses—not to mention a forest-full of pine and cedar boughs—enough to turn the Arctic Building's ball-room into one big Christmas card.

Boris signed the estimate impatiently, then drew me into his studio. This was a high, brick-walled space, banked with flower coolers and ranked with shelves of wire, ribbon, foam, and other necessaries for making floral magic.

Down at the far end, two of Boris's darkly handsome as-sistants—all named Sergei, as far as I could tell—were work-ing with lilies and stephanotis. I closed my eyes and breathed in the heady scent that floated above the smoky va-por from the grand gilt samovar in the corner. Everything about the space—the delicious perfumes, the tender shapes and textures, the heart-lifting colors—was as far as could be from the cold white chamber where I'd last seen Jason Kraye. I could happily have stayed for hours.

On the long table in the middle of the room, Boris spread a series of colored sketches for Sally's flowers. We needed only two bouquets and a few corsages, because the ceremony itself would be small and private: just the bridal pair and one attendant each, plus the four parents and Frank's sister. They would gather at six P.M. on New Year's Eve in a judge's chambers at the King County Courthouse, and then dine in a private room at an elegant bistro farther uptown. All very discreet and intimate.

The reception to follow would be quite another kettle of martinis: an all-night party at Neurolux, a trendy new Belltown club that we planned to decorate in high, not to say startling, style. Other brides chose soft, girlish color themes for their weddings: dusty rose and powder blue, or peaches and cream. But not Sally Tyler. Sally had opted for black and silver. She was even wearing a black gown, a long bias-cut number in silk charmeuse that made her look like a 1940's movie siren. As Eddie would put it, *va-va-voom*.

I had to admit, it was fun getting away from pastels for a while—and from Bonnie's relentless red and green. I planned to drape the interior of the Neurolux with black velvet hangings, and set the tables with silver candelabras holding ebony tapers. At midnight of the old year, the guests would be showered with glittering confetti, dazzled by a laser light show, and serenaded by an African percussion ensemble. At Sally's insistence, the guest list was long on stylish young people and short on her famous mother's business colleagues. The buff bride would have the limelight all to herself.

As always with a Nevsky Brothers wedding, the bride's bouquet was both gorgeous and unique: against her black satin, Sally would carry a scepter of enormous white calla lilies, each bloom as pale and shapely as the bride herself, the long stems braided with black velvet ribbon. For the Neurolux, Boris had designed silver pedestals draped with thick garlands—he called them flower boas—of anemones and roses in deep burgundy and indigo, with wandering strands of bird's-foot ivy and dangling clusters of fat black grapes. Very Deco, very decadent.

I *ooh*'d and *aah*'d over the sketches, as I always did. It was our little ritual, and Boris and I both enjoyed it. But then came a less-enjoyable interrogation.

"So, Kharnegie, you don't speak of Aaron anymore. Why is this?"

"I told you already, Boris, he was spending a lot of time in Boston. He's back now, but we've agreed that it's not working out. It wasn't serious, anyway."

"Bah!" Boris swept up his sketches, almost toppling his ever-present, ever-potent glass of tea. Russians must have asbestos stomachs. "Not serious, she says to me! First her eyes light up like candle when she speaks of him, and now she says not serious. Did he break your heart, my Kharnegie? I will break his head!"

"Leave it alone, Boris, would you? Aaron just wasn't the right kind of guy for me."

"And what is right kind, eh?"

I answered quietly, half to myself, as I tucked the estimate and sketches in my briefcase. "I don't know, exactly. Someone more straightforward, not such a smooth talker. Someone *solid*."

Boris clamped a brawny arm around my shoulders.

"Then you should come back to me! There is no one more solid than Boris Nevsky!"

I laughed aloud at the thought. Then I noticed that the Mad Russian wasn't laughing. *Uh-oh*.

"Come on now, Boris, we settled all this."

"But we should settle again, different!"

"I don't think so."

I began to put on my coat, but Boris snatched up my hand and kissed it. I pulled it away, more roughly than I meant to, and took a few paces back. We stared at each other, wordless, uncertain. The Sergeis, I realized, had made themselves scarce.

Boris wears his heart on his face. He glowered, but only for a moment, and then I saw a flicker of regret, which gave way in turn to a crafty grin that gleamed through his thicket of black beard.

"Kharrnegie! You don't know joke when you see one!"

He laughed, a little too heartily, and I joined in, much relieved. I liked Boris, and the way things were going, I couldn't spare any friends. Besides, Nevsky Brothers was one of my best vendors.

We ended the encounter with smiles that were only slightly forced, back on the safe shore of friendship. Good old Boris. I gave him a quick bear hug of my own, then I fetched Vanna and headed north out of Seattle, to what I blithely expected would be a routine appointment at Habitat Coffee.

Chapter Eleven

DOES ANYTHING ON EARTH SMELL AS GOOD AS COFFEE? NO. Not bacon, not lilacs, not even new bread. As I waited for Kevin Bauer in Habitat's front office, I was getting a contact high from the dark-roasted atmosphere, and loving every deep breath. Now that I had a bed for the night, my trip out of town was feeling like a mini-holiday.

The roasting plant was nestled in a forested area near the little town of Snohomish. (The Snohomish River is fed by the Skykomish and the Snoqualmie, not to be confused with the Skagit, or for that matter, the Klickitat or the Dosewallips. I love Washington State.)

I got off the freeway early, just for the change, and drove north through the odd jumble of development along Highway 9. One minute you're cruising past some ticky-tacky housing development called Ridgecrest Meadowview Estates, next minute there's an outlet mall, and then you're back in deep stands of Douglas fir and big leaf maple, and the occasional Christmas-tree farm.

The maples were bare this time of year, of course, but in spring the Habitat property would be positively sylvan. A grassy field surrounded the series of low, interconnected buildings, and a towering Doug fir made a backdrop for a massive steel silo.

Most of the complex was drab and industrial—no photo op there—but the front office doubled as a visitor center, with a wooden porch and an old-fashioned air of welcome. Inside, I was greeted by a smiling woman in her early forties, wearing long handmade earrings and her brown hair in braids. She took my name, offered me a candy cane from the little decorated tree on her desk, and asked me to wait just a moment.

The visitor center was a single large room, painted in Habitat's signature red and white, and crammed with fascinating coffee-themed paraphernalia. A row of fine old cabinets in glass-fronted oak held displays of coffee cans and bags going back decades, like a general store for caffeine fanatics. Above them hung a long row of framed burlap coffee sacks from Costa Rica, Panama, Indonesia, all with exotic names and eye-catching folk-art logos.

On the opposite wall, a series of lively posters illustrated the whole shade-grown issue. Coffee that's farmed in the open, they declared, forms an ecological desert, shunned by wildlife and greedy for oil-based fertilizers. Indigenous shade trees, if left in place over the coffee bushes, will fix nitrogen in the soil, discourage weeds and erosion, and provide shelter for the billions of warblers, orioles, and other songbirds that funnel through Mexico and Central America every winter.

Hmm. I'd always passed on Habitat beans because of their price, but now I made a mental note to pick up a bag. *Who can say no to a homeless warbler?*

The far end of the room was a sort of coffee-roasting museum, with antique scales, grinders, and roasters bearing neatly-typed cards explaining their use and history. One glass-topped display was missing its card, and the contents were puzzling: an array of bent nails, bottle caps, gum wrappers, pebbles, keys, even a lottery ticket, printed in a language I didn't recognize. Also a small pen knife, nicked and dirty. I was bending closer, curious, when I heard a gruff voice behind me.

"Imagine finding those in your mug."

The man who spoke was fortyish and six foot one—funny how fast we gauge these things—with arresting blue-gray eyes in a square, weathered, notably unsmiling face. He was a redhead, though not a copper-top like me. His short, straight hair was the color of chili powder, the dark smoky kind, and it continued down into a matching, neatly-trimmed beard. Crisp corduroys and a pressed flannel shirt completed the effect: casual, but controlled.

"In your *mug*?" I repeated.

"That's what I said. All that debris was found among the beans, sometime in the last few years. We sieve stuff out or snag it with a heavy-duty magnet along the line from the warehouse to the final package. I'm Kevin Bauer. Come on up to my office and we'll start your tour."

Upstairs, with his door discreetly closed, Bauer changed his tour-guide tune. "This press party is a lousy idea, you know that?"

"I . . . I guess that's something you'd have to discuss with Ivy."

"I *have* discussed it with Ivy, at length. The woman's a goddamn brick wall." He scowled at his telephone, as if she were still at the other end of the line. "The buyout's a good move for Habitat, I'm not saying it isn't, but I don't need a bunch of freeloading reporters and MFC management types spilling chips and dip all over the damn place and attracting vermin to my beans."

"Aren't you a management type yourself?"

Bauer glanced at me sharply. "I suppose I am, but my job is roasting coffee, not putting on a show for the *Wall Street Journal*."

"Well, my job is to plan successful events for my clients, and my client wants to hold a reception and press conference here. So can we get on with it?"

He scowled again and yanked open a desk drawer. First he handed me a sample bag of Habitat coffee beans; apparently, even unwelcome visitors got one. Then he pulled out a small paper envelope and tossed it to me. "Hair net. We're a food-processing facility, we've got rules. Are you wearing any rings?"

I showed him the hammered-silver band that I'd bought myself the week before in the Market.

"Not a problem," said Bauer. "We just worry about stones that could come loose, earrings that could fall off, that kind of thing. You see what I mean about a bad idea?" He didn't wait for me to answer. "And for God's sake, keep quiet about MFC out there. I don't want to tell my people till next week, after our company Christmas party."

"I'm just a casual visitor," I said solemnly, scooping my hair into the industrial-strength net. "I won't say a word, and if you give me your home number, I'll call you there with any questions I have about the arrangements. Fair enough?"

"Fair enough," he allowed, and we set off on our tour.

It was fascinating, really, even with my ill-tempered companion—and Bauer warmed up as we went, his pride in the operation gradually overcoming his annoyance at my errand.

We began by going outdoors and entering the Habitat

warehouse from the gravel parking lot, the way that party guests would arrive. And what a sight would greet them when they got inside: the vast space, open in the center, was surrounded by row upon row of shelving units that ran at right angles to the warehouse walls, like the stacks of a giant's library.

The units rose in lofty tiers that stretched up from the concrete floor at our feet to the shadows of the girdered roof above our heads. Some of the shelves were crammed with stacks of unassembled cardboard boxes, or huge spools of laminated bags destined for the supermarket, in Habitat's signature red-and-white design. But most of the space around and above us was filled with rough burlap sacks, fat with coffee beans. Thousands of sacks, billions of beans. Just looking up at them made me feel caffeinated.

The aisles between the tiers were barely wide enough for a single one-man forklift. Three or four of the toylike, bright green machines were grunting and whining their way around the area, busy as ants, bearing unwieldy-looking pallets of coffee sacks that looked far too top-heavy for their little electric motors. Bauer called them "VNA reach trucks, VNA meaning 'very narrow aisle.'" But they looked like forklifts to me.

As we walked, Bauer reeled off more facts and way too many figures: 132 (pounds of beans in a sack), 600 A.D. (when coffee was first consumed in ancient Ethiopia), three billion (cups the world now drinks in a day). I made the appropriate interested noises, but statistics bore me. I was thinking party.

A red-and-white color scheme, of course, with some of those nice bright posters, and maybe stacks of Habitat boxes. The boxes could wall off a space inside the warehouse for the speeches and the buffet, and I could give strict orders to keep refreshments inside the perimeter, and out of the coffee. That ought to satisfy the dour Mr. Bauer.

The forklift operators, like the rest of the workers, just nodded nonchalantly as we went by. No putting on a show of extra effort for Mr. Bauer. In fact, the atmosphere throughout the plant was brisk and upbeat, a happy, hard-working family, with good-humored chatter and lots of personal snapshots and funny clippings taped here and there. I wondered how these folks would feel about joining the MFC family, with Ivy Tyler as the stepmom. *Not my problem, thank goodness.* Sometimes managing Eddie was all I could handle.

Beyond the warehouse, but connected to it, was the large, windowless roasting area. It felt like a submarine movie, if the sub had high ceilings: steel walls and bare light fixtures, hoppers and catwalks, pneumatic ducts and tubes snaking everywhere, moving the beans from one stage of processing to another. Amid the constant thrumming roar of machinery, I half-expected to hear a sonar *ping,* and some square-jawed actor shouting, "Dive, dive!"

But submarines don't smell like fresh coffee, and they probably don't have parts labeled "Made in Perugia, Italy." One wide upright duct, thus labeled, caught my eye. It had a square transparent panel in it, and behind the panel a swarm of dark brown coffee beans raced in blurring, ricocheting flight *upward,* like furious bees from a shaken hive.

"Cool!"

I'd broken my vow of silence, but Bauer smiled for the first time. "That's what everybody says. They're coming from over here, where the actual roasting takes place."

He pointed at a huge, gleaming tank with an octopus of pipes and tubes emerging from it. We walked over, and he pulled on a handle sticking out from the tank's side wall. The handle drew forth a steel cylinder, open along the top, with a cluster of dark beans nestled inside. The warm, intense fragrance rising up from them was nearly erotic.

"This is called a 'tryer.' Every roaster has one, from the oldest to the newest. You can computerize all you want, but you still have to—"

"Wake up and smell the coffee?"

The smile broadened. "Exactly. You listen to the beans pop as they heat up, and then you use the tryer to look at them again and again, until they're just the way you want them. This batch needs a few seconds more."

He reinserted the tryer, winked at the roaster operator, and went on with his technical spiel, while I went on with my imaginary reception. It had become an imaginary wedding reception, to tell the truth, a mental habit I have whenever I find an intriguing venue. *We could put huge tubs of champagne on the forklifts, and dress the tables in those cool burlap sacks, and serve espresso mousse cake studded with coffee beans . . .*

"This is the nerve center of the whole place," Bauer was saying. "Hang on to the rail, OK?"

He led me up a narrow set of steel stairs to a glassed-in office overlooking the roasting floor. The glass walls were hung with venetian blinds, swiveled open at present, and the single large desk in the middle was surrounded by panels of dials, lights and switches, and three different computer monitors.

"We've got a PC at every workstation," said Bauer, "and Lou Schulman here is the network mastermind. Aren't you, Lou?"

The brawny, broad-shouldered young man named Lou

looked up from his work. He wore a dingy sweatshirt, a Habitat baseball cap on backward, and, once he saw me, an expression of intense surprise.

Well, well, well. I took in the lantern jaw, the beady eyes, and the thick-fingered hands that lay slack on his keyboard. *If it isn't Mr. Garlic from the bachelor party.*

"You've met?" said Bauer into the uncomfortable silence.

"Briefly." No point embarrassing the guy. And besides, if Lou was a friend of Jason Kraye's as well as Frank Sanjek's, then he'd just had some bad news. *What's a little drunken groping, compared to murder?*

The network mastermind rose from his rolling desk chair in a clumsy fluster. Apparently, all the leering bravado of Sunday night had come out of a retsina bottle. In the daylight, he looked older than I had thought—thirty at least, maybe more.

"I-I heard about Jase." He was blinking rapidly, and he spoke in an awkward mumble. "I heard that you, that you were the one—"

"I identified the body," I said gently. "Were you and Jason close friends?"

"No!" The vehemence of the denial startled me. Lou began to fidget with the coiled cord of his telephone, not meeting my eyes. "I mean, we were friends, but not real good ones, you know?"

Kevin Bauer glanced from his employee to me and back again, his wide brown forehead creased in concern. "A friend of yours died? Listen, if you want some time off, you just—"

"*No,*" said Lou again. "I'm telling you, I barely knew him."

He lifted his hands in protest, but his fingers were still tangled in the phone cord. The cord lassoed Lou's empty coffee mug, yanking it to the edge of the desk, and the mug did a half-gainer off the edge and landed right at my feet. Instinctively, I reached down to try and break the fall.

Too late. Instead of the mug, my fingers met the spray of broken fragments that ricocheted from the concrete floor. When I stood up again, I had a deep gash on my left hand, and blood gushing all over my best dove-gray suit.

Chapter Twelve

"HELL AND *DAMNATION!*" I SAID, AND I'M AFRAID I DIDN'T stop there. My father was in the merchant marine, after all.

Both men reacted instantly. Lou gave a horrified shout of alarm and shrank back from the gore. Kevin Bauer, in contrast, whipped out a folded handkerchief, pressed it to my palm, and raised my arm above shoulder level, to stem the blood flow. I just stood there and let him, while continuing to express my displeasure in the language of the sea. I'm an awful baby about pain, and my hand hurt like a bitch.

"I'll call 911!" said Lou, coherent at last.

"Don't be silly," I snapped. "It's just a cut."

But a crimson stain had already soaked through the handkerchief. Bauer let go of me and rummaged in a nearby locker for a first-aid kit. Some gawking workers appeared in the office doorway but he waved them off, and let the blue plastic kit clatter to the floor as he grabbed out a roll of sterile gauze.

"Let me see ... no, don't move the handkerchief, just keep this on top of it ... Can you hold it there while we drive?"

"Drive where?" But I knew where. I had a rendezvous with some needle and thread.

Fiona, the pleasant post-hippie from the office, did the

actual driving, while her boss sat in back with me and held my hand. Literally. I had stopped swearing by then and gone into stiff-upper-lip mode as I stared unseeing at the woods and the ticky-tacky houses rushing by. I was chiefly aware of two things: the determination not to cry, and the warm, reassuring feel of Kevin Bauer's hands clasped around mine.

"Here we are," Fiona announced, pulling into a shopping plaza near the freeway. "It's small, but they know what they're doing."

The Snohomish Community Clinic was a storefront squeezed between a running-shoe emporium and a discount eyeglass place. Once inside, Fiona sat with me in the examination room while her boss filled out paperwork at the front counter.

"I don't think it's too bad," she ventured, watching me wiggle my fingertips beyond the gauze pad.

"Just a flesh wound," I said, mock-heroic. "At least I didn't bleed in the coffee. He would have thrown me out on my ear."

"Kevin's not quite *that* fanatic."

"But almost?"

"It's his life," she said simply. And then, gingerly testing our newfound camaraderie, "You're from MFC, aren't you?"

I was caught off guard. "That's supposed to be—"

"A secret, I know. But you can't have a series of nighttime meetings with the great Ivy Tyler and not have it get around!"

"Fiona, I'm sorry, I can't talk about this."

"I don't expect you to, really. We all know what's coming. There have been rumors for months, and everyone's worried about layoffs." She smiled tolerantly. "We figure Kevin's waiting until after Christmas, so everyone can have their holiday and get their year-end bonus."

"Nice of him."

"He's a nice guy. Did he tell you how he got into the business?"

"No, how?" She was trying to distract me from my injury, I could tell, but I was quite willing to be distracted.

"About ten years ago he got an inheritance from his grandfather, and went bumming around South America for a while. He'd done graduate work in ornithology, so he was interested in songbird migration and the whole biodiversity issue. When he got back, he wanted to do something practical to help, something beyond research."

"Something like Habitat?"

She nodded, her braids swinging. "He used the rest of grandpa's money to buy a roasting plant and convert it to a strictly shade-grown operation. He's absolutely passionate about it."

Passion for a good cause; very appealing. But I needed information about a less appealing man. "And Lou Schulman, is he a crusader, too?"

Fiona grimaced. "Only for beer and women. He was the star techie at some dot-com that went under, and according to Kevin, he's a brilliant programmer. But he's Clueless Lou in the social skills department. Kind of crude, in fact." Then, trying to be fair, she added, "He's an asset to Habitat, though, and that's what counts. And he felt terrible about your accident."

"Tell him I'll live."

That was the doctor's opinion, too. One tetanus shot and a fancy bandage later, with the throbbing in my hand nicely blunted by a stiff dose of painkillers, I was ready to go home.

Fiona went out to warm up her car—it was almost dark already, and quite cold—while Kevin paid the clinic bill and helped me on with my coat.

"I called Ivy," he told me. "She said she'll be waiting for you at her apartment, in case you need anything tonight."

"I'll be fine. It didn't even need stitches. If you could just drop me back at my van—"

"Fiona will drop both of us," said Kevin Bauer in a no-nonsense tone. "I also called a friend of mine who lives in Snohomish and commutes to downtown Seattle. He'll give me a ride back up here after I deliver you and your van to Ivy's place. No, no arguments. I'm driving you home."

I might have resented the take-charge tone if I'd been feeling better. And not exiled from my houseboat. And not on the outs with my best friend. As it was, I had no objection to someone else taking charge, at least for the next hour.

Traffic was heavy, as it always is on I-5 these days, and between the glare of oncoming headlights and the warmth of Vanna's heater, I was half-asleep for most of the trip. My chauffeur drove skillfully and kept a companionable silence—a skill in itself—until we exited the freeway.

"Where shall I park?"

"What? Oh, there's an overnight garage on First Avenue. I'll show you."

He docked the van neatly in her new berth, and insisted on paying for parking and walking me to my door. We even made some small talk, admiring the Christmas lights that twinkled all around. I paused at the entrance of Ivy's building, not sure if she would welcome a business associate like Kevin inside her personal domain. Kevin and I stood facing each other on the sidewalk, suddenly awkward.

"Well," I said intelligently.

"Well," he concurred.

"Thanks for the ride, and the tour . . ."

Kevin laughed out loud, a nice deep laugh. "And the blood and the pain? Thank you for being so reasonable. Of course, you're stealing company property . . ."

He reached out a hand, as if to touch my face, and I held my breath. *What's happening here? And do I want it to happen?* Then he slid the forgotten hair net off my head, and slipped it into his pocket.

I laughed myself, a little nervously, and shook my hair loose. "You should talk! I could sue you for dangerous factory conditions."

"We can't have that. Can I bribe my way out of it?" The streetlight made a spark in his blue-gray eyes. "Say, with dinner tomorrow night? I'll bring my own car this time."

I took a deep breath, and exhaled some of the tension that had been building up somewhere between my shoulder blades ever since Sunday. "I'd like that. I'd like that very much."

"Wonderful. I'll meet you here at seven."

"Sounds good. Although . . ." I said impulsively, and then once the word was out I had to keep going. "Although if you came earlier, we could walk around and listen to the carolers? Tomorrow's the Figgy Pudding event, it's a fund-raiser for the food bank?" *Hell, I'm talking like a teenage girl.* "People dress up in costumes and sing on the street corners, and then there's a big finale on an outdoor stage. It's really fun, I mean, it is if you like Christmas, because if you *don't* like Christmas, I guess it's kind of corny . . ."

"I was born corny," said Kevin Bauer. "And I love Christmas. See you at six."

Ivy had given me a spare key to her apartment, but being

one-handed, I just knocked, still smiling about Kevin's last remark. Ivy drew me inside with a warm but careful hug, the mentor giving way to the mother.

"Here, I'll take your briefcase. Does it hurt? Let me get you a drink, you poor thing..."

She steered me to the living room, and my smile froze. Ivy's angular steel coffee table and her eggplant-colored couch were strewn with files, photographs, and newspaper clippings. Sitting there in the midst of the them, shutting off a tape recorder and tapping rapidly away on a laptop, was Aaron Gold.

"Hello there, Carnegie." He glanced up at me, outwardly friendly, but his chocolate-brown eyes were expressionless. "Ivy mentioned you were staying here. I was just telling her that we have some friends in common. Sorry about your hand."

"Small world, isn't it?" said my hostess. She seemed quite pleased about it.

"Very small. I . . . need to change my clothes. Excuse me."

When I returned, in jeans, Ivy was emerging from the kitchen with a round teak tray. It held a plate piled with sandwiches, a bottle of expensive-looking Scotch, and three generous glasses of ice.

"New Zealand cheddar," she announced, "from De Laurenti's downstairs. And a single malt, much deserved after all this talking. Aaron, my friend, I'm talked out. Let's call it a night. Carnegie, did I tell you that Aaron's doing a book about Meet for Coffee?"

"I think you did, yes." I lowered myself into a chair that matched the eggplant sofa. Pain meds or no, a drink suddenly seemed like a good idea. "It must be quite a saga."

"With quite a main character." Aaron grinned at Ivy. He

seemed perfectly at ease, but then, he'd been forewarned I was coming, the bum.

I sipped some Scotch and attempted some ESP. *Go away, Aaron. Finish your drink and go home. I don't want to see you or think about you. Or think about us. Go away.* That's the trouble with being a guest; you can't throw the other guests out.

"Remember," said Ivy, "some of those stories *don't* go in the book. Like the one I just told you about the governor..."

They chuckled and ate sandwiches and chatted, winding down from their interview for what seemed an interminable time. I'd lost my appetite, so I went on sipping and beaming thought waves. No dice. The man was rooted to the sofa—as I seemed to be myself.

Finally they were done eating, and Aaron pulled a pack of cigarettes and his trusty stainless-steel lighter from a shirt pocket. I hated his smoking, and he knew it, but I was surprised at his discourtesy to Ivy. Then Ivy surprised me by holding up two fingers in a V. Aaron lit a cigarette and gave it to her, then lit one for himself. They'd obviously done this before. Ivy caught me watching them.

"I'm trying to quit," she said sheepishly, "but you know how it is."

"I don't think Carnegie does know," said Aaron, with a damnably innocent expression. "You don't smoke, as I recall?"

"No, I don't. What a good memory you have."

I meant it as an exit line, but as I began to excuse myself, Ivy got a call on her kitchen phone. The moment she left the room, Aaron set down his glass and spoke to me urgently.

"Stretch, we need to talk."

"We're done talking," I said. "And don't call me that. Acquaintances don't have nicknames."

"Well, what did you want me to tell her? That I've never heard of you?"

"Of course not," I conceded. " 'Friends in common' is fine. But let's just leave it at that. I don't want any more arguments."

"Neither do I. In fact, I'd never have . . . said what I did, if I hadn't been drinking at that damn party." He frowned at the memory. "I owe you an apology for barging into Solveto's in the first place."

"Apology accepted. So why—"

"I'm sorry." Ivy reappeared, her face bleak. "I have to get back home."

"Charles?" said Aaron.

She nodded, and a look of understanding passed between them.

"Please, stay and have another drink." Ivy was trying hard to sound matter-of-fact. "Carnegie, will you be all right? I'll touch base with you tomorrow about Habitat. Aaron knows about the acquisition, by the way, so he's safe."

That's what you think. I assured Ivy that I'd be fine, and within moments I was left alone with the mysteriously married man.

"I need to talk with you," said Aaron once again.

I shook my head, but the room whirled around me, so I stopped. "I told you, apology accepted. Now if you don't mind, it's been a long day. A long week, for that matter. What's today, Wednesday?"

"Tuesday. Now would you listen to me? It's about Darwin."

"How did you know—?"

"Lily's my friend, too, remember? She called me this afternoon, half out of her mind. Darwin hasn't been charged with murder, but they found some dope in his car. Not much, but enough to hold him on. She asked me to find him a lawyer."

"Oh, Lord." I put a hand to my now-throbbing forehead. "Is she still blaming me?"

Aaron shrugged an eloquent Jewish shrug. "Bound to, isn't she? Without your testimony, Darwin's just another guy who drank too much at a bachelor party. Now the police want to know where his clothes went, and whether he owns a knife."

"And does he?"

"He says not. He also says he stuffed his clothes in a trash can because he threw up on them while he was driving around in a stupor. And he put on some new clothes that he just happened to buy the day before and leave in his trunk. And he can't remember where the trash can was. Between a half-assed story like that, and the fight you saw outside the Café, it doesn't look good."

"It wasn't that much of a fight. I don't think." I sighed and closed my eyes. It was difficult to open them again. "But I couldn't lie to the police. I just couldn't!"

"I understand that. And Lily probably does, too. She just needs a target right now, and you're it."

"But can't she see . . . No, of course she can't."

I slumped back in my chair and stared at the little oil painting on the wall above the sofa. It showed a luminous twilight sky in shades of violet over a rocky headland. Within the headland's sheltering arm were a cluster of fishing boats, their hulls glowing lapis and garnet and turquoise against the dusk. Wistfully, I imagined myself sitting at the water's edge, watching the sky darken, listening to the whisper of the waves . . .

"Hey, Sleeping Beauty!" Aaron was standing over me. "You're fading out on me here. Did they give you pain pills when they fixed up your hand?"

"Um, yeah."

"And you inhaled all that booze anyway. Smart. Come on, up you go." He got an arm around my shoulders and hauled. "I think the bedroom's down here."

"Thanks." I stretched out on Ivy's guest bed, grateful to be horizontal, and didn't move as Aaron slipped off my shoes and pulled the bedspread over me. "Thank you, Aaron. Really. You're being so nice—"

"Don't mention it. Go to sleep."

"First Kevin was so nice, and now you . . ." My voice sounded far away.

"Kevin?"

"Someone I'm dating," I said. In my altered state, it seemed important to be accurate. "I mean, we haven't even had our first date yet. But he—"

"Frankly, my dear . . ." said Aaron from the doorway. He was silhouetted by the hall light, his face unreadable, his voice cold. "Frankly, I don't want to hear about it. You get some sleep, and tomorrow we'll try and figure out who killed Jason Kraye."

Chapter Thirteen

WAKING UP IN A STRANGE BED—AGAIN—WAS BAD ENOUGH. At least Ivy's guest room was an orange-paisley-free zone, and I didn't have to check out by ten o'clock. But waking up Wednesday morning still in my clothes, with a sore hand, a worse head, and a vague memory of having said something stupid to Aaron, was considerably disorienting.

Things didn't get much more oriented once I got to Solveto's, either. My office was full of Buckmeisters.

"They said they wanted to wait for you," said Kelli with a giggle. "I hope that was OK? Eddie's not here yet."

Lucky Eddie. The Buckmeisters were friendly folk, but they didn't help a headache, being very Texan and very loud. The phrase "three's a crowd" might have been coined for the Buckmeister clan.

"There she is!" boomed Buck, the bigger-than-life patriarch of the threesome, rising up from my desk chair like a force of nature in a checkered suit. Buck, who made his pile as the hot-tub king of El Paso, was the kind of man who never met a stranger; to know him was to be embraced by him, as he embraced me now. Along with the suit, he wore a gaudy bandanna tied pirate-style around his high red forehead. The bandanna was different every day; today's was turquoise with yellow dots. "I swear, girl, you get prettier every time I set eyes on you!"

"Carnegie, what happened to your hand?" asked Bonnie, the bride. Midway in size between her hefty father, Buck, and her petite, rosy-cheeked mother, Betty, she had curly black hair and a girlish enthusiasm that was leagues away from Sally Tyler's ice-princess disdain.

"Just a cut," I told her, as Momma Betty patted my shoulder and made cooing sounds. "Really, it's nothing. What can I do for you folks today?"

"We had this wonderful idea!" said Betty.

I tried not to whimper. The Killer B's always had one more wonderful idea. "Listen, guys, the wedding is less than a week away—"

"But that's perfect!" Bonnie chimed in. "Because we're hoping he'll still be in Seattle."

"He, who?"

"Beau Paliere," said the blushing bride, blushing. "We watched the two of you on television. Isn't he *wonderful*? And he said if he was invited to a wedding in Seattle, he'd go."

"I don't know about that," I said, groping for a good solid objection. *This isn't fair. I haven't had breakfast yet.* "I mean, I really don't know the man, and besides, he's used to movie stars—"

"Bull puckey!" roared Buck.

"Language!" chided Betty.

"Sorry, Mother. But there's not a movie star around prettier'n my Bonnie! And I bet that Frenchman's never seen a Christmas blowout like ours is gonna be. So what do you say?"

"Let's just think about it, all right, folks? I'm really awfully busy right now—"

"Carnegie, look what came for you!" Kelli stood in my
doorway, half-hidden behind an enormous bouquet. There
were three dozen roses, at least, in the tenderest shades of
pink and ivory and coral. Even the vase was extravagant: a
huge and ornate urn in vintage milk glass.

The Buckmeisters gave forth glad cries; Kelli set the bouquet on my desk, and I held my breath and reached for the
enclosure card. *Kevin Bauer? But we just met . . . and Aaron
would never—*

But Aaron hadn't, and neither had Kevin. The card was
from Beautiful Beau. "So charmed to meet you," it read.
Even his handwriting was beautiful. "I'm at the Alexis Hotel.
Shall we talk?" His full name and a phone number followed.

I swallowed my disappointment. Flowers from Aaron
wouldn't have changed my mind about him, of course. *Or
would they?* Meanwhile, the Buckmeisters were reading the
card over my shoulder.

"Well, there you go!" said Buck. "The man wants to get
to know you, all right. I'll just call him right now."

Before I could protest, Buck punched in the number on
my desk phone and, in his best Texan French, asked for
"Monsoor" Paliere. As he launched into his introduction,
and extended his invitation, I smiled weakly and subsided
behind the roses. The Killer B's have that effect on me.

"Well, that's just great!" Buck trumpeted at last. "Mercy
boocoo to you, too!"

Then he gave me a broad wink and handed me the
phone.

"My dear Carnegie!" Beau's voice was cognac-smooth.
"How delightful that I'll be seeing you again, and observing

you at work. Perhaps after this wonderful Christmas wedding we'll have a nightcap here in my suite. We have so much to talk about, you and I."

I couldn't imagine what, but with a passel of Texans gazing at me, I wasn't about to ask. I made a vague reply, thanked him for the flowers, and rang off. As the Buckmeisters made their way to the elevator, noisily thrilled about their date with destiny, I slumped back in my chair, and Joe poked his head in my door.

"My darling redhead, did I hear the Killer B's talking about Beautiful Beau?"

"Don't call them that! They might hear you."

He strolled over to the roses. "I doubt they can even hear themselves in all that uproar. Nice people, but they need a mute button. Who are these from?"

"Are you telling me that Kelli didn't read the card, and you didn't worm it out of her? Joe, you're slipping."

"All right," he laughed. "Next question. Why is the fabulous Frenchman sending you roses?"

"Damned if I know. I'll ask him at Bonnie's wedding."

Joe went on red alert without moving a muscle, like a cat who hears the can opener and is pretending not to care.

"Beau Paliere will be at Buckmeister/Frost?"

"Yep." I sat up and made a note for my file. "Just what I need is his snooty criticism of my—"

"How interesting," said Joe, leaning down to sniff a rose. A lock of his sandy hair fell fetchingly across his forehead. "Carnegie, remember how you asked me to run some of my vintage Lionel trains at the reception?"

"I do, and I remember that you refused, even though I asked you ever so nicely. You're more worried about those trains than all your crystal and ceramics."

He straightened up and smiled sweetly. "Not anymore. Where shall we set them up, the buffet table or the hot chocolate bar?"

It was my turn to laugh. "Joe, you're shameless! You think the paparazzi are going to shadow Beau Paliere at Buckmeister/Frost, and you want the unique arrangements provided by Solveto's Catering to figure prominently in the background of their pictures."

"Damn straight I do, if you'll forgive the expression."

"What if there aren't any photographers there except Bonnie's?"

"Oh, no fear of that." He drifted toward the door. "Excuse me, I've got some phone calls to make. . . ."

At that point my cell phone chirped from the pocket of my coat. No cognac smoothness from Aaron. More like black coffee.

"So, Stretch, you ready for your third degree?"

"My what?"

"Come on, you weren't that far gone last night. You're going to help me spring Darwin, remember?"

"Of course I remember. But I'm at work. I have a meeting in an hour, I keep getting interrupted, and I still need to eat breakfast—"

"Hey, me too. I'll be at the Daughter in ten minutes."

I was there in five. The Fisherman's Daughter was just up the block from Joe's building, a brand-new place trying a bit too hard to evoke funky old Fremont, with distressed lumber and fishing nets and such. But they served four-egg omelets and pepper-cured bacon, so what the hell.

Best of all, the Daughter's waitresses fill your coffee cup before they even hand you a menu. This was critical today, because back at Ivy's apartment I'd been completely flummoxed by her built-in home espresso contraption. Built-in! What if I pushed the wrong button and injected hot milk into the drywall? I had taken one look and fled the scene.

So I was eagerly dosing myself with caffeine when Aaron arrived, notebook at hand, in a navy-blue pea coat and white scarf. He looked gallingly wide-awake, the eager newshound hot on the trail.

I decided to get the hard part over with right away. "About what I said last night . . ."

"You mean, about your new friend Kevin?" He sat down and gave me a tight smile. "I don't want to hear about it. I'd rather tell you about your old friend Aaron, and why—"

"Why you lied to me about your wife?" I could be brusque, too. In fact, I needed to be, to remind myself to stick to my guns. "No, thanks. We're discussing Jason Kraye's murder and nothing else."

He rolled his eyes. "All right, me proud beauty, be that way. But one of these days you're going to hear me out. Maybe not today, and maybe not tomorrow . . ."

"I'm not kidding, Aaron! Just drop the whole subject. Case closed."

"All right, Stretch." He had taken out his steel cigarette lighter and was tapping it on the table, end over end, a habit he had when he was thinking hard. "All right, tell you what. I won't bring up my sordid past until you ask me to."

"You mean, *unless* I ask you to."

"Whatever. Deal?"

"Deal."

Aaron put away the lighter and held out his hand, to

shake on it, which got us a funny look from the waitress bringing our menus. But it cleared the air, at least for me, and soon we were diving into breakfast. It was—it used to be—one of the fun things about being with him. Good food and lots of it, and don't spare the ketchup. Some of my friends liked haute cuisine, but Aaron and I liked to eat.

"Here's what I've got so far." Aaron was well-practiced in operating a notebook with one hand and a fork with the other. He swallowed a mouthful of salmon hash and flipped to a page of scribbled notes. "The police haven't recovered the weapon yet, and there are no witnesses except you. No criminal background on Jason Kraye, no obvious motive for his murder. So the working theory is that Kraye was slashed in a drunken fight, maybe even unintentionally, and that the killer was one of the men at the bachelor party."

"Darwin, you mean."

"Well, they've been grilling everyone who was there, me included. But yeah, Dar's the prime suspect. Whether they book him or not, they'll keep on questioning him until he slips up. Or cracks up. I sure couldn't stay sober at a time like this."

"And it's all my fault!"

"Jeez, I get first prize for tactless, don't I?" He put a hand on mine, then withdrew it when I stiffened. "What's done is done, Slim, and it's nobody's fault. The best way to help Darwin is to find out what really happened."

I squared my shoulders, feeling the coffee take effect. *Bless those ancient Ethiopians, anyway.* "OK, where do we start?"

"Let's put together what we know for sure. You first. Tell me everything you saw going on outside the Café that night, every little detail." He poised a pencil over a fresh page and crooked one eyebrow. "You can skip the musical entertainment. I saw that from inside."

"I bet you did." I wondered if the memory of Santa's dance number was still as vivid for him as it was for me. *Never mind that. Remember the scuffle.*

I closed my eyes and it all came back: the flailing shadows, the two men struggling, the third man kneeling in the frozen grass. But even with Aaron's interruptions, it didn't take long to describe the whole episode. I simply hadn't seen all that much.

"So you didn't watch Darwin leave the premises, or Frank Sanjek, either? You're sure?"

"Look, I'd love to be able to say that Darwin left the party by himself, while Jason Kraye was still alive. And I'm sure that's what did happen. But I didn't *see* it. I didn't see anyone leave except the stripper, going up the street on foot, and someone going downhill toward the bike path."

"No guesses as to who that was? Height, build?"

I shook my head. "He was down in the bushes, I couldn't really tell."

Aaron nodded, frowning, and reviewed his notes. "But you definitely saw that both Darwin and Kraye had empty hands? No glint of a knife?"

"No. They were shoving at each other, and then punching in a sort of half-hearted way. But I didn't see a knife. I told Mike that. I just hope he told Lily."

"He's not telling her squat." Aaron waved to the waitress for more coffee, then looked at me ruefully. "She's the sister of a homicide suspect, for God's sake. The department's shorthanded, so Graham is still on the case, but he's not going anywhere near her till it's settled. Conflict of interest."

"Poor Lily! I hate to think of her dealing with all this alone. I should go see her."

"Bad idea, Stretch. Really. She's so strung out, seeing you now would do more harm than good. Leave Lily be for a while, and I'll tell you the minute that changes, I promise. Meanwhile, she isn't alone. She's got me."

"She's got both of us," I insisted. "Whether she likes it or not. But I'll keep away until you think she's ready to talk with me. So, it's your turn. What went on *inside* the Café, that might have led to murder?"

"That's what I can't figure out." Aaron glared at his coffee, then shook his head as he dumped in some sugar. I wondered if he was yearning for an after-meal cigarette. "See, I just wasn't picking up any bad vibes there. Not that bad, anyway. Kraye was being a macho jerk, as I gather was normal for him. After you left, he goaded Darwin into drinking some retsina, and then some more. But Dar seemed like a sloppy drunk, not a dangerous one. Same goes for Frank and the other guys. I swear, it just didn't feel like the kind of party that ends with a knife."

"But it did, though. And you're only one observer. Maybe someone else at the party got a different impression. We could start by asking them. Though of course, the police already have."

"That's assuming they told the truth," he pointed out.

"I bet Lou Schulman didn't."

"The guy who groped you? What makes you think that?"

"Well, he—wait a minute! You *saw* him groping me and you didn't say anything?"

Aaron, all innocence, hoisted shoulders and eyebrows.

"Seemed like you were handling things just fine by yourself. Besides, I had to finish my pool game. I was winning. What makes you single out Lou?"

"I'm not sure," I said, swallowing my indignation along with my coffee. Cream, no sugar. "I ran into him at the Habitat roasting plant, where he works, and he got awfully emphatic about not knowing Jason very well."

"So you think Schulman doth protest too much? It's worth checking out." Aaron jotted down the name. "It's worth checking everything. What does he do at Habitat?"

"Some kind of computer stuff." I told him what Fiona had said, about Lou being a programming wizard with poor social skills.

"Typical," said Aaron, still jotting. "I wonder how Schulman and Kraye got to know each other? I'll see if I can find out. And I'll call the other guys at the party, too. I can say I'm doing a piece for the *Sentinel*. Can you get me a guest list?"

"Sure."

"Good. Something about Jason Kraye, good or bad, past or present, made somebody at that party want him dead. We have to find out what it was and who it was."

"Just that simple."

"Well, look at what we've got going for us." He dropped a credit card on our bill. "Excellent access to the suspects, for one thing. Most of the guys at the party were Frank's coworkers at MFC. So between me researching the book on Ivy, and you doing Sally's wedding—"

"Damn!" I jumped up from the table. "I'm supposed to be at Meet for Coffee headquarters right now, for an appointment with one of Ivy's people. I'll pay you back, OK?"

"My treat," said Aaron. "Just be sure and pump them

about Kraye. I'll drop by Solveto's later and you can fill
me in."

"OK."

But I didn't have to pump Madison Jaffee. She ended up
pumping me.

Chapter Fourteen

"MS. JAFFEE WILL BE WITH YOU IN A MINUTE," SNIFFED THE angular, sour-faced secretary guarding MFC's marketing department. Her nameplate said Nora, but her eyes said Wicked Witch of the West. She sighed, in the perpetually put-upon tone of the chronic complainer. "She's running late, as per usual."

"No problem." *Especially considering I'm late myself.* I gave Nora a cheery smile, but she didn't have the energy to respond. It's a hard life, being grumpy.

I settled into a chair to wait, but I'd barely made it to page three of MFC's latest annual report when Ivy's "whiz kid" came out to greet me. Madison Jaffee was about my age, with short black hair and a taut, coiled energy in her stride. Her angled green eyes were shrewd and skillfully made up, and a short upper lip gave her mouth a curious look—of surprise or anticipation. Her lip curled just a little at the secretary's frosty glance, then she shook my hand and steered me down the hall to a small conference room.

If Madison's vigor contrasted cruelly with Nora's burned-out lassitude, her sophisticated taste in clothes made me feel raw around the edges. Most of the staff I'd passed on my way in were dressed Seattle-casual, lots of khakis and sweaters, but Madison looked more like Manhattan. Her hair clasped her temples like a cocktail hat from the forties, and above her cropped trousers and Italian boots she wore a wide-shouldered jacket, obviously one of a kind, made from panels of jewel-toned brocade.

"Great jacket," I said as she shut the door. We were forty stories up in a glass tower downtown, far from the MFC roasting plant in South Seattle. Unlike the heady atmosphere at Habitat, the only coffee aroma in this room came from the paper cups we brought with us.

"Thanks. It's antique kimono fabric. I just got back from Tokyo yesterday, testing the waters for MFC in Asia. Have a seat."

The MFC lobby and hallways were decorated in conservative Corporate Yule, lots of holly and ribbon, nothing at all religious. The conference room, in contrast, was crammed with the bright and blatant signs of summer. There were sunshiny travel posters taped to the walls, a display of picnic baskets and beach paraphernalia, and a couple of easels pinned with ink and watercolor sketches of tropical shorelines and tall, cool drinks.

"Creative Services is concepting our summer promotion for next year," explained Madison, brisk and impersonal. "We wrapped up Christmas back in August. Now, I don't have much time, but Ivy filled me in on Made in Heaven and asked me to brainstorm a little. . . ."

Storm was the right word. In one tempestuous, buffeting burst, Madison analyzed the Seattle wedding market, critiqued my promotional efforts thus far, and sketched out a six-month branding plan for Eddie and me to embark upon, starting with "Identify relevant opinion leaders" and ending with "Continue to cultivate press contacts."

We even came up with a phrase for me to work into interviews, to support the idea that my events were affordable without seeming cheap. The way Beau Paliere used *Beauty and perfection in every detail*, I would use *Fairytale weddings for real-world brides*.

Or something like that, anyway. Eddie would gag at the fairy-tale bit, and I wasn't sure I liked it myself. Still, by the time Madison was done, my brain was hurting, but I was thoroughly impressed. And grateful; you can pay a lot for this kind of advice.

"I can't thank you enough," I told her at the end of our allotted half hour. "If you ever need a wedding planner yourself, count on me."

"Doubtful," she said curtly. But then her poise seemed to waver, and she gathered up our scattered paperwork with inordinate care, not meeting my eyes. "I . . . heard you were at the bachelor party, and that you found the . . . you found Jason. Everyone's talking about it."

"Well, everyone's got it a little wrong. I was at the Hot Spot that night, but only briefly. And then the next day I identified the body. But I didn't find it."

"Oh." Madison drummed a nervous tattoo on the table with the fingers of one hand. Like Ivy, she wore no nail polish, and like me, no wedding ring. She frowned abruptly. "But you saw *something* that night, something about Darwin, and that's why he was arrested. So you must think he's guilty."

"Absolutely not," I told her. "In fact, I'm trying to prove his innocence."

"And how do you expect to do that?"

How, indeed. "Well, by asking around, talking to people who knew Jason. I know this reporter—maybe you've met him—Aaron Gold. He's got sources at the police department."

"I want to help." Madison pushed the papers aside and locked her hands together on the tabletop. "What has Aaron found out?"

"Hang on," I said. This was moving a little too fast. "Can I ask why you want to get involved?"

"Well, why are you involved?" Her nostrils flared, and her knuckles were white. "What makes you so sure Darwin didn't do it?"

"Because I know him," I retorted. I wasn't going to tell her I was spying on the Hot Spot that night. "His sister is my closest friend."

That seemed to take the wind out of Madison's sails. She crossed the room to an easel and began straightening the sketches on it, her back to me. I waited. I had the sense that she was assessing factors unknown to me, with the mental swiftness she had shown in setting out my marketing plan. When she turned back to face me, it was clear she had come to a decision. A difficult one.

"Carnegie, can I be honest with you? In confidence?"

"Of course."

She returned to the table and sat, closer to me this time. "I believe Darwin's innocent, too. Everyone here does. He puts on a show of being tough, but you can tell what a gentle person he really is. He shouldn't be in jail. Someone else was the killer, and I have to find out who."

"But why? I mean, why you in particular?"

She swallowed, and spoke in an undertone. "Jason and I were lovers."

"*Oh.*"

She hurried on. "We kept it secret because I was his boss.

In fact, I hired him. That's not why I hired him, but the whole thing was totally against company policy, and my career is so important to me. Do you understand?"

"I think so," I said slowly.

What I didn't understand was how anyone could feel amorous about Jason Kraye. But if there's one thing I've learned in my line of work, it's that you can never, never fully understand what's going on between two people in love. They're living deep inside the Republic of Two, and the borders are closed. Jason had been repugnant to me, but behind her polished façade, this woman was shaken to the core.

"Madison, I'm so sorry for your loss. You must be devastated, especially if you can't talk about him with anybody here. But listen, now that Jason's, um, gone, maybe you could confide in Ivy. I'm sure she would sympathize—"

"*No!*" Madison gripped my hand; she was remarkably strong. "I don't want anyone here to know about this, and . . . and gossip about us. I couldn't stand it. I just want to help you find out who killed him."

How could I deny a need so intense, from someone in such pain?

"All right," I said. "We'll work on it together. But I'll have to tell Aaron about you and Jason, you know."

She hesitated, biting her lip. "All right. He'll be discreet, won't he? You trust him?"

Interesting question. Trust Aaron with my heart? No, never again, much as I might want to. But trust him not to ruin Madison's reputation? That was different.

"He'll be discreet."

"All right, then. Tell me everything."

I described what I'd seen through Eddie's binoculars, and what Aaron had gleaned about the police investigation.

"Their theory is that one of the guys at the party, probably Darwin, had a knife and used it. But Aaron was there that night and he didn't pick up any sense of hostility from anyone. Of course, it could have been a random attack, a mugging, but the way Jason was slashed was so deliberate and brutal, it seems like—" I caught myself. "I'm sorry, I shouldn't have said that."

But Madison was one tough, unsqueamish cookie, and she dismissed my apology with a wave of her hand. "So, you didn't see anyone else? The police don't have other suspects?"

"Not so far. They're interviewing everyone from the party, and checking into Jason's background. Did he have, well, enemies?" Detectives always ask that in the movies, but here in the prosaic atmosphere of marketing paraphernalia and fluorescent light, it sounded absurd.

"I think he gambled a lot," said Madison thoughtfully. The green eyes were preoccupied, miles away. "Maybe he had debts . . ."

"You think? Jason didn't tell you?"

"What?" She snapped back to the present. "Well, he was secretive about certain things. Some people keep different parts of their life walled off from each other. You know how that is."

Do I ever, I thought. A gambling habit wasn't much compared to a wife back in Boston. "Well, maybe Aaron can mention it to some of the guys around here, and find out more. Did you ever hear any details?"

"Just a name, Noble Pearl. It's a restaurant in the International District."

"Hmm." Exotic Chinese gambling dens sounded awfully melodramatic, but how dramatic is murder? "Anything else in Jason's past, maybe?"

"Not that I can think of—"

The door opened then, and Ivy Tyler leaned into the room. She wore a skirted suit in dark gray—a gesture of mourning?—with a large garnet brooch on the lapel. No, make that ruby. Easy to forget that my down-to-earth mentor was a multimillionaire. "Maddie, we've got that conference call in ten minutes. Hi, Carnegie. Getting some good ideas?"

"Tons," I said, rising. "Madison, thank you again . . ."

But Madison was already gone, brushing past Ivy without a word. What a tightrope she was walking. I still thought she should confide in her boss, but it wasn't my call.

As I moved into the hallway, Ivy stopped me with a hand on my arm. She wore a subtle, expensive perfume, and more makeup than usual. I wondered if a murdered employee also made for photo ops; there had been a lot of press about the Canal Killer. But her next words put my cynicism to shame.

"I just wanted you to know," she said, "Darwin James is on full salary while this gets settled. And MFC is going to cover his legal fees."

"That's very generous of you. Darwin has a sister in town, she'll be glad to hear it. I can give you her number—"

"I just got off the phone with Aaron, he'll tell her. He says you're a friend of Lily's, too. Is that how you met him?"

"Sort of."

Ivy's eyes were mischievous. "He speaks pretty highly of you, for a casual acquaintance. I think you've got an admirer there."

I tried for a smile, though it felt like a grimace. "Just friends."

"That's what they all say."

She looked past me down the hallway and beckoned to someone: a large, square-shouldered man in his forties who approached us with the brisk, easy stride of a natural athlete. I recognized the thick, prematurely gray hair and the craggy features, irregular but quite appealing. This was Ivy's go-to guy.

"Simon, come meet Carnegie Kincaid," called Ivy. "She's the one who checked out Habitat for the reception. Simon's the logistics guru around here, so you two have a lot in common."

"You're handling Sally's wedding, too, if I remember." Simon Weeks's voice was rough, almost harsh, but his tone was friendly. "That's a bigger operation than most of mine."

I laughed. "At least I don't have Wall Street looking over my shoulder. If you have a minute, I'd like to talk with you about setting up at the roasting plant."

"Gladly."

Ivy excused herself, and Simon led me back into the meeting room. As we reviewed my plans for the reception, he made some sensible suggestions about running in power for the food prep and the band, and even an idea or two about decorations. But mostly Simon answered my questions, approved of what I had in mind, and showed a real appreciation for my work.

As we exchanged business cards on my way out, it struck me that if I hadn't just met Kevin Bauer, I'd be wondering whether Simon Weeks was single.

I returned to Joe's building feeling flattered by the attention and full of things to think about, from marketing strategies for Made in Heaven to how to keep my "just a friend"

Aaron at arm's length. I badly needed some quiet time at my desk.

I would have gotten it, too, back on the houseboat. But a catering company has a kitchen, and kitchens have prep cooks, and prep cooks have tempers. Alonzo and Filipo were at it again, and they were at it in my office.

"Twenty-five minutes! I am spending twenty-five minutes to peel and to mince my shallots, and you stole them! Thief! *Hijo de cabrón!*"

"*Your* shallots! What of *my* chopping knife? You steal my knives, and complain about shallots! I have sea bass going late into the oven and Casey shouting and not one moment to spare—"

Alonzo and Filipo—whether these were first names or last, I never knew—were kitchen demons who hailed from Brazil and Venezuela, respectively. They were both small and wiry and unshaven, and when they weren't flirting extravagantly with me or Kelli, they both took up permanent residence on the very edge of hysteria, each darkly convinced that the other was his treasonous foe.

From time to time Casey Abbott, the executive chef, threw them out of the kitchen, and then Kelli would shoo them out of the reception area, and they'd end up having histrionics in my office. The first few times I found it amusing, and consented to referee. But this was far from being the first time.

"Gentlemen, *please*! I've asked you before, find somewhere else. I mean it!"

"He followed me here," spat Filipo, "crying like a baby about his miserable shallots. *I* have business with you, Carnegie. Private business."

Alonzo muttered something dire in Portuguese and made

his exit, and I sat wearily behind my desk. "What is it, Filipo?"

The cook's demeanor transformed itself on the instant, from violent fury to conspiratorial glee. "I have brought your toys, Carnegie! Don't worry, I tell no one."

With that, he set a Solveto's carrier bin on my desk, and began to remove a layer of packing paper from inside. It took me a moment to remember the platter I'd rescued at the Hot Spot on Sunday night, and brought back to the kitchen in a bin like this one. Or apparently, in this very one. But I hadn't realized it held anything but more dirty dishes.

"Filipo, if there was something in there—what is *that*?"

The question was rhetorical. My Venezuelan friend was holding up a recognizable plastic object of enormous size and specific sexual function. Grinning, he set the thing in front of me, and reached back into the bin to draw forth a lacy black garment with some very interesting cutouts. I felt myself blushing, even as I realized what had happened: some gag gifts from the bachelor party had been tossed into the bin, and I'd set Joe's platter on top of them.

"Dean tells me these are yours," said Filipo, with an insinuating smirk, "but he forgets and they stay in the kitchen. I knew that my beautiful redhead wants her toys back!"

Dean, a sweet but slow-witted youth, was Solveto's dishwasher and general cleanup man. Perhaps he really had believed that the bin held my personal belongings, but obviously Filipo did not. He just couldn't pass up the opportunity to tease me.

"Put that down, for heaven's sake!" I said, as the cook began to laugh uproariously. "You know perfectly well those things don't belong to me. I'll have to return them to Frank and—oh, hell."

Filipo, following my eyes, turned to the doorway with the length of black lace still fluttering from his fingers. At least it wasn't a client standing there, but it was bad enough: Aaron Gold. Aaron cocked his head, and with a wide-eyed, captivated gaze took in the cook, the negligee, the vibrator on my desk, and the great sheaf of roses on my credenza. Then he gave a long whistle of appreciation.

"That's it! I know when I'm beat." He reached out to shake hands with the puzzled but still smiling Filipo. "I bow to the competition. You've got a class act here, mister—"

"Would you shut up!" I snapped, still blushing. "Filipo, get back to work, would you please? And leave Alonzo's shallots alone."

I whisked Frank Sanjek's gifts back into the bin. There were nongag gifts in there as well—a silver hip flask, a digital camera, a small cigar box—and probably more, but I didn't want to look. *It's all client property, whatever it is, and I've got cooks playing around with it.* I covered the stuff hastily with the packing paper, and set the whole ridiculous thing in a corner.

I called Frank's work number and began to leave a curt message, asking him to come fetch the bin. Then I realized how brusque I was sounding. It wasn't Frank's fault, after all.

"Or I can drop it off with you," I added lamely, far too aware of Aaron's amused gaze. "I'll probably be at MFC tomorrow. Or I could give it to Sally next time I—no, I guess that's not a good idea. Um, I'll call you back. Bye."

I hung up and looked over at Aaron. He was leaning back in my visitor chair, arms clasped behind his head, grinning broadly.

"Not one word," I warned him. "That was stuff from the

bachelor party, and you know it. In fact, you're probably responsible for some of it."

"On the contrary," said Aaron, feigning offense. "I have far better taste. I gave the young man a box of particularly nice cigars. Only minis, I'm afraid, but Cuban minis. Better a little of the best than a lot of the not, don't you think?"

"I don't think I know what you're talking about, and I'm sure I don't care. Do you want to hear about my conversation with Madison Jaffee?"

"Of course I do. Nice roses, by the way." Aaron's voice was casual, but not casual enough. "I don't recall seeing them at the Hot Spot."

I should have told him about Beau, I suppose, in case he thought the flowers were from Kevin. But I couldn't resist a little payback. Sparring with him was much more comfortable than yearning after him.

"They are pretty, aren't they? A friend of mine sent them. . . . But never mind that. Guess who Jason Kraye was having an affair with? Madison Jaffe."

Once I'd told him the details, Aaron gave a low whistle, thoughtful this time.

"That's tough on Madison, losing him and having to keep it secret. Well, it can only help us, and Darwin, to have an MFC insider like her looking for information. I had thought about asking Ivy, but I don't think she knew Jason all that well. Besides, the CEO never hears all the good gossip." He slipped a rubber band around his ever-present notebook. "Let's go."

"Go where?"

"Noble Pearl, of course. I'm still full from breakfast, but there's always room for Chinese, right?"

"Wrong." I gestured at my chaotic desktop. "I have work to do. I'm running behind as it is."

"Tonight for dinner, then."

"I can't."

"Of course." Aaron stood up, pulling out his gloves and tossing one end of his white scarf over his shoulder. "You've got a date. Have fun."

"Thanks," I said evenly. "I intend to."

Chapter Fifteen

"FUN" WAS NOT THE WORD FOR MY FIRST DATE WITH KEVIN Bauer. The word, as it turned out, was "magic."

Sure, I was feeling easy to please, what with Aaron's deception, Lily's resentment, and not being able to sleep in my own damn bed at night. The shock of the murder, and the strain of managing two big weddings within a week of each other, had me yearning for friendly company and wide open to the chance for romance.

But setting all that aside, who could be difficult to please when the night was clear and frosty, the gentleman sincere and attentive, and dozens of good-hearted people in ridiculous costumes were caroling their hearts out on the street corners?

Kevin met me at Ivy's building right on time, wearing a handsome chestnut-colored leather jacket and bearing two tall paper cups of steaming cider. Even there in the Market, I could hear music and laughter echoing down Pine Street from the Westlake Mall. Driving "home" after work, I'd seen the gaily decorated Figgy Pudding stage out in front of the mall, awaiting the grand finale of tonight's songfest.

As I drove past it, I had looked through my windshield at the old-fashioned carousel that appears downtown each December. The candy-colored wooden horses rose and fell and circled, bearing gleeful children and grinning adults. The store windows shone bright and vivid, and for blocks in every direction the filigree branches of the street trees sparkled with white lights like diamond stars against the falling dusk.

I can't help it; I love Christmas.

"Oh, perfect," I said now to Kevin, accepting a cup from his gloved hands. Large hands, to go with his large, square frame and his rugged features. With his leather jacket, dark red beard, and breath puffing white in the cold air, he might have been an Alaskan bush pilot setting off for adventure.

All right, so I was absurdly easy to please. But I hadn't had a date, a proper date, in a long time.

I was well bundled up myself; luckily I'd brought my long camel's-hair coat from the houseboat, and a fetching moss-green beret to pull down over forehead and ears. The hot, spicy drink added just the right glow of internal warmth. We crossed Pike Place and headed up Pine, sipping cider and eyeing each other sideways, faintly but happily nervous. *No wonder teenage girls talk funny.* Just as well that the first part of our evening didn't call for much conversation.

Every year, the Figgy Pudding Caroling Competition seems to attract more participation by downtown businesses, more spectators willing to donate to a good cause, and more hilariously elaborate song-and-dance numbers. This year there were rapping tax accountants, tap-dancing mortgage bankers in reindeer hats, and silver-haired lawyers waving cardboard palm trees in a conga line. There were kids dressed as elves, men dressed as women, and one bunch of women dressed as giant cloves of garlic.

And all of them caroling, lifting their voices in joyous song, which ranged from an exquisitely harmonized "God Rest Ye Merry" by a choir in full Victorian getup, to a baseball-themed "Twelve Days of Christmas" raucously rendered by some beer-fueled guys in Mariner Moose costumes, who counted down from "Twelve bases stolen" to "And a home ru-un in the cheap seats." I'd never seen so many smiling faces per square block of Seattle.

Kevin and I drifted with the currents of people from one corner to the next, joining the little audience at each performance, dropping our dollar bills in the donation pails, singing along on the carols we knew. Kevin had a thin but true baritone, and he seemed to be having a wonderful time. I certainly was.

"All we need now is the dogs barking out 'Jingle Bells,' " I said, raising my voice a bit above the hubbub. Then, at his blank look, "You know, that you always hear on the radio this time of year, along with the Cheech-and-Chong routine about Santa's old lady?"

My date smiled politely. "I just listen to the classical station."

"Never mind." I laughed, and we drifted on for another half hour. All too soon, the carolers were packing up their props and making for the main stage, thronged now with spectators many dozens deep.

"This has been great," said Kevin, stamping his booted feet for warmth. "I think I've got a new holiday tradition. But do you mind if we skip the final show? I've got a long drive back—"

"Of course! Anyway, I'm starving. Where shall we eat?"

We ended up settling into a booth at Etta's, a lively bistro down near the Market. There we warmed ourselves with a glorious seafood chowder, and exchanged the obligatory first-date life stories. He sketched out the founding of Habitat Coffee, and I related the history of Made in Heaven Wedding Design. Just as with Ivy Tyler, Kevin and I were operating on very different levels, but there's a kinship among entrepreneurs that you don't quite feel with folks on a regular salary. Doubts, triumphs, and obstinate bankers make for good stories, whatever the size of your enterprise.

We talked about our other interests, too, theater and day-hiking on my part, classical music and bicycling on his. My childhood in Boise, his in Tacoma. My plans to visit Sun Valley, his trip to Portland the previous weekend, where he'd immersed himself in the legendary Powell's bookstore and had to drive home in the wee hours of Monday morning.

I did most of the talking, spurred on by the appreciative questions and smiles of my companion. No needling, like I got from Aaron, no thrust and parry of smart-alecky remarks. If anything, Kevin Bauer was a bit on the quiet side. A quiet man, I decided, was a nice change. The fact that he was burly and handsome, with his russet beard and his nubbly gray fisherman's knit sweater, didn't hurt a bit.

"Are you sure your hand is OK?" Kevin asked at one point. "It bled so much—"

"It's fine," I assured him. "I changed the bandage this morning, just like they told me. I think Lou Schulman was more upset than I was."

He agreed, then after a moment's hesitation he said, "You mentioned a friend of Lou's, who died. Was that the body in the canal, the man from Meet for Coffee?"

"How'd you know Jason worked at MFC?"

I asked it casually, but Kevin frowned. "It must have been in the newspaper. Does it matter?"

"Not at all. I thought maybe you'd met during the merger talks—"

"Shhh! That's still confidential." He glanced around, but it was obvious the clamor of the other diners more than masked our conversation. He smiled an apology, and reached over to top up my wineglass. "Ivy's got me so paranoid...She's a remarkable person, though. What's her daughter like?"

I rolled my eyes. "Well, Sally's my client, so that makes her a lovely girl with exquisite taste, doesn't it? Let's just say she can be very explicit about what she wants, and how she wants it. Brides always have some kind of vision about the perfect wedding, of course, but Sally—"

But Sally, apparently, was not the member of the Tyler clan that Kevin really cared about. He leaned forward, interrupting me. "And Charles Tyler, what's he like in person? His compositions are so powerful and so...He's a genius, that's all there is to it. Has he talked about his music at all?"

"I hate to break it to you, but I've never even met the man." *Aw, don't tell me,* I was thinking. *Don't tell me I'm having this enchanted evening because Kevin is a Charles Tyler groupie.* "I take it Ivy hasn't introduced you?"

He shook his head in regret. "I was hoping, but no. They live near Habitat, too, by a lake just outside Snohomish. Can I tell you a secret?"

"Please."

"Charles Tyler is the reason I first agreed to talk with MFC." Kevin said it quite sheepishly. He really was starstruck. "They'd been putting out feelers, but I ignored them till I found out who Ivy's husband was. I was there that night, at the Kennedy Center." It was my turn to look blank, so he added, "His last appearance. It was heartbreaking."

"What happened, exactly?"

"No one really knows, except Ivy, I guess." My quiet man grew voluble. "Tyler was conducting one of his own works, and he started to lose the tempo. The orchestra tried to follow him, but the concertmaster, that's the first violinist, had to finish conducting from her chair. It was horrible, all the musicians craning around to watch her, and Tyler up there in his tuxedo, waving his arms. At the end of the piece he just stood perfectly still, until someone led him away."

"How long ago was that?"

"Twelve or fifteen years, maybe more."

"And Ivy has taken care of him ever since?" I remembered her expression when he called the apartment, that intense concern, and her daughter's air of respect. "She must be devoted to him."

"Almost too much so, according to some people. When he's doing poorly, she sometimes neglects the business." Kevin took a deep breath. "Well, that's enough about my hero worship. Tell me, what's it like to live on a boat?"

"On a houseboat, you mean. My place isn't going to sail away anywhere. But I love it, being right down on the water. It's, well, it's hard to describe. You have to visit sometime, once I've moved back in."

"I'd love to. And *you* have to come back to Habitat, so I can make up for the way your first visit ended. The company

Christmas party is Saturday night. It's just cookies and punch and a boom box, but . . . Be my guest?"

I wondered if Ivy would object. I must have wondered that for two, maybe even three seconds. Then I said yes. "I do need to check on something, though. Ivy's putting on a dinner party for Frank's parents and she had to reschedule. I'm invited, but I'm pretty sure it's going to be Friday night, not Saturday."

"I hope so." Kevin touched my hand—there was that warm glow again—and the conversation flowed smoothly onward, helped along by the cool topaz wine, the hot rich coffee, and Etta's famous coconut cream pie, two forks please.

Suddenly it was late, and Kevin was walking me back through the Market. A brief hug, affectionate but not intimate—all the winter clothing saw to that—and I was alone in the elevator of Ivy's building, smiling a big moony smile and humming: *One coffee roaster, Two dates in one week, Three . . . three . . .*

I gave up on "three" and dug out my key. I didn't notice anything at first, as I stepped into the hallway, but once the elevator closed behind me I was blind; the hallway light was out. I groped along the wall toward the apartment door, making a mental note to tell Ivy so she could call maintenance.

I didn't reach the apartment. In the unfamiliar darkness I bumped painfully into the corner of a table, recoiled, and stepped sideways—right into someone who swore in a low rough voice and shoved me violently to the floor.

I gave a shout as my head glanced off the wall, and then my flailing arms brought a lamp crashing down on top of me. I shoved it aside, knocking off the shade as I did so. The bulb shattered somewhere near my shoulder and I turned my face away, instinctively horrified by the thought of glass near my eyes.

Meanwhile, a door at the end of the hall swung open, offering a split-second impression of a man in dark clothes, disappearing down the fire stairs.

Chapter Sixteen

"WHAT DO YOU MEAN THE POLICE DIDN'T CARE? YOU WERE assaulted!" Aaron angrily rattled the laminated menu he'd been perusing as he waited for our table, and for me.

"It's not that they didn't care, exactly," I said, pulling off my gloves and flexing chilly fingers. Not that I minded Aaron springing to my defense, but I wanted to be accurate. "It's just that when I suggested that there might be a connection to the murder, they looked at me like I was crazy. They wouldn't call Mike Graham, either."

"Why the hell not?"

"They said it was only attempted burglary. He didn't even get the dead bolt open on Ivy's door. Nothing taken, no description of the guy, there's lots of street people around the Market, blah, blah, blah. I spent half the morning waiting for them and the other half arguing with them, and all I got was, 'Don't call us, we'll call you.'"

As I spoke, I tried to focus on Aaron's indignant face, but I was distracted by another face looming over his shoulder: a beady-eyed, fat-lipped fish who resembled Alfred Hitchcock to an alarming degree. Of the two of them, the fish had a better reason to be indignant; it was waiting to become someone's lunch.

Aaron and I were wedged into a corner of the Noble

Pearl's tiny foyer, surrounded by cloudy tanks of live fish, crabs, lobsters, and something eelish that I tried not to look at. Also by hungry office workers in heavy coats, all perusing their own menus and debating the merits of General Tso's Chicken versus Jumbo Shrimp Hunan Flower Basket.

Someone in hiking boots trod on my foot and I edged away, trying to keep my distance from Aaron and the electrical effect he sometimes had on me. Well, most times. But I was blocked by someone else who wore not only boots, but an enormous down parka.

"I won't bite, Stretch," said Aaron mildly. I took a reluctant step closer and he chuckled. "Not in public, anyway. So, what did Ivy say about all this?"

"I couldn't reach her directly. She's meeting with her board all day. But I'll call her tonight."

"Gold, party of three!" called a brisk male voice.

Our third person was Madison Jaffee, who was running late. The plan, formulated by phone this morning, was to get some lunch, case the joint, and interview the owner of the Noble Pearl about Jason Kraye, gambling man.

"That's the owner's son," murmured Aaron as we extricated ourselves from the crush and approached the front counter. "Dad's supposed to arrive soon and talk to us."

The son, a handsome young fellow chewing on a wad of gum, checked us off his list and turned us over to a waitress. She was a small, pretty girl, surely still a teenager, with rounded Chinese features and a port-wine birthmark on one cheek. Shyly averting her eyes, she showed us to a table and brought a pot of tea and three thick white cups.

Noble Pearl hardly looked like an ill-omened gambling den. The high square dining room was painted Pepto-Bismol pink, an unfortunate association for a restaurant, and hung with gaudy red and gold decorations, to mark the Chinese New Year coming up in January. Above the clamor of the lunch crowd, pop music played inexorably from the speakers bolted up in each corner.

"I shouldn't do it," said Aaron, tapping his menu indecisively on the edge of the formica table, "but the Dungeness crab in ginger and scallions sounds really good."

"Why shouldn't you do it?"

"Crabs don't have cloven hoofs."

"Huh?"

He smiled. "Jewish joke. Shellfish isn't kosher."

"I didn't know you kept kosher."

"Stretch, the things you don't know about me would astound you. Take my checkered past, for example—"

I held up a hand. "Hey, we had a deal."

"Right, right. I just thought, since you were so interested—"

"I'm not! I'm just interested in, um, in people's food preferences generally. For my work. Tell me, is that the right phrase, 'keeping kosher'?"

"Exactly right. Although personally, I don't. I observe certain holidays and certain customs, and, as far as I'm concerned, bacon is not food. But I've got a jones for crab meat and—hey, there's Madison. Over here!"

The marketing mastermind was dressed in black once again, this time topped by a long double-breasted wool coat in a deep wine color. She looked smashing, but her green eyes were guarded and her lovely mouth was set in a flat, fixed line. I wondered what it was costing Madison Jaffee to maintain that poise in the wake of her lover's death.

Aaron rose from the table to embrace her. I kept forgetting that he'd been working with Ivy for a while now, and would naturally know her senior people better than I did. She had certainly never smiled at me the way she was smiling at him.

"How you doing?" he murmured, helping her off with her coat, as he hadn't helped me.

"I'm fine, thanks. I'll be fine." Her hand lingered on his shoulder, then she slipped into her seat. "But she told you it's not public knowledge? That's important to me."

"Absolutely. But if you ever want to talk about him—"

"No," she said flatly. "No, I can't, not yet. I just want to find out who did it."

"OK, Maddie." Aaron patted her hand, and then took on a brisker tone. "Well, for starters, Carnegie had a weird thing happen last night . . ."

As we ordered lunch, I described my encounter with the would-be burglar again, and we puzzled over its significance. Or lack thereof. Madison irked me by brushing off the whole incident.

"I don't see that it necessarily means anything," she said. "Apartments do get burgled, after all, and the Market isn't the safest neighborhood at night."

"But why Ivy's place, and why now?" I protested. "Don't you think it's quite a coincidence that someone broke in there so soon after Jason Kraye's murder?"

Whatever Madison thought, she didn't get to say it, because at that point a wave of Lucky Three Jade Vegetables came cascading across the tabletop and into my lap. Our timid young waitress stood horrified, the serving dish still in her shaking hands.

"Excuse me!" She spoke in a strangled whisper. "It slipped . . ."

I had jumped to my feet, and suddenly a white-haired

gentleman with fierce black eyebrows was beside me, giving the girl a furious dressing-down in low, rapid Chinese. Her eyes, huge in the childish face, began to brim with tears.

"It's all right, really," I told him, and gave her a reassuring smile. "You should have dropped the Egg Drop Soup! That's a joke—"

But her gaze was on the floor now, and stayed there.

"I am Peter Yan," said the white-haired man. He glanced at the business card he was holding. "Mr. Gold, you wished to speak to me? You will not be charged for your meal, of course. This clumsiness by my niece is inexcusable. Li Ping has not been here long—"

"Honestly, it's not a problem," I said. "Where's the ladies' room?"

He snapped something at the girl and she trudged away. I followed, and soon I was mopping at my skirt with a paper towel. I expected the girl to vanish, but instead she lingered, casting furtive glances at me in the mirror. The bathroom walls were queasy pink as well, and we both looked pale and off-color against them.

"There, no harm done," I said brightly. "I'm sure your uncle will—"

"You knew Jase?" she blurted. Rushed together like that, the three syllables sounded almost Chinese, and it took me a moment to interpret.

"You mean, Jason Kraye?" She nodded. "I knew him slightly. He's been . . . I mean, did you know that he was . . ."

"Dead!" she whispered, and now the tears came in earnest. "It said in the newspaper. Someone killed him."

"Yes. Yes, I'm afraid so. How did you know him?"

Her face lifted and contorted, as a baby's does when it's about to wail in distress. "He loved me!"

"Oh, *honey.*"

I reached out to hug her—what else could I do?—but she shook me off, her eyes wide and frightened. There were voices approaching, and the door to the room began to swing open. She whispered something, so low I could barely make it out.

"Uwajimaya, one hour."

Chapter Seventeen

Uwajimaya was the vast Asian food market a few blocks away. As a group of women entered the rest room and Li Ping locked herself into a stall, I had a sudden urge to go shopping there. Say, in about an hour.

Back in the dining room Peter Yan was seated at our table, speaking seriously, but with no suggestion of restraint or hostility. Aaron was taking notes, and Madison was frowning into her teacup.

Lord, I thought, *I've got to keep her and Li Ping apart. What on earth did these women see in Jason Kraye? I wouldn't have touched him on a bet.*

"I explained all this to the police." Peter Yan rose courteously at my approach, then sat again. The place was still packed, but he seemed unconcerned about being overheard. "Some of my customers play cards after dinner, in a private room upstairs. It is not a cardroom, there are no fees. A social game only. Mr. Kraye would sometimes participate. There is nothing illegal here."

"Of course not." Aaron made a show of consulting his notes, but I could tell he was puzzled by all this candid cooperation. "And you think some of Jason's coworkers gambled with him, but you don't know their names?"

The restaurateur sat perfectly still, blinking slowly as an

owl. Then he made a slight sideways inclination of his silver head.

"Unfortunately not. Some prominent gentlemen enjoy relaxing here in private, therefore we use courtesy names: Mr. Smith, Mr. Jones. I was shown a photograph of the dead man, or I would not know his name, either."

He gazed at each of us in turn. "A tragedy, a young man like that. I said so to the police. I must return to work now, but of course you may call me if you have more questions. Once again, I apologize for my niece. She has not been long in this country. I think she may return to China soon."

Out on the sidewalk, squinting in the low winter sun, I had a quick decision to make: bring Aaron to interview Li Ping, or not? But Madison made it for me, by asking Aaron for a lift uptown to the MFC building. She could easily have walked, I thought cattily, but maybe her stylish Italian boots weren't all that comfy.

"You two go ahead," I told them. *Just as well, Li Ping is skittish enough already.* "I've got some errands to run down here. Madison, you take care."

"I will." With her pale impassive face, black hair, and dramatic eye makeup, she looked ready to go onstage. But then she was already playing the role of a woman who wasn't bereaved.

Aaron, for his part, made a sudden detour into romantic comedy. He tugged at my coat sleeve as I turned away and brought his face close to mine. "Remember, we'll be getting together soon for that bite."

"In your dreams, mister."

He laughed and turned back to Madison, slipping an arm around her shoulders and murmuring something sympathetic. She leaned into him gratefully and they walked off, looking for all the world like lovers.

I meant to stride purposefully away, just to keep up appearances, but they never glanced back. So I just stood there and watched them go, trying not to feel the way I was feeling. Then I pulled out my phone.

"Hi, Eddie. I'll be out for a while yet. Did Sally call about the dinner party?"

"Yeah, Friday night for sure, seven o'clock. And Frank Sanjek's coming over at three today, to talk about a new best man."

"I'll be there. See you."

There was just one problem about a rendezvous at Uwajimaya: The place was enormous. This being the week before Christmas, it was also mobbed. As I made my way through the cars crawling hopelessly around the parking lot, I was glad I'd left the van at a meter near the restaurant.

Under the blue-roofed Uwajimaya entrance, I paused to watch the constant stream of people in and out, and wondered how to find my small, shy waitress amid the holiday crowds. Even here the Salvation Army Santas were ringing their bells, and why not? Besides its exotic edibles, Uwajimaya housed a sizeable shop full of housewares, clothing, and gifts from all over Asia, as well as a large book, music, and video store. For Christmas shoppers seeking something unique, it was just the ticket.

Inside, the food store itself seemed to spread out for acres, with ranks upon ranks of fluorescent lights marching across the ceiling into the green-painted distance. Suspended beneath them was a huge Chinese dragon, big as a parade float, and below that were long grocery aisles offering everything from the most prosaic milk and eggs, to bento box lunches and elaborate sushi platters. In honor of the new year there were racks of tasseled red decorations like the ones at Noble Pearl, and rows of potted orange trees and pussy-willow bouquets. These last, I knew from a Chinese-American friend, were traditional New Year's gifts whose colors represented the gold and silver of prosperity to come.

After a few minutes of wandering in admiration, I did the logical thing and returned to the main entrance. Li Ping would have to find me. I stationed myself just inside, by a wall of twenty-pound rice sacks, and hoped that my height and hair color would make me easier to spot. I was certainly the only close-to-six-foot redhead studying the labels on the Yinzhu Extra Fancy Short Grain and the Thai Gold Jasmine Long Grain. Not to mention the Dynasty Dehraduni Basmati. I had just about exhausted my interest in the infinite variety of white rice in the world, when I heard a hesitant voice behind me.

"Come, quick!"

Li Ping was wearing a cheap acetate jacket in a hideous mustard color—*Too big for her. A hand-me-down?*—which I had no trouble following along a busy aisle and around a corner display of rice cookers. We ended up near a deep cooler full of packages, all of them variations in the key of tofu. The girl stared into it for a moment, catching her breath, then looked up at me between the curtains of her black hair.

"My uncle will be angry." Her voice was breathy and her accent thick, though it sure beat my mastery of Mandarin or my command of Cantonese. "He told everyone at the restaurant not to talk of Jase, to anyone."

"Why did you want to see me, then?" I asked gently. "Li Ping, you can tell me. Do you think your uncle had something to do with Jason's death?"

She looked entirely taken aback, and even affronted. "No, no! They were friendly, most friendly. He loaned money to Jase."

"To cover his gambling debts?"

She nodded, and went on with a rush, "Jase was going to pay it back, all the money, on Sunday night. Then he would come to me, but in secret. You cannot tell my uncle!"

"Of course I won't." Whether Jason Kraye had really cared for this girl, or had simply preyed on her naïveté, she was as much bereaved as Madison Jaffee, and with far fewer resources to help her recover. "What happened on Sunday night? Did your uncle go out to meet Jason?" *And perhaps to kill him?*

But Li Ping's next words blew that theory right out of the water. "No, he waited and waited, after the restaurant closed. He waited all night! I know, I waited also, upstairs."

"But Jason never came."

Her breath caught on a sob. "Never. He will never marry me."

I touched her arm in sympathy, and she gripped my hand with both of hers and squeezed it with all the desperation that she was trying to keep out of her face, here in this public setting. But she needn't have worried; all around us shoppers moved past without a glance, mesmerized by the bountiful merchandise.

"You were his friend," she whispered. I shook my head, afraid of what was coming, but she didn't raise her eyes. "You were friendly to me. Tell me, did Jase talk of me before . . . before he died? Did he say we would marry?"

At that point I damn near broke into tears myself. Only a monster would destroy her illusions now. "Li Ping, you have to understand, I only knew Jason slightly. He wouldn't have confided in me, not about something so . . . so secret and important. I'm sorry."

She bit her lip forlornly, as I tried to think my way through this tangle. *Do I have to report all this to the police, like I reported on Darwin? But look at what happened to him. Peter Yan is obviously not the killer, and this poor kid would get into such trouble . . .*

"Listen, I think it's better that you don't ask other people about Jason."

"I understand," she said, and released my hands. "I will go home."

"To your uncle's?" I thought she meant today, this afternoon, but I misunderstood.

"To Hong Kong." She drew a long uneven sigh. "I did not want to come to the United States. I am a student of music, not a waitress. I do not want to be American. My uncle will send me home."

That brought me back to my own problem with a jolt. "Li Ping, wait! I'm trying to find out who killed Jason. Can I ask you some questions?"

She looked at me dully. Jason was gone, that was all that mattered. She didn't even seem to wonder why a mere acquaintance would want to solve his murder.

"What questions?"

"Well, first of all, who did Jason gamble with? Your uncle mentioned 'prominent gentlemen.' Did you recognize any of them, maybe from the newspaper or the TV news?"

I talked fast, in case she took flight, but Li Ping seemed rooted to the spot, listless in her despair.

"My uncle said they were very important men." She sighed. Only one of the men had been important to her. "Some were on TV. I don't know the names."

I remembered the Smith and Jones business. "Well, never mind. Did Jason ever bring friends with him?"

A nod. "One friend, sometimes two."

"Can you describe them?" *If someone knew he'd be carrying a lot of money, someone who was at the bachelor party . . .*

"Men," she said, frowning. "Young men."

"What did they look like?"

At first we hit a road block; just like Westerners who can't tell a Chinese face from a Korean from a Japanese, Li Ping could only tell me that the two men were "tall like Jase." Given how diminutive she was herself, that could mean anything. But when I described a few of the taller guys from the bachelor party, and watched her nod or shake her head in turn, it was clear to me which friends the dead man had gambled with: Frank Sanjek and Lou Schulman.

"But Jason didn't ever bring a black man with him? You're sure?"

"I am sure," she said, her black hair swinging. "No black men there, only white and Chinese."

"And how much money was Jason supposed to deliver to your uncle?"

"Many thousands of dollars."

My informant was getting restless, and I was close to giving up, when one last question occurred to me. "How did Jason get so much money, anyway? Why was he suddenly able to pay back the loan?"

This sparked more of a response. "Jase was very smart! He had investments."

"Investments in what?" The stock market had been moribund for months.

Another frown, as Li Ping groped for the words. "High . . . technology. Big investment in high tech, he told me. He would be wealthy, and we would marry." Her eyes went dreamy, and then—I could actually see it happening—she dragged herself back to the cold, comfortless present. "I must shop for my uncle. I must go back."

She drew herself erect, and unfolded a slip of paper covered in Chinese characters. The top of her dark head didn't even reach my shoulder, but she was tapping some kind of inner strength, strength that would take her back home to China, and away from the memory of Jason Kraye.

Touched by her courage, I pulled out a Made in Heaven card and pressed it into her hand. "Listen, if you have any problems with your uncle, or if you just need someone to talk to, you can call me, all right?"

She pocketed the card without looking at it, and turned away without another word. As I watched her go, my cell phone sounded. I answered on autopilot, my thoughts all on Li Ping and her journey, but the caller got my attention fast enough.

"Carnegie, are you going to condescend to come to work today or not? It's like Grand Central Station around here!" Eddie sounded nearly unglued. My partner is not a people person, and working in Joe's busy establishment was getting on his nerves.

"Take it easy, Eddie. What's going on?"

"Every damn thing you can think of. I got Ivy Tyler raising hell, something about a confidential situation showing up in the newspaper. The Sanjek kid and his new best man, fellow named Schulman, are on their way over and they want some box from the bachelor party, but I don't see any damn box. And then this girl shows up without an appointment and wants a new-client pitch from you personally. Won't even talk to me."

Clever girl, I thought, as I hurried out of Uwajimaya and down the block toward Vanna. "Ask Joe to make nice to the bride, down in the tasting room, give her a glass of wine, whatever. I'll deal with Frank when he gets there. Meanwhile, put Ivy in my office. She'll cool off."

He snorted. "Fat chance."

Chapter Eighteen

WHEN I WAS A KID MY MOTHER, AT HEART A GENTLE SOUL, would sometimes lose it. If my father had been out to sea for months, and my brother and I were raising more than our share of Cain, she would sometimes round on us with a fierce eye and a tight mouth and snap, "Just *stop* it, both of you! I Am In No Mood."

That's how I felt when I got back to Solveto's and faced Ivy Tyler. On the one hand I'd seen a brokenhearted Li Ping, her suitor slain and her dreams despoiled, trudge off into her lonely future. On the other I saw a beautifully groomed multimillionaire fulminating in my office, accusing me of leaking her secret deal to *The Seattle Times*. This on top of the fact that my best friend wasn't speaking to me and the man I—well, the man I liked a lot—was not only married but was now off somewhere consoling the lovely and talented Madison Jaffee, was just too much.

I was in No Mood.

"It must have been you!" said Ivy. Her throat was mottled red above the cowl of a lush white cashmere sweater. "I told you to be discreet out at Habitat, and then someone saw you dining at Etta's with Kevin Bauer, for God's sake!"

"My dinner with Kevin is in the *Times*?"

"Of course not. But this is, and I want to know how it got there!"

She slapped the business section on my desk, and I glanced at the headline: "MFC Gulping Down Habitat? Ivy Tyler Won't Rule Out Holiday Layoffs." Then I looked up at my accuser with a fierce eye and a tight mouth.

"Sit down! Right now."

It wasn't the response she expected; fear and trembling would be more like it. But she dropped into a chair, looking startled by my tone, and maybe by her own outburst. Maybe playing coffee mogul and mother of the bride simultaneously was getting to be a bit much, even for her. I sat behind my desk and took a deep breath.

"My professional reputation is of the utmost importance to me." I measured out the words, quiet but emphatic. "Betraying the privacy of my clients would destroy my reputation. Ivy, you and I have been working together for months, and I'd like to think we've become friends. Now either you trust me or you don't. Which is it?"

Ivy began to bluster, but she ran out of steam almost immediately. "We've kept a lid on the merger all this time, and when I heard you were out with Kevin, naturally I thought..."

"Which is it?"

A pause, but only a brief one. "I trust you. Of course I trust you. I just hate being blindsided...and things have been difficult lately." She slumped in her chair, massaging her temple with the fingertips of one hand, suddenly looking her age.

"I live in a fishbowl, Carnegie. The success of MFC depends far too much on my personal image. Rags to riches, the mom who made good, America's hostess. This story makes me out as a coldhearted bitch, when all I'm doing is behaving like any normal CEO. *Male* CEO. But that's my problem, not yours. I apologize."

"Accepted." I opened my calendar, trying to hide my relief that she hadn't fired me on the spot. "So where does that leave us? For whatever reason, the merger isn't secret anymore. Do you still want a January press conference at the Habitat plant?"

She shook her head in resignation. "The whole thing will be old news by then. I've lost control of the story."

"Then take it back!" I had a sudden bright idea, the kind that goes straight from my imagination to my mouth without due diligence on the part of my brain. "Habitat's Christmas party is Saturday. Why not make the official announcement then, with a big show of holiday cheer and an assurance that everybody's job is safe? That would make a terrific image. You could pick up the tab for the party, bring in some fancier food and drink, and invite a couple of reporters."

"Wait a minute, who said all the jobs are safe? Layoffs don't look necessary at this point, but I like to keep my options open."

I took an even bigger chance then, and stepped right over the wedding planner line. "Ivy, your options are these people's livelihoods. You know what the job market is like right now. The Habitat employees are one big family. If you want to make this look like a change for the better, then firing family members at Christmas, or even leaving them in limbo, isn't exactly the way—"

"All right, already, we'll have a party!" She was laughing at me now, but fondly. "Kevin must have swept you off your feet. And here I thought you and Aaron had some potential. Which one sent the roses?"

"Neither," I said, scribbling furiously to cover my blush. "It's just, um, floral samples. From a colleague. OK, once you get the go-ahead from Kevin about the party, I'll contact who-ever's planning it . . . probably Fiona . . . let's see, music, bev-erages, food . . . Joe can put antipasti together on short notice . . . oh, hell!" I'd forgotten that Joe was downstairs in his tasting room, baby-sitting a bride. "Ivy, I've got a prospec-tive client waiting for me. Can we go over this tonight at the apartment?"

"Of course." Mention of the apartment raised the specter of last night's intruder, for both of us, and Ivy's brow fur-rowed in concern. "Carnegie, I should have asked right away, are you sure you're not hurt? My secretary said you weren't, but getting bowled over in the dark like that must have been so upsetting."

"I wouldn't care to repeat the experience," I said ruefully. "But I'm perfectly OK."

"Thank God. I had new locks put in this afternoon, and the Market management is beefing up security. Still, I'll un-derstand if you don't want to stay."

The thought of moving once again was more than I could bear. "I'll be fine. I should have my houseboat back soon, but meanwhile, if it doesn't inconvenience you, I really ap-preciate having somewhere so nice to hang out."

"That's the spirit. Here's a key for you, then." Ivy rose and took the key from her purse, a designer item costing more than everything now on my body. "It's no inconven-ience in the least. I'm spending most nights in Snohomish anyway. You go tend to your new bride, and I'll see you this evening before I drive home. Don't forget, my dinner party for the Sanjeks is tomorrow night. Come early."

Of course, she should have been apologizing again, instead of issuing instructions. But people like Ivy, self-made successes, rarely apologize the first time. I shrugged it off, grabbed some new-bride paperwork, and headed down the back stairs.

Solveto's tasting room was a smaller version of those you see in wineries: a pleasant, hospitable space on the ground floor of the building. Joe had conceived it as an elegant mini-restaurant, complete with two-burner stove, warming oven, and a walk-in cooler in one corner. The cooler was an old one Joe had salvaged and installed as an afterthought, but even then he'd had it paneled in tongue-and-groove white cedar to match the rest of the room. Tall French windows faced the Ship Canal, a doorway opened to the sidewalk, and a staff-only inside passage led through from the back stairs and the kitchens. At the long bar or the scattered tables, clients could sample a new entree, compare various wines, or just review their menus and contracts.

The new bride seemed quite at home, perched at a table in the soft, warm lamplight that was artfully calculated to stimulate the appetite. Joe himself was emerging from the cooler as I entered, with a split of champagne and a small plate of what I recognized as Alonzo's best appetizers. *I owe you one, Joe.*

As he presented these goodies, I did a quick scan of my visitor: tall, blonde, model-thin and model-pretty, with expensive clothes and—even more expensive—bionic breasts. Her left hand bore a diamond ring the size of a compact car. *I owe you big.*

"Carnegie, this is Andrea. I'll leave you two to talk." Joe poured our bubbly, and gave Andrea a smile that conveyed his infinite regret at parting. Joe was good.

"*So* nice to meet you," I said. "What a gorgeous ring..."

First consultations with brides are my favorite part of the job. But with so much else happening today, I wasn't at the top of my form. Fortunately, my visitor took the lead, asking about my qualifications and methods in some detail. That was fine with me; I gave her the rundown about Made in Heaven, and showed her my "look book" of happy couples, splendid receptions, and glowing letters of gratitude from various brides and their mothers.

"Very impressive," said Andrea coolly. "You must be one of the most successful wedding planners in the area."

I made a diplomatic reply—arrogance tempts the gods— and put forth questions of my own. These fell into various categories, beginning with the basics: budget, preferred type of venue, possible length of the guest list, and whether a date was already selected.

Andrea had those down cold: she wanted a wedding weekend for two hundred people sometime next autumn, with a church ceremony, a formal dinner, and various subsidiary events. The budget was—sweet music to my ears— open-ended. *That would satisfy even Eddie,* I thought. *Maybe we could finally upgrade our computer system.*

"We'd need to start looking at locations soon, to get the best choice," I told her, "but since you're flexible about the exact date, I'm sure we could come up with something wonderful."

I sketched out my fee structure and showed her an outline of the general planning process. I also presented a breakdown of my services, from interviewing vendors to adjusting her veil to depositing her relatives back at the airport. If she hired me and Eddie, the buildup to Andrea's special day would be a major part of our working year.

"Let's do it," she said. Rather casually, considering she'd just met me.

"Wonderful! I'll draw up a letter of agreement for us to sign."

She nodded and sipped her wine. "So, what colors do you think for the bridesmaids' dresses?"

"Well, before we get that specific, let's daydream a little." I personally was daydreaming of my bank balance, but that's not what I meant. "Tell me off the top of your head, if you could spend a day and night exactly as you wanted, anywhere in the world, what would it be like?"

She frowned prettily. "What's that got to do with the wedding?"

"It's a way for me to get a sense of your personal style. Also, it helps you to step back from your preconceptions about weddings, and think about the things that are really meaningful and joyful to you. Then we try to incorporate some of those elements into your wedding. I always ask my brides about their favorite books and movies, landscapes that speak to them, periods of history they find intriguing, things like that."

"Oh." She seemed nonplussed. "I thought we could talk about dresses."

"We can, of course. It's just that—excuse me just a minute, would you?"

Kelli was in the doorway, beckoning wildly. She drew me out into the hall and whispered, "You better come upstairs!"

"Can't you see I'm with a client?"

"I know, but does Eddie have high blood pressure?"

"What?"

"Because he's yelling at Filipo and turning kind of purple, so I wondered—"

"I'll be there in one minute. Go."

I made a smooth apology to Andrea and charged back up

the stairs two at a time. Eddie and the prep cook were squared off in the reception area, steam issuing from all four ears. My partner was purple, all right. He was used to peace and quiet when he worked, and Solveto's offered neither. Especially today.

"He calls me thief!" Filipo appealed to me, his Latin melodrama at full throttle. "Carnegie, defend me to this man!"

"Hang on, would you? Eddie, what's happening? Make it quick, I've got a bride downstairs."

"Well, you've got a groom up here," Eddie retorted, hooking a thumb toward my office, "and he's asking for the box of gifts left behind at the Hot Spot after his bachelor party. Kelli says this character here stole it."

"Borrowed!" said the cook, his hands swooping through the air like distressed Venezuelan birds. "I see the sexy things in the box so I borrow it, for a small joke on *mi amigo* Alonzo."

"Never mind about the joke," I said sternly. "Where's the box?"

He shifted guiltily. "At Alonzo's apartment. I arrange a few things, you see, and when his girlfriend come home she will be mad at him. Very funny!"

I closed my eyes. *I'll rent*, I thought, exasperated almost to tears. *If Eddie and I don't get back in the houseboat soon, I'm going to rent an apartment and an office both. This is intolerable.*

"No, Filipo, it's not funny at all," I said. "The things in that box are private property, and you took them without permission, which is called theft. I want you to go to Alonzo's right this minute and bring everything back."

"But I am cooking—"

"*Now*, Filipo. I'll fix it with Joe. Now!"

He made his exit, still gesticulating, and I entered my office to deal with Frank. The young bridegroom seemed calm enough, even a little embarrassed about the fuss. But Lou Schulman was distinctly ill at ease, pacing the few steps back and forth that my quarters allowed, flexing his meaty hands and blinking his small, dull eyes. I remembered what Fiona said about him: a genius with software, clueless with life in general. Some best man.

"Hi, guys," I said in a breezy, no-big-deal voice. "Frank, your party gifts were . . . misplaced, but we'll have them back shortly. Sorry about the delay."

"No prob," he said. "I guess you heard about Lou being best man now."

"Indeed, I did. Welcome to the wedding party." I extended my right hand, but Lou caught up my left one instead.

"Is your cut OK? I'm really sorry."

"It's fine!" I said, disguising a wince of pain. I'd replaced the large bandage with some small adhesive strips. The gash was healing, but still tender.

"I want to make it up to you," he said. "I'll take you out to dinner tomorrow night, OK?"

"Not necessary, really." I proceeded quickly, torn between curiosity about these gambling buddies of the late lamented Jason, and eagerness to return to the well-diamonded Andrea. "Besides, tomorrow night is the rehearsal dinner at Ivy's house in Snohomish. Do you need a map?"

Lou favored me with an insinuating smirk. "Are *you* going to it?"

"As a matter of fact, I am."

"I'll drive then, and you can give directions. I've got a brand new Porsche. A 911 Turbo."

He offered this thrilling news with a leer, and I realized that Mr. Garlic was hoping for a replay of the bachelor party incident. Only without the slap. *Right, bucko, the minute hell emerges from its next ice age.*

"Thanks anyway. Here's the map, and I'll get you the tuxedo rental form, and the schedule—"

"You can take me and Sally," said Frank. "You said I could drive the Porsche sometime, and she can fill you in on the wedding stuff."

Lou nodded sourly, and I changed the subject. "Frank, can I ask you something about Jason?"

"Sure." His eyes were guileless.

"Did you ever go gambling with him? Either of you?"

For a single suspended moment, the room fell silent. I could hear the *click-clicking* of Kelli's keyboard out in reception, and the flat blast of an air horn from the Ship Canal, as some pleasure boat requested passage under the Fremont Drawbridge. Then both men spoke at once.

"No!" said Lou.

"Sometimes," said Frank.

The groom gave his best man a puzzled look, then I heard a quick intake of breath as he read the unspoken message on Lou's face.

"Sometimes," Frank amended, "but a long time ago. Not anytime recently. Um, we'd better go now."

"What about your box of gifts?"

"Could you just bring it tomorrow night? Only, um, maybe you could—"

"Put a lid on it, so no one sees what's inside?"

He nodded thankfully, and they hustled out of Solveto's.

I left the elevator to them and clattered down the back stairs, pondering several new questions. Frank Sanjek was the world's worst liar, but why lie about gambling with Jason? And was Lou just anxious about his role as best man, or had something else been preying on him?

I stopped at the tasting room door to catch my breath and switch my brain to wedding mode. But the questions lingered. Why hadn't Frank, or Lou either, asked the reason for my probing into Jason's gambling? Why not tell me to mind my own business? Then I pushed open the door and another question arose.

Where the hell was Andrea?

Her coat was gone, her wineglass stood empty, and a ball-point scrawl on the paper napkin beneath the glass said only, "Had to run. I'll call you."

My lucrative new client, no, my lucrative new *potential* client, had vanished. And I, too mired in Jason's death to truly mind my own business, didn't have a letter of agreement from her. In fact, I didn't even know her last name.

Chapter Nineteen

AFTER THE ANDREA FIASCO, I HAD A BLESSEDLY QUIET NIGHT IN Ivy's guest bed, and then I swore to spend all day Friday hard at work. My *own* work—like placing reminder phone calls to Bonnie Buckmeister's vendors, and arranging all the embellishments to the Habitat Christmas party. Kevin Bauer had agreed to an early announcement of the merger, Ivy's secretary Jenna had told me, so I should go ahead and shoot the works. Money was no object. I love it when money is no object.

I made a good start on both projects, even though my partner had gone AWOL. When I got to my borrowed desk Friday morning, I'd had a message from Eddie, couched in his own inimitable style.

"Look, sister, I'm not getting a damn thing done around there, so I'm taking some time off, at least a week. You know where the files are, and you can call me if you need to." A pause as he began to hang up, and then a postscript: "I might not answer, though. Merry Christmas, anyway."

His bailout was annoying, but not entirely unreasonable. Eddie's half-time work for me often stretched to full-time, while his paychecks—when he agreed to cash them—didn't stretch at all. He was never sick, as a matter of principle, and he'd taken a vacation maybe twice in the three years of Made in Heaven's history.

Well, I could handle the Habitat party on my own, and his behind-the-scenes work on Tyler/Sanjek and Buckmeister/Frost was all done. Still, I'd miss his grumpy company. I'd thought about inviting him out to Christmas dinner. I sure wouldn't be welcome at Lily's house.

Maybe by next week, I thought, erasing the message, *I can welcome Eddie back to the houseboat and then take some time off myself. We'll get Andrea's wedding on the calendar, then I'll take a day trip with Kevin . . .*

But I set aside that agreeable thought. Better not jinx it by getting ahead of myself; better to see how things went at the Habitat party first. Feeling virtuous and resolute, I plowed into my phone calls, and when I received a call from Aaron, eager to compare notes, I put him off until lunch and kept working.

"I don't have much time," I told him, over the same table at the Fisherman's Daughter where we'd had breakfast two days before. We even had the same waitress, a stark brunette with Unemployed Actress written all over her. She gave Aaron a sultry, welcome-back smile, though she seemed to have forgotten me entirely. Funny about that.

I was still debating whether to tell Aaron about Li Ping. He was a newshound, after all, despite his current role as author, and I was afraid he'd insist on following that particular trail, with disastrous results for the girl. I put off the decision by asking about his calls to the other bachelor-party guests.

"Not much luck," he told me. "The guys who were sober enough to remember had the same impression I did, that the atmosphere was rowdy but not dangerous."

"Did you talk to Lou Schulman?"

He flipped through his notes. "Let's see . . . left the same time as some other guys, drove home alone, didn't notice anything out of the ordinary. Apparently, no one saw Kraye's scuffle with Darwin except you. Frank doesn't remember it. Too busy puking."

"So the police are still fixated on Darwin?"

"Yeah. Mike Graham is doing what he can. He's got a search going for Darwin's discarded clothes. Of course, the killer wasn't necessarily splashed with blood, but finding the clothes *without* blood on them would at least support his story."

"Darwin still can't remember where he drove on Sunday night?"

He shook his head. "Complete alcohol blackout. Mike's got people showing Dar's picture around, and also a picture of his car. So far, no luck."

"Aaron, have you talked to Lily? How's she holding up?"

"Not well. She's gone back to work, and of course the boys are a distraction, but it's going to be a lousy Christmas." He sighed, and then got back to business. "What makes you zero in on Schulman? The fact that he groped you once?"

"He doesn't want to stop at once. Yesterday he offered me a ride in his Porsche."

"So, did that make you go all weak at the knees? I'd better start saving up." Aaron drove a banana-yellow Volkswagen Bug with an extensive collection of rust spots.

"Very funny. But listen, I asked Frank and Lou straight out if they ever gambled with Jason. Frank's such a Boy Scout that he started to say yes, but then Lou gave him the sign and he switched to no. They were obviously lying!"

"Obvious to you is one thing," said Aaron. "Conclusively

proved is another. And besides, a casual game of cards here and there doesn't mean much."

"I wouldn't call thousands of dollars 'casual.'"

Oops. His tuna sandwich stopped in midair.

"Who says they were playing for thousands of dollars?"

"Never mind. I don't want her involved."

"Her? Madison? She would have told me..." His eyebrows rose. Aaron was very, very quick on the uptake. "The little waitress! The one who dumped lunch on you. I *thought* you looked secretive when you came back from the rest room. Was she pouring the Tsing Tao at these card games?"

"What's Tsing Tao?"

"Chinese beer. Quit stalling. Was she?"

I bit my lip. "It's more than that. She was in love with Jason."

Aaron put the sandwich down in disgust. "What is it with these women, that they'd fall for a slimy type like him? I can understand the girl, she must be, what, nineteen? But Maddie's an alpha female if I ever saw one."

"Excuse me?"

"Well, look at her! She's beautiful, she's sophisticated, she's got a hotshot job, why would she bother with Jason Kraye?"

"I can't imagine." I was shooting for a tone of utter indifference, but apparently I missed.

"Hold the phone, Stretch, is that *jealousy* I'm hearing?" Aaron left off theorizing to peer at me, his chocolate-brown eyes full of amusement. Very irritating amusement. "Because if you care enough to be jealous, then there's hope for me yet, and I don't need a Porsche. You're saving me a bundle here!"

"Oh, shut up. I agree with you, Madison's extremely attractive—"

"Yes, she is." He reached over and brushed the back of

my hand. Just once, but the sensation seemed to linger. "She's also in mourning. Carnegie, Madison's boyfriend just died. I don't think they were soul mates, from the way she's acting, but it must have been traumatic. I would hardly come on to her at a time like this, OK?"

I reached for my bag and fussed around paying the check. There were any number of things I could have said at this point, like "Does that mean you'd come on to her at some other time?" and "What's it to me anyway?" and oh, all kinds of sensible things like that. Instead, once the busboy was out of earshot, I just muttered, "OK."

"Now," said Aaron, sitting back and slapping the table. "Let's get Noble Pearl on the phone."

But a conversation with the gum-chewing son told us we were too late. Yes, Li Ping used to work there, but no, not anymore. Li Ping had returned to Hong Kong. A phone number? No, they didn't have a phone number for Li Ping. She planned to go traveling for a while, somewhere in China. No itinerary, no forwarding address. No deal.

I was remorseful. "I should have told you right away, and Mike Graham, too. But I just couldn't. She was so young, Aaron, and so brokenhearted."

He touched my hand again, and this time I began to turn my palm up to meet his. But he'd already withdrawn it, to get out his notebook, and I got hold of myself, instead. No doubt he held hands with his wife, too.

"Don't beat yourself up," he was saying. "I might have done the same thing. Just tell me exactly what she said."

"All right, but then I really have to get back to work." I related my conversation with Li Ping, word for word where I could. It was little enough, except for the bit about investments.

"High tech, huh?" Aaron underlined the phrase twice, then a third time. "So Kraye is due for a windfall from some kind of technology deal, and then he gets killed. The two things might be related."

"Or he might have been lying, to impress a girl."

"Maybe," he said, flipping backward in his notebook. "But wasn't Schulman at a dot-com? Yeah, your friend Fiona said so. Of course, if it went belly-up, nobody's investing in it these days . . . hmm. Not much of a connection, but you never know. Let's go over all these notes at dinner, OK?"

"I can't. I'm working tonight." I explained about Ivy's dinner party, and Lou's new role as best man.

"That's perfect!" Aaron shrugged into his pea coat. "You run along and be charming to Schulman, and see what you can worm out of him. Wear something sexy. Get the name of the dot-com, find out if Kraye worked there, too, and sound him out about high-tech investments."

"Forget it!" I said. "I'm not going to encourage that oaf. Can't Madison snoop around in Jason's personnel records?"

"I am *shocked* that you would suggest something so unethical. Good idea, I'll ask her. But you should still see what you can pick up from him in person. Scope out Frank some more, too, though I'd be surprised if it was him."

"I'd be astonished. Nobody's that good an actor."

Back at the office, I settled down to review the guest list for tonight's gathering: the bridal couple, all four parents, the groom's one sister, the best man and maid of honor, and me. Ten people in all. Although, for once, the exact head count didn't matter; Ivy, loath to host a stilted formal meal, had taken my suggestion to engage a sushi chef for the evening. Now there's an ice breaker for you.

Tonight I'd be meeting Charles Tyler for the first time,

and also Frank Sanjek's sister, Erica. I'd already met his parents, a pair of small, soft-spoken people from Spokane whose transposition of their own first names to their children's—Frances and Eric begat Frank and Erica—was apparently the only walk on the wild side they'd ever taken. They were proud of their boy. To be marrying not just an heiress, but the daughter of the famous Ivy Tyler, well, that was really something. I liked the Sanjeks.

I couldn't say the same for Sally's maid of honor, Brittany, a chattery girl obsessed with celebrity gossip. But she was going to look fabulous on New Year's Eve in her shorter version of Sally's black gown. This was one bridesmaid's dress that could definitely be worn again . . .

Yikes! Suddenly, in midlist, I remembered the one detail I'd overlooked: fetching my trusty jade-green silk—my own dress for tonight's dinner—from the cleaner's. It was almost time to leave anyway, given the drive ahead of me, so I gathered up my things and called ahead to make sure it was ready.

"I'll just put it out front for you," came the cheerful voice of the Qwik-Kleen proprietor. She was used to my dashing in and out. "I'll hang it by the register . . . hmm . . . where do you suppose . . . wait a sec, would you, honey?"

The receiver at her end clattered down; the Qwik-Kleen didn't run to HOLD buttons. I pressed the phone to my ear, straining for the distant noises of the mechanized clothes rack as it ground along, the suits and shirts swaying, imagining my jade silk coming around on the next pass . . . *please?*

"Well," she said, "it is just not here. Isn't that funny?"

"No," I said plaintively, "not really. Could you look again?"

"I'm still lookin', honey, but if it isn't here, it isn't here.

I'll call you tomorrow, OK, and if we can't find the garment, we'll replace it a' course, it's in our guarantee—"

"Fine, whatever. Call me."

Damn, damn, damn. Most of my clothes were at the houseboat, and the dove-gray suit was still bloody. Well, didn't I deserve a new dress once in a while? I checked my watch: just enough time to dash downtown, make a quick but hopefully wise selection, and change at Ivy's apartment. And if I saved the tags and didn't spill anything, I could always return the dress tomorrow.

What with running orange lights and having good parking karma, twenty minutes later I was on an escalator in the Bon Marche, heading up to Better Dresses. I was gazing vaguely at the back of the woman above me on the escalator when I came to with a little start.

"Lily?"

The woman turned around. My dear friend looked like hell, with puffy eyes and drawn complexion, but she actually smiled. If I had telephoned, I bet she would have hung up on me, but appearing face-to-face like this was too immediate for either of us to resist.

"Oh, Carnegie, I . . . I'm so *sorry.*"

"So am I, Lily, more than I can say. And I miss you!"

"I miss you, too. So do the boys. 'Where's Aunt Carrie?' I hear it twenty times a day."

Her eyes were bright with tears. We half-hugged, me reaching up and Lily down, and then we were startled into laughter when the escalator dumped us off at the top. We moved out of the stream of shoppers we were blocking— honestly, people can be so cross at Christmas—and stood among the racks of glittery holiday dresses, first embracing and then stepping back, holding on by both hands. Holding on to friendship.

"They let Darwin go," she said, her voice tremulous.

"That's wonderful! So the police found out who did it?"

She shook her head emphatically. "No, they still suspect him. They just didn't have enough of a case to charge him with murder, and there was some kind of time limit. But Mike says they can always rearrest him."

"I see. Lily, this must be hell for both of you."

"We'll get through. He's staying at my house for now. I want Marcus and Ethan to see that he's still their Uncle Dar." Marcus was six years old, and Ethan four. Too young for abstract explanations.

"That's good, Lily. And you're seeing Mike?"

"Just talking on the phone, and he shouldn't even be doing that. Aaron comes over a lot, though." She squeezed my hands. "He told me where you're staying, and that you're helping him figure this out."

"I'm trying. We'll do what we can." I thought about the mission Aaron gave me, to charm Lou Schulman, and sighed. "Everything we possibly can."

"Bless you both," she said. "I just called Aaron, to tell him Dar was home. He said he'd have some research for me to do soon, on a dot-com or something. Listen, I was just on my break, trying to find this one last gift for Ethan, but I've got to give up for now. Can you walk back to the library with me?"

"I wish I could, Lily, but I've got a rehearsal dinner in Snohomish in . . . Ack! In two hours. I've got to grab a dress and get going. What's the gift, though? Maybe I can find it for him later."

"Are you ready for this? Ethan wants a toilet for his superhero action figures!" She laughed out loud, that wonderful throaty laugh of hers, and it did my heart good to hear it again. "He was so proud of using the potty on his own last year, and now all of a sudden he's decided that his guys should do the same thing!"

I joined her in laughter. "That's Ethan all over. Listen, I'll call you tomorrow, OK?"

"You do that." She hugged me again. "And you come for Christmas like we planned. Promise?"

"Promise. Tell the boys."

She took the down escalator. I watched her descend out of sight—she glanced up and waved—and then I started to search for a dress that would knock the socks off Clueless Lou.

Chapter Twenty

THE DRESS WAS STUNNING BUT THE TRAFFIC WAS CRAWLING, and I was late for Ivy's dinner.

At least gridlock gives you time to finish doing your makeup, and call ahead to say you'll be late. And to slurp some coffee, too; I always crank up on caffeine before a big client event, and with time so short, it had to ride with me in a thermos. So I sipped and painted and fumed and sipped some more—Habitat coffee was excellent—at about nineteen miles an hour. When the traffic thinned out, just past the commuter cutoff for the Mukilteo Ferry, I put aside the thermos and gunned it.

I thought I was home free at the exit for Snohomish, but I hadn't realized how far out in the country the Tylers' country house was. After miles of secondary roads and a couple of wrong turns, I came at last to a private gravel lane winding through the darkness. It delivered me to a three-story mansion secluded in its own private woods, the proud residence of some turn-of-the-century timber baron. I parked Vanna and hurried across the wide cobbled courtyard, groaning to see all the cars there already.

The front door was a massive oaken affair, flanked by coaching lanterns. I rang the bell and waited, grateful that the air was less icy than it had been lately. Looming high above me, the walls of age-softened gray shingle sprouted bay windows and corner turrets and a cedar-shake mansard roof, complete with widow's walk. The baron didn't fool around.

An imperturbable middle-aged woman in a maid's uniform let me in and took my coat, leaving me garbed in nothing but goose bumps and a flimsy scrap of purple satin. Not exactly indecent—I was working, after all—but having my hemline and my neckline in such close proximity was way beyond my comfort zone. *No spilling tonight,* I vowed, *and this rag goes back to the Bon tomorrow. Boys and girls, can you spell "slut"?*

Clicking along on my highest heels, I followed the maid through a lofty front hall and past a grand staircase, its banisters and newel posts carved in dark, gleaming wood. Beside the stairs stood a Christmas tree, twelve feet tall at least and decorated in high Victorian style. Marcus and Ethan would have loved it.

We came to a set of fine paneled doors, from behind which came voices and a burst of laughter. The doors opened to the living room, where the first faces I saw were Ivy Tyler's, looking furiously at her watch, and Lou Schulman's, looking at my dress like he'd been hit from behind with a two by four.

"Nice of you to drop by," Ivy muttered through a gritted-teeth smile. She seized my elbow and turned her back to her guests. "I told you to come early!"

"I'm awfully sorry, Ivy. Traffic. I'll go check in with Andy."

Andy was Andrew Mikami, private chef, master of sushi and showmanship, and a pleasure to work with. He was busy at the marble-topped prep island in the middle of Ivy's kitchen, arranging a display of slicing knives, rice paddles, and immaculate raw ingredients on black porcelain dishes. I recognized *gari*—pickled ginger—and *nori*—the sheets of seaweed for rolling—and of course the rice, but the ice-filled tray of seafood held some mysteries. The tuna and shrimp were familiar, and even the squid, but the remaining items were beyond my ken.

As I walked in, Andy looked me up and down and gave a wolf whistle. "Carnegie on the half-shell, very nice!"

I blushed. "Too much?"

"Not at all. A different look for you, but a good one." Then he turned businesslike. "I need fifteen minutes, OK?"

"You got it. I'll put out the flowers." I had decided on orchids for tonight, in lacquered vases that the ladies could take home with them. I'd also rented high stools and tables for better viewing of the culinary performance, and was relieved to see how well they fit into an arc around the island. I adjusted each delicate spray of orchids to just the perfect angle, and straightened the inlaid teak chopsticks at each place.

"Can I help?" asked the maid from the kitchen doorway.

"I think we're set," I told her. "If you'll just—I'm sorry, I don't know your name?"

"Eleanor."

"OK, Eleanor, if you'll just check in with Andy from time to time, to see if he needs anything. I'll be out with the guests."

The living room was long and gracious, with cream-colored plaster walls and mahogany picture rails, hung now with evergreen garlands. At the far end, an immense field-stone fireplace was guarded by a brass fire screen in a peacock's tail design. Most of the party was clustered there, but Lou was waiting by the doorway. The minute I entered, his beery breath was on my cheek. At least our hostess served a classy brand of beer.

"Man, you look *hot,*" he said, in a hoarse but fortunately low voice. "I really dig redheads."

I did some gritting and smiling of my own, but I had fences to mend with Ivy before I started charming Lou. I gave her the high sign, that everything was on track in the kitchen, then went to the fireplace and scraped Lou off on Frank's parents like a horse leaving its rider on a low-hanging tree limb.

"Mr. and Mrs. Sanjek, so nice to see you again." Small and washed-out and quite unremarkable-looking, they were nibbling on hors d'oeuvres like two modest little mice. "You've met the best man, I'm sure. Lou, tell the folks about that new car of yours, why don't you?"

I left the three of them together and went over to Brittany, the irrepressible maid of honor, who was chatting gaily to a young woman who must be Frank Sanjek's sister.

"Carnegie, this is Erica. Doesn't she look just like Frank?"

I had to agree. Erica shared her brother's bland good looks, with curly gold-brown hair and wide, sparkling eyes. She also shared his open, ingenuous manner.

"I'm glad you're here!" she burbled. "I've been trying to figure out about a dress for the ceremony. I have this really pretty one, but it's white, and I know you're not supposed to wear white to someone else's wedding, only Sally's wearing black, isn't she? Is she *really* wearing black? That's so . . . well, I guess it's sophisticated, isn't it? So could I wear white or would that still be rude?"

"You and your mother can wear whatever you like," I reassured her. "Black or white, or anything else, so long as it's on the formal side, to go with the gentlemen's tuxedos. I'm sure you'll look lovely, Erica. Did Sally tell you about the flowers? They're going to be gorgeous."

As the wedding talk flowed along, I scanned the room for Frank and Sally, but they were elsewhere. At first I thought Ivy's husband was absent as well, but then I turned toward a leather wing chair drawn up to the fire, and found myself in the presence of Charles Tyler.

Presence was precisely the word. It wasn't just that I recognized him from old pictures and broadcasts: the narrow bald head and the eyes dark as onyx under snowy brows. No photograph, not even a film, could have captured how it felt to be in the same room with him. Even seated, even aging, even in weakened health as he clearly was, Charles Tyler was commanding.

Admittedly, I would have taken him for a man of seventy-five, not the sixty-something that Joe had mentioned to me. Tyler's skin hung loose on his face, as if he'd lost weight in some harsh fashion, and he slumped back in the chair as if he was grappling with gravity, and gravity was winning.

But his brooding gaze, from eyes so dark that they seemed all pupil, arrested me where I stood. His shoulders were wide and unbowed under the rough tweed of his old-fashioned jacket, and his hands were preternaturally large, with long powerful fingers. He waved a hand at me now, and I excused myself to Erica and Brittany.

"You're the wedding planner," Tyler said, as if pronouncing a foreign phrase. His English accent gave an aristocratic lift to the raspy voice. "My girls talk about you constantly. Sit, sit."

I sat, wondering about "girls" plural, then realized that he meant Ivy as well as Sally. Odd to think of Ivy Tyler as anyone's girl. The mahogany piecrust table between us held a carafe and water glass. I set my sherry down beside them.

"I've been looking forward to meeting you," I began, tritely but truly.

"Because you're such a fan of my music, I suppose?" The onyx eyes were mocking. "I'll wager that you prefer something sweeter. Let's see, Strauss waltzes? Pachelbel's *Canon*?"

"I'm sick to death of Pachelbel!" I protested. "And I'm not crazy about Strauss, either."

"Then whom do you prefer? Quickly now, your very favorite."

Somehow the small talk had become a challenge. I glanced around—the other guests were occupying themselves just fine—and turned back to my inquisitor. If he thought I was going to name some obscure composer just to impress him, he was wrong. I don't know much about classical music, but I'm damn sure I know what I like.

"Beethoven," I declared. "The string quartets."

"Hah!" He pointed a long finger at me, his hand twitching just a bit. "But which one?"

"The first Rasumovsky." Maybe that was trite, too, but I'd loved that piece since the first time I heard it, at a concert back home in Boise.

"*Really.*" The dark eyes narrowed in appraisal. "Well, well, well."

And the old devil actually hummed the first few notes of the quartet's cello theme. He was testing me! I hummed right back at him, completing the theme, and he tilted his finely modeled bald head and laughed, an unexpectedly young and hearty sound.

"You'll do," said Charles Tyler, and I felt like I'd been

knighted, or damed, or whatever it is that women get. "You'll do very well."

"May I join you?"

The voice was familiar, but not one that I expected to hear tonight: Kevin Bauer. He wore the same gray fisherman's knit sweater as the other night, and he was gazing at Tyler like a kid meeting Santa Claus. Then he focused on me, apparently for the first time, and almost dropped his teeth. "Carnegie! I didn't see you come in. That's . . . quite a dress."

Chapter Twenty-One

KEVIN'S TONE WAS LUKEWARM, WITH A NOTE OF SOMETHING—disapproval?—that left me hovering between embarrassment and irritation.

"Thank you," I said, mildly defiant. "I just bought it."

"And *I* applaud it," said Tyler roguishly. "It shows off your, ah, charms, very nicely. Very nicely, indeed."

"Well, Kevin," said Ivy, coming up behind us, "are you satisfied with your part of the bargain?" She caught my puzzled look and laughed. "Habitat agreed to announce the merger at their holiday party tomorrow night, *if* the CEO here got an invitation to meet a certain composer. Kevin, come have a drink with me and talk business. You can schmooze with Charles over dinner."

As she led Kevin away, Tyler looked at me shrewdly.

"A particular friend of yours, I take it?"

"Y-yes," I told him. "Yes, he is."

"I approve." He patted my knee and I felt his hand twitch again, a sudden sideways jerk that we both pretended not to notice. "Mr. Bauer knows his music. What's more, he knows mine, and I'm not above a little flattery."

"Kevin's talked a lot about you. I mean, about your career."

"And did he tell you that my career is over?" His entire

arm twitched this time, and he imprisoned one hand in the other, to still it. "My body is proving quite disloyal."

"I'm sorry," I said, matching his bluntness with my own "It must be very hard."

Tyler looked around. Sally and Frank were just entering from a side door—I could have sworn their clothes were disheveled—and the other guests gathered around them. The group moved away, everyone talking merrily and refreshing their glasses at the handsome drinks cabinet across the room. The hiss and crackle of the fire lent the two of us a sense of privacy.

"It's hellish," he said softly, and stared into the flames his onyx eyes gleaming. Then he sat up straighter. "But my girls take excellent care of me. You'll help me get through my daughter's wedding, won't you? I'm really quite sound for the moment."

"Of course I will!" Respect, not pity, was called for here "Please let me know about anything you need, anything that will make you more comfortable. A wheelchair? . . ."

"I have one, my dear, though I rarely need it." Tyler': smile was youthful as well, a charismatic smile. "Now, now don't look so stricken! In truth, my doctors are adamant that I get my exercise. I drive myself to a park by the river almost every day, and take my constitutional. Ivy confers with my doctors constantly, you know, and enforces their edicts to the letter. Exercise and a battery of medications, to assist my equilibrium and coordination. Though I draw the line at 'counseling.'" He gave a comic shudder of distaste. "I always tell her, I keep my own counsel, thank you very much But she harries me out of love, I know."

This was happier ground. "Ivy seems devoted to you."

"And I to her, young lady, and I to her. After all these

years, we would do anything for each other. I wish you the same good fortune with Mr. Bauer." The devilish note was back in his voice. "If he's your eventual choice, that is. Your dress suggests, how shall I put it, that you're keeping your options open?"

Blushing hotly, I said, "All right, Mr. Tyler, no wheelchair. What can I do to help?"

"Charles," he said. "Just have an ordinary chair nearby at the ceremony, in case I need to sit. And if you would, a spare dress shirt somewhere at hand at the dinner. I occasionally spill something."

The valiant dignity of the man had me almost in tears, so that Ivy's brisk announcement came as a relief.

"Into the kitchen, everyone. Andy's ready for us."

The mansion's original Victorian kitchen was long gone, but the marvelously modern new space held all of us easily. We found our seats, guided by place cards of handmade rice paper: Frank and Sally at the far table with Lou, then Ivy between Frances and Eric, then Charles and Kevin at a table by themselves, as promised. I had Erica and Brittany on either hand, and a good view of the whole party.

Once we were settled, Eleanor brought cups of warm sake to each orchid-bedecked table. Then Andy delivered a lively commentary on the art and science of sushi, all the while slicing, rolling, and forming his creations. It made quite a show, just as Ivy and I had planned. And the food was amazing, even the mystery fish.

Sally, a raging fiend of perfectionism about her wedding and reception, had left this dinner entirely to her mother and me. Even now she seemed oblivious, absorbed as she was in conspiratorial and apparently hilarious murmurings with Frank. You expect some of that from an engaged couple, but this was bordering on insolence.

Lou, on Frank's other side, was left with nothing to do but stare across the kitchen at me, and tell the occasional heavy-handed joke to the group at large. After he'd favored us with a gem about an Englishman, an Irishman, and a Scot who—what a surprise—go into a bar, he pressed his advantage. "So this rabbi goes to visit the Pope—"

"I believe we've heard that one," said Charles in a loud, quelling tone. Lou subsided, but Charles continued to eye him with cold dislike throughout the evening. An old-fashioned gentleman, especially one who had to reserve his strength for special occasions like this, couldn't be expected to suffer fools like Lou gladly.

Ivy, meanwhile, was trying to drag her daughter back into the social circle. "Sally...Sally...I was just telling the Sanjeks about the wedding supper. What's that steak the Dahlia Lounge is so famous for?"

"How am I supposed to know?" Sally looked vaguely annoyed, and returned to her tête-à-tête.

Happily, the conversation grew general at that point. As we nibbled on Andy's delicacies and chatted about restaurants, I actually began to relax. But not for long. When Frank's sister left the stool beside me, to take some family snapshots, the seat was quickly occupied by Lou Schulman, plate in hand.

Showtime. I knocked back my sake, took a bite of tuna roll, and asked Lou to explain what made the 911 Turbo so darn special. Greater love hath no woman than to lay down her evening for her best friend's brother.

As long as Lou didn't want me to lay down anything else. He kept edging his stool closer to mine and urging me to try some of his flying fish roe. Kevin frowned at us over his shoulder, then turned all his attention to Charles, who had launched into an anecdote about the London Philharmonic.

I'll explain later. I projected the thought at the back of Kevin's handsome russet head. *Just give me the benefit of the doubt for another twenty minutes. . . .*

It took far less than twenty minutes to get Lou talking about his dot-com experience. The abundance of sake on the table, and the scarcity of fabric on my dress, did the trick in five.

"Dark Canyons," he slurred at me. "Darkcanyons-dotcom. You heard of it, right?"

"N-no, I can't say I have. What did you sell?"

"Not selling," he said with disdain. "Leveraging. Leveraging connectivity to, uh, optimize vertical marketing channels. Or something. Jase made up all the bullshit like that."

"You worked with Jason Kraye, then?"

"Yeah, so what?"

I backpedaled. "So, nothing. What does that mean, exactly, leveraging connectivity?"

He grinned slyly. "We made pop-up ads. It was so cool, because if you program them right, they keep coming up on the screen even if the target computer has lockouts. See, this is how it works. . . ."

As Lou was explaining the coolness of it all, Andy set down his knives with a final flourish and bowed to our applause. Then he came forward to be personally introduced to Eric and Frances, the guests of honor, who plied him with eager questions. Ivy, I could see, was glowing over her success as a hostess.

"... so either way, they've got to read the ads! Smart, huh?"

I know little enough about Internet technology, but I know what I hate, and that's pop-up ads. Still, I wasn't wearing this purple number for nothing. I leaned close and dropped a hand on Lou's arm.

"Very smart!" I said. Softly, so maybe Kevin wouldn't hear. "So, do you invest much in tech stocks, since you're such an expert?"

"Nah. Stock market's for suckers. When I make money, I like to drink it or drive it."

Ivy was leading the guests back into the living room, but I stayed in my seat. "You must have made a lot of money at Dark Canyons, then."

"I did OK." Lou leaned forward and ran a hand up my bare arm to my shoulder. "I'm doing better now. In fact, I guess you could say I'm investing in technology."

"Really!" There was a revelation coming, I could feel it. "I'd love to hear—"

"*Excuse* me." Ivy, damn her, spoke coldly from the doorway, and Lou's face closed down. She gave him a venomous look—*jeez, his jokes weren't that bad*—and then addressed herself to me. "Carnegie, if you're not too terribly busy, could you get your butt in here and help me serve the green-tea sorbet?"

Chapter Twenty-Two

THE GREEN-TEA SORBET WAS A BIG HIT, BUT I REMAINED IN THE doghouse with Ivy. I had company, too; over dessert by the fireplace, Ivy became more and more exasperated with her errant daughter. But the more she bristled, the more Sally acted up, giggling uncontrollably and repeatedly trying to unbutton her fiancé's shirt. At least Frank had the grace to look embarrassed when Ivy snapped at him. She even snapped at Charles once, when an anecdote went on too long for her taste.

Well, I'd seen worse behavior in the run-up to weddings, and poor Ivy had a wedding and a merger colliding on her calendar. So I did my best to make the remainder of the party a success, drawing everyone into the conversation and answering questions about the plans for New Year's Eve. Unfortunately, this meant neglecting Lou for a while. I was impatient to hear more about his financial dealings—if I hadn't lost the moment for good.

"Would you all like a tour of the house?" asked Charles after a time, setting down his glass. "Come, my dear, let's show these people our little castle."

We all went with him eagerly, Andy Mikami included. Charles walked well enough, and our admiration of the grand rooms seemed to please him. We saw the library, and the enclosed terrace looking out to the lake, invisible now in the winter darkness.

We were on our way to the conservatory when I noticed uneasily that Sally was missing. I dropped back, and found the petulant princess in the living room, standing by the fire. As she jabbed at the flames with a long antique poker, I took the opportunity for some gentle diplomacy.

"Sally, I think your mother needs you to be a little more involved with the guests tonight."

"What?" She peered at me, her milky skin flushed and her pale eyes glassy.

"Are you all right?"

She smiled slowly, seraphically, and I realized with a sinking heart that my bride was more than all right. She was stoned out of her gourd.

"I'm just wonderful," she said, dropping the sooty tip of the poker to the floor and letting it drag along the carpet. "I am won-derfully won-derful. Hey, where's Frankie?"

"Frankie will be back in a minute." I removed the poker from her limp fingers and restored it to its place. "Why don't you come with me to the kitchen and we'll get you some coffee? Come on, that's a girl..."

She came with me, docile enough for now, and perched on a stool with her pretty little heart-shaped face propped in her hands. I almost liked Sally better this way; at least she wasn't sniping at me.

Eleanor poked her head in, but I waved her away. Then I got out two cups and brewed a French press of MFC's finest. *If I can just send her home before she does anything outrageous... and if Frank is high, too, I'll drive them both myself...*

"Dammit, Carnegie, you keep disappearing—Sally! What the hell is wrong with you tonight?" Ivy entered the kitchen and bore down on us with blood in her eye. "I've been cutting you slack for months now, but this is too much."

Then the pot perfume reached her and she stopped dead.

"There's nothing wrong," Sally began, but her words trailed away as Ivy erupted.

"Not *again*! You are the most thoughtless, inconsiderate...Do you have any idea how upsetting it would be for Charles, to have some kind of scandal in the family? I'm a public figure, Sally, do you know what that means? I told you after the staff party, for someone in my position to have illegal drugs on the premises is just begging for trouble!"

"Oh, screw your position," the girl muttered.

I quit edging my way out of the room. *Better stay and prevent domestic violence.*

"Young lady, my reputation pays for the clothes on your back, and every room in this house, and every goddamn dollar of your very expensive wedding, and if you can't show some common sense and some discretion, you can pay for it yourself!"

"Discretion?" said Sally, goaded out of her lethargy. "Oh, like you're so discreet, with your little hideaway in the Market. People at the company talk about that, you know, Frank told me. Half the time when I call you there, Simon Weeks answers. What's up with that? What if Charles called?"

Ivy caught her breath in a startled gasp. Then she laughed, a little wildly. "Charles knows perfectly well why I need that apartment, and he knows I sometimes meet with Simon there."

And with Kevin Bauer, and with Aaron, too, I thought. *The girl's being absurd. Or is she?* I'd found Simon quite attractive myself. He and Ivy were two vigorous, ambitious people who spent a lot of time together. And Charles was older, almost an invalid . . .

"You let me take care of my own affairs," Ivy continued, regaining command of the situation. "You concentrate on behaving yourself. You have no idea what kind of scrutiny I'm under right now. If I catch one whiff of this on you at Habitat tomorrow night, I'll cancel the wedding, I swear I will."

Sally jutted her lower lip. "Frank and I aren't going tomorrow night. It sounds like a big bore."

Ivy strode around the table then—it was as though I'd become invisible—and put her face very close to her daughter's.

"You will both be there." She bit off each word. "You will speak cheerfully to the reporters, and smile for the cameras, and do nothing, *nothing,* to harm my reputation. Is that clear?"

A dangerous pause, and then Sally nodded, her blonde hair swinging. "Whatever."

"You're damn right, whatever. Now, Carnegie, let's get these people on their way." She looked back at her daughter, clearly having the same thought I had, about Frank's possible condition. "These two will stay here tonight."

The party had begun to break up, with handshakes and hugs and Eleanor bringing coats. Ivy and I pasted on smiles and did our duty. Lou and Andy had already left, but I showed Brittany and Erica out, enjoying their lighthearted chatter after the drama in the kitchen.

As I closed the door behind the girls and turned back to the hallway, I saw Kevin standing by the Victorian Christmas tree. He looked old-fashioned himself, in his beard and his top coat. Old-fashioned and solid, a serious man.

"Can I talk with you a minute?" His face was impassive, but he had a pair of leather gloves in one hand and he kept slapping them softly against the palm of the other. *Nervous? Annoyed with me?*

"Of course, Kevin." With Lou gone anyway, I could please myself. "I'm sorry we haven't had much time tonight—"

He lifted a hand. "Carnegie, this is awkward, but . . . are you involved with Lou Schulman? I know it's none of my business, we've only been out once, but I am his boss, and—"

"No!" I blurted. "No, unh-unh, absolutely not! It's just . . ."

Just what? How could I explain my behavior without divulging my suspicions about Lou? Kevin was looking at me quizzically. He really did have the handsomest eyes. I took a deep breath, and took the plunge. Aaron wouldn't approve, but to hell with Aaron.

"Kevin, can I tell you something and ask you not to repeat it, not to anyone? Because I might be completely wrong about this."

"Of course I won't repeat it. Wrong about what?"

"About Lou. I think he might know something about Jason Kraye's death."

Kevin's gloves dropped to the floor, and he bent to retrieve them. "What makes you say that?"

"Well, I think they knew each other better than Lou lets on, and they might even have had some investment scheme going on. I don't know what it is yet, but I'm going to find out. Well, me and some other people."

I told him briefly about Lily, and how this reporter friend and I were trying to clear Darwin. I didn't mention Madison or Li Ping, and I sure as hell didn't go into my strange situations *vis-à-vis* Aaron Gold.

"I might talk with Lou again tomorrow night, but all I'm looking for is information, not . . . not anything else. OK?"

He frowned. "Shouldn't the police—"

"Anything I find out I'll take straight to the police, believe me. They just need a little help with this part."

He shook his head. "You're amazing. So you're still my date for the party?"

"Absolutely."

"Good, because this nice little wine bar just opened in Snohomish, and I'd like to take you there."

And I'd like to be taken, I almost said, and then rephrased it. "Sounds great."

We might have kissed then—a good kiss, I could see it coming—but Eleanor appeared out of nowhere.

"Is this your scarf, sir?"

"No. I mean, yes." He smiled at her. He had an excellent smile. "Thank you."

Then, when she showed no signs of disappearing again, he murmured to me, "It's a nice private wine bar. Good night."

Back in the living room, the host and hostess were at the fireplace, still conversing with the Sanjeks. *Oh, good, the in-laws have connected.* That was half the battle, sometimes. Frank had apparently been dispatched to deal with Sally in the kitchen.

I approached the foursome. "Ivy, is there anything else I can do?"

"You've done plenty already," she retorted, but I realized with relief that she was teasing me. The storm had blown over. "Go on home and I'll talk with you tomorrow."

Eric and Frances chimed in with their compliments on the dinner, and I made my farewells. Outside in the courtyard I ran into Andy Mikami, having a cigarette before he drove away. In the light from the front door, his white chef's jacket showed pale beneath his dark parka.

"My wife hates smoke in the car," he explained.

"But she doesn't mind you smoking? I mean, the health issues?"

He shrugged. "It's my business, isn't it?"

"I guess it is." That was certainly Aaron's attitude. But it still wasn't mine. "Andy, you did terrific work tonight. Thank you."

"Thanks for the gig," he said. "How's Joe doing these days?"

We went on talking shop for a few minutes, until the cold got to me. "I'm getting Popsicle toes, Andy. See you soon."

I had to walk around a big SUV to get to Vanna, thinking as I did that the Sanjeks must have rented it for their visit. The rest of the courtyard was almost empty, and presumably Ivy kept her vehicles in a nice warm garage. *But is that a Porsche over there under the trees? I thought Lou already—*

"Hey!" There was someone fiddling with the driver's door of the van. "What are you doing?"

"Oh, hi." Lou turned toward me with a sheepish smile. "Uh, Frank said you'd have that box of stuff for him. I was going to put it my car for him."

"I don't have it yet," I told him. Filipo hadn't returned to work yesterday, so now Joe and I were both furious at him. "Besides, Frank's staying here tonight."

He nodded ponderously. "Guess I'll go, then. G'night."

"Lou, wait." My toes could get a little icier, and he was much more likely to spill the beans now than at a crowded party. "You were telling me something, remember? About your investments? You really got me curious. . . ."

He moved closer. "You got me curious, too. About you."

My big mistake was to hesitate, wondering how to fend him off without blowing the chance to question him. Before I knew it, I was on the receiving end of the kiss that I'd wanted from Kevin and most certainly did not want from Lou. His embrace seemed to go on forever, but in fact, in a spectacular example of bad timing, it lasted just long enough to embarrass Frances Sanjek.

"Oh!" she squeaked, coming around the back of the SUV. Her pinched little face peered out from the fur-trimmed hood of her jacket like a squirrel from a tree hole. "Oh, I'm so sorry!"

Lou dropped his stranglehold at the sound, and I stepped quickly away from him. My coat was all askew, and I was still straightening it when Eric Sanjek appeared behind his wife—and Charles Tyler right behind him.

"I didn't mean to barge in on you two," Frances simpered. "I guess you just couldn't wait to be alone! Come on, Eric, let's us older folk go home."

She pulled a cute, conniving grimace at me—I wanted to slap her—and hopped into the passenger seat of the SUV. Eric, amused, shook his head and turned away. But Tyler stood his ground, staring at me, his face stiff with fury. If he had been Jove, I'd have had a thunderbolt clear through my forehead.

I closed my eyes and swore under my breath. Of all the people in the world, suddenly Charles Tyler was the one whose respect I most cherished. When I opened them he was gone, and Lou was retreating to his Porsche, with a muffled "See ya!" tossed over his shoulder.

I climbed wearily into Vanna and started up the heater, waiting for the Sanjeks to drive away. My fingers were frozen, too, by now, and I was deeply sleepy. At least there was one small comfort left: my coffee thermos was still lying on the front seat. I unscrewed the cap and tilted it to my lips to get at the last warm, shade-grown mouthful.

But the demons of mischief weren't done with me yet. There were three mouthfuls. One went into me, and the other two ran down the cleavage of the goddamn purple dress.

Chapter Twenty-Three

JUST WHEN YOU THINK THINGS CAN'T GET ANY WORSE, THEY don't.

Sometimes, anyway. Saturday morning was one of those times. I slept blissfully late, and then received three phone calls, each one more welcome than the last.

The first came from my contented client Ivy. "Last night went great, Carnegie. I have to tell you, I wasn't sure about the sushi business, but Eric and Frances raved about it."

That's what made Ivy my kind of millionaire. She genuinely cared about being hospitable to her future son-in-law's parents.

"Glad to hear it." I rolled out of bed and stretched. "How's Sally today?"

"Oh, we made up," she laughed, answering my real question and easing my mind. Mother–daughter feuds make for difficult weddings. "She promised to behave herself tonight, and I put the fear of God into Frank about it, too. Got a pen? I have the names of the reporters who'll be there. Maddie lined up some TV coverage, along with the papers."

We ran through the details of the party, from the antipasto buffet to the strolling carolers to the "Welcome to

MFC" gift packs for the Habitat employees. All the while I was debating whether to ask Ivy about that awkward little scene in the driveway.

"One last thing," she was saying. "I decided to invite some of my marketing department. Once the merger is in place, they'll be cooking up a campaign for our new shade-grown products, and I want them to network with the Habitat folks. So figure on another dozen guests."

"I'll take care of it." I hesitated, and then ventured, "Charles seemed to enjoy himself last night. I, ah, saw him walking the Sanjeks out to their car."

"Yes, I thought he'd be exhausted by then, but he insisted. He insists on making an appearance tonight, too, to show the whole family together. We should get some nice press out of it."

So Charles hadn't said anything about me and Lou. Good. I mulled this over as I wandered to the kitchen and munched a bagel. Maybe I was worrying too much, and that thunderbolt look Charles gave me had been more surprise than anger. Still, Sally wouldn't be the only one on her best behavior tonight. I'd have to come up with a substitute for my long-lost jade silk. . . .

I kept hoping to hear from the elusive Andrea, but the second call, right after the bagel, was from Lily. We'd been on the outs for less than a week, but it felt far longer, and it was delicious to catch up. She avoided the subject of Darwin, except to say that the two of them were leaving shortly to take the boys to a Christmas matinee.

"Tell me fun stuff," she said. "Girl talk."

So I told her everything, from the big things (Kevin Bauer) to the more routine (the sushi party) to the kind of minutiae that no one would care about except your very best friend.

"It was your shade of purple, Lily, but the style was outrageous! And of course I can't return it now, with coffee stains all down the front. It did the job, though. Lou Schulman got pretty forthcoming."

"You think Schulman knows something?" End of girl talk.

"Well, not necessarily. But he was involved with Jason Kraye in some way, and he's been trying to conceal the fact. It's the only real lead we've got. Is Mike getting anywhere with retracing Darwin's route that night?"

"Not yet. But he's not giving up. And the lawyer Aaron found for me says that unless they come up with new evidence *against* Dar, he probably won't be rearrested."

She paused, and I could read her thoughts. "Probably" wasn't all that comforting. And not being arrested for murder isn't the same as being exonerated.

"Lily, we're going to work this out, I promise. Listen, Schulman used to work for a dot-com named Dark Canyons. It's defunct now, but maybe there's still information available."

"If there is, I'll find it," she said. "It'll be a relief to have something to do."

"That's the spirit. Hey, what can I bring for Christmas dinner, besides an action figure toilet? If I can locate one."

"You can forget about that," she chuckled. "I've convinced Ethan that superheroes use a special men's room in another dimension."

"Ooh, you're good."

"Mothers know everything. You could just bring some

nice crusty bread from the Market, since you're right there these days."

"Done. And I'll probably see you before then, anyway. You take care, my dear."

"You, too."

I had just gotten dressed when the phone rang again. Third time's the charm, and this call was utterly charming: my landlady, telling me I could go back to the houseboat. My exile was over.

"I'm sorry it's been so long," she quavered. "But I wanted everything safe and sound for you."

"Thanks *so* much, Mrs. Castle. I'll be home for Christmas! I'm going over right now."

I called Joe with the good news.

"That's marvelous, Carnegie! Not that you weren't welcome at my digs, but it was getting to be a bit much, wasn't it? Eddie will be thrilled, of course."

"Well, yes. But you've been great, and so has Kelli and everyone else. Can I keep my keys for a little while, till I get everything moved?"

"No problem. By the way, I've got a little surprise for you."

"Tell, tell."

"Remember we talked about doing a panini bar sometime, where guests pick out Italian ingredients at a buffet and the chef grills them on ciabatta bread?"

"Joe! Did you arrange for panini at Habitat tonight? On this short notice? You're a magician."

"I believe I am. Enjoy your homecoming."

Better and better. Happily humming, I scooped up my stuff, revved up Vanna, and was soon pulling into the little parking lot for houseboat owners on the east shore of Lake Union.

I hurried down the dock, enjoying the familiar hollow sound of my footsteps on the worn wooden planks, and admiring my neighbors' Christmas decorations. There were wreaths on many of the doors, garlands of lights and greenery along the weathered railings, and even a life-sized Santa doll propped up in someone's canoe, swaying gently as the canoe bobbed at its mooring.

My houseboat held the coveted position at the end of the dock, with a panoramic view of the lake. From the Made in Heaven office upstairs, or my narrow front porch down at water level, you could see all the way from the downtown towers to the south, past Queen Anne Hill and the Fremont Drawbridge on the west shore, to the green slope of Gas Works Park to the north. I wouldn't have traded that view for all the mansions in Washington State.

As I paced the dock now, my lungs expanded with the thrilling, unmistakable scent of a large body of water, and I felt my spirit expand as well. *Welcome home.* I strode up the gangplank, instantly adjusting my gait to the slight sway of the platform under my feet, and looked around.

Aside from the patches of new lumber here and there, showing raw and clean against the faded old boards, the place didn't look much different. Inside, as I went happily from room to room—there weren't many, but I loved each one—my cell phone sounded.

"So how'd it go, Stretch?"

"Oh, hi. It went fine."

"What did you learn, and what'd you have to do to learn it?"

"Ha, ha. Lou and Jason both worked for an outfit called Dark Canyons. They made on-line pop-up ads."

"I hate those things!"

"Me too. But listen to this. When I asked Lou about high-tech investing, he said he never played the stock market, but that he's got something going on now that's going to make him a lot of money."

"Now that's interesting," said Aaron. "What kind of something?"

"I don't know, but I'm going to see him at a function tonight, and I'll try to find out more."

"You do that. Meanwhile, I've found out something interesting myself, about Jason Kraye's gambling companions. It might be nothing, but—"

"Can you tell me quick, Aaron? I want to unpack. I'm back home in my houseboat!"

"Hey, congratulations. You know, I've got something to show you, too. I'll come on over."

"But—"

But he'd already hung up. Aaron lived at the Lakeshore Apartments, a low-end development not far from me, so I was still putting clothes away when he arrived. He wore his navy pea coat, and was brandishing a large manila envelope.

"Here it is, Slim!"

"Here what is?"

He slapped the envelope down on my kitchen table. "Go ahead, open it."

Curious, I drew out a thick sheaf of documents. *Commonwealth of Massachusetts . . . Judgment and Decree . . .* I slid them back inside and closed the clasp.

"Aaron, we agreed not to talk about this."

"I'm not talking, I'm just showing you."

"I don't need to see your divorce papers."

"Sure you do. You made such a big deal about trust, so here it is, documentary evidence, absolutely legal. Trust me, I'm a born-again bachelor."

"But that's not the point!" I rubbed my forehead; big headache coming on. "You're divorced, fine, I believe you. But am I supposed to forget about what happened?"

"What do you mean, what happened? Nothing happened." He tried to take my hand, but I pulled it away and walked into the living room. He followed, raising his voice. "Just because I didn't tell you every detail of my life story the first day I met you—"

"Being married is not a detail!"

I felt my face flushing, and turned away toward the sliding glass door of the porch. I hated being put on the defensive like this. *Am I being unreasonable? No. Honesty is honesty, I have my principles.* I'd been burned too many times lately; I refused to risk it again.

"When were you going to tell me, after we made love the first time? Just mention it in bed one morning: 'That was great, honey, and by the way, I'm married'?"

"But I'm *not* married, not anymore! And I'll tell you anything you want. If you remember, I've been trying to tell you the whole story for the past week. You won't listen."

"I don't want to listen!" Not to some lame tale about how his wife didn't understand him. "Aaron, this is pointless. It wouldn't have worked out for us anyway."

"Why not?" He approached me at the glass. "Just tell me that."

"We're not compatible. We argue all the time. I can't stand your smoking. And besides," I added, turning petty in my resentment, "you're too short for me."

He flinched, and I wished the words unsaid, while they still hung in the air.

But Aaron wasn't hurt, he was angry. "Are we back to that? Honest to God, Stretch, for a smart woman you can be so stupid."

"There's nothing stupid about it! I'm just not comfortable being taller than the man I'm with."

"And why exactly is the man you're with supposed to be bigger than you? You want equal pay and equal rights and equal everything, but the guy is supposed to be able to drag you to his cave?"

"Don't be silly. It's only that—"

Something happened then, but even afterward I wasn't sure exactly what. I remember he pulled on my left arm, and gave a little shove to my right shoulder, and before I finished my sentence, I was lying on my living room carpet with Aaron on top of me, his hand cushioning the back of my head from the fall and his face inches from mine.

"If I wanted to drag you somewhere, Slim," he said, not even breathing hard, "I would."

Chapter Twenty-Four

Now, there are a lot of ways that a situation like that could go.

I could have said—I almost did say—"How dare you?" In which case, Aaron could have made an equally melodramatic reply and covered my heaving bosom with burning kisses, or my burning bosom with heaving kisses, or something to that effect.

Alternatively, I could have screamed my head off and brought charges for assault.

As it was, I just gulped air and gazed into the warm brown eyes above me, entirely perplexed. A moment passed. Aaron smiled slightly. I opened trembling lips.

Someone started banging on the houseboat door and calling my name.

"That's Larry," I said.

" 'That's *Larry*?' Aaron's eyes widened, then he rolled away onto his back and, to my considerable annoyance, began to laugh uproariously. "I just pulled off the coolest maneuver I've ever tried on a woman and all you can say is 'That's Larry'?"

You had to hand it to Aaron Gold. He had a slight stature and a huge ego and an irritating way of asking endless questions, but he also had a lead-lined, armor-plated, bulletproof sense of humor. The man could laugh at anything. Right now he lay on the floor chortling, then rose smoothly to his feet and reached down to help me to mine.

"And who is Larry, pray tell?"

"My neighbor." I brushed myself off. My hands were trembling, too. "He fixes things for me, so behave."

When I opened the kitchen door Larry Halloway bounced in like a beach ball, buoyant and spherical and cheerful as ever. He was over thirty and under sixty; premature baldness and a baby face made it hard to tell much else. He'd been my neighborly neighbor since I moved in, always ready to clear a drain or trace a short circuit.

Today Larry was clad in corduroys and a down parka, but he also carried a fancy ski jacket, all zippers and flaps and garish black and yellow stripes, like a huge hornet.

"Carnegie, the prodigal daughter returns! I thought those workmen would never leave. Country music all day long, I almost went crazy. They had some great tools, though. This is yours." He pushed the jacket at me and smiled over at Aaron. "Howja do! Larry Halloway, and you are?"

"Aaron Gold. Pleased to meet you."

"Pleasure's mine! Did you see the new siding they put in on the north wall? Nice neat job—"

I broke in. "This isn't mine, Larry. Where'd you find it?"

"Oh, I didn't find it, someone gave it to me to give to you. A Chinese girl, I didn't catch her name, but I figured you would know. She had your business card, anyway."

Aaron went very still, and the hair on the back of my neck stirred.

"Crying like a baby, too," Larry continued. "I invited her inside but she was in a tearing hurry. Said she couldn't take the jacket with her and she didn't want anyone else to have it. At least I think that's what she said. Heavy accent. Mind if I look around? Hope those guys did a good job for you."

"Sure." I waved him absently toward the living room, and laid the bulky garment on the kitchen table, on top of Aaron's manila envelope. "Aaron, do you think this belonged—"

"To Jason Kraye? Must have." His hands, quick and deft, checked the inner collar and patted down the pockets. "No name tag, but from what you told me, Li Ping wasn't exactly overrun with gentlemen callers. Gloves...tissues...aha! What do you suppose this is?"

He held up a piece of white cardboard. The size and shape was familiar: a compact disc mailer. It bore an uneven line of postage stamps, and a blue sticker that said Priority Mail.

But the FROM and TO lines were blank.

We both stared at the mute, unrevealing white square. Then Larry returned, full of grudging approval for the repair job, and Aaron slipped the mailer out of sight.

"Not bad, not bad. Got to go. Aaron, pleasure to meet you. Carnegie, let me know if you find any loose wires or anything. Sometimes these guys mess things up while they fix things up!"

"I'll do that, Larry."

He bounced away and I closed the door behind him. Immediately, Aaron pulled out the mailer again.

"Shouldn't we give that to the police?" I asked.

"But then we'd never know what was in it, would we, Stretch? And that"—he tilted the mailer and shook out the silver disc inside—"would spoil the fun. Besides, it wasn't even sealed. They'll never know."

Apparently the fun of tumbling me to the floor was forgotten for the moment, so I tried to forget it, too. For now. Besides, I was busy being eaten up with curiosity. This wasn't a music CD, some late Christmas present that Jason meant to mail. This was an unmarked, unlabeled disc, an electronic missive from a dead man, meant for some unknown destination, and possibly full of revealing clues about a hideous murder. Clearly, it should be turned over to the authorities as soon as possible . . .

The PC upstairs in my workroom took a few minutes to power up. Aaron spent the time pacing along the windows and jingling the change in his pocket. When I inserted the disk and opened the CD folder on my screen, two icons appeared. He hung over my shoulder and jingled some more.

"Would you quit that? I'm trying to figure out—"

"Look, there's a document file called READ ME."

"I *see* it."

Two people cannot operate one mouse and keyboard simultaneously. As I tried to open READ ME, I kept getting error messages and Aaron kept pointing to the screen and hovering his hands over mine.

"Try right-clicking—"

"Let me do it, would you? It's my computer."

"OK, OK, but if you just—"

"Just what?" I gave the mouse a final click and a document sprang into view. "There! I told you I could—oh, my God."

It was a blackmail note, vicious and crude.

```
You saw the pictures, now see the
movie!!! You think you know who we are
now, so what? You can't prove anything,
and if you try to, this video goes
```

straight to the Internet. All those
people watching the two of you screwing
over and over and over. Everywhere you
go, anybody you meet will have seen you
naked and crazy.˙If you don't believe
it, watch it yourself with the decrypt
we sent. Get the money together the way
we said, or else.

I stared at it, horrified, and as I stared, the words suddenly blinked off and on. Once, twice, and with the third
blink they disappeared entirely. "What'd you do?" demanded Aaron.

"Nothing! I didn't even touch the keys."

"Well, get it back!"

"I'm trying..." I closed the blank file, but then the icon
itself disappeared. I removed and reinserted the disk, even
restarted my computer, but READ ME had vanished. The only
icon remaining on my screen was a tiny camera, presumably
the video file referred to in the note. And it stubbornly refused to reveal its contents, no matter what I tried.

Finally I yielded the keyboard to Aaron. He downloaded
various programs from the Internet, growing more frustrated
by the minute, but none of them worked on the video file.

"It's encrypted all right," he said at last. He'd shed his
coat and rolled up the sleeves of his shirt. Oxford cloth, in a
cornmeal color that set off his olive skin. "And the note was
programmed somehow to delete itself. Quick, let's try and
reconstruct the wording. We should have done that right
away. The details could be important."

But the details, as we recalled them, didn't tell us much.
Two people, maybe more, had pictures and a video of two

other people having sex, and they wanted money to keep it out of the public eye. The victim knew, or thought he knew, the identity of the blackmailers, but the blackmailers didn't care. Or said they didn't.

"Also, this is part of a series of messages," Aaron reasoned, "because there were references to something already sent."

I nodded. "A decrypt, whatever that is. A decryption program? And without it, we can't watch the video. Not that I want to."

"Me, neither," he said with a grim scowl. "Blackmail is the ugliest, most cowardly crime . . . But watching it is the only way to find out who Kraye was blackmailing. Though I think I can guess."

"What do you mean?"

"I had something to tell you, remember? I've been talking to Peter Yan's son, the gum-chewer at Noble Pearl. Those 'eminent gentlemen' who gamble there after hours are pretty damn eminent. Judges, a couple of state senators, possibly the governor when he's in town."

"The son *told* you all this?"

A quick grin. "He doesn't hold his liquor very well. I'd want to confirm that last bit with another source, though. The gov's a little flighty, but he's not stupid."

"And he surely wouldn't kill anyone, or have them killed. It's unbelievable!"

"Murder is unbelievable, Stretch, but Jason Kraye is still dead." Aaron went back to pacing. His hair was tousled, his forearms brown and sinewy. "What are the odds he was killed in a random bar fight, right in the middle of a blackmail scheme? No, I think our murderer was either his partner in crime, or else his victim."

"Or victims," I said glumly. "There could have been several."

"True. We'll have to keep following up—" He was interrupted by another knock. Someone had come up the outside staircase and was waiting on the landing. "Tell me that's not Larry again."

The second floor of my houseboat has two parts: the good room, where I met with clients, and the workroom beyond it, with a connecting door in between. I crossed the good room and opened the door to a Venezuelan bearing gifts.

"Apologies!" cried Filipo, setting the ill-fated carrier bin down on the adorable wicker love seat that pleases brides and makes grooms fidget. "Apologies to Joe, and now to you. A thousand thousand apologies."

"Where were you yesterday?" I demanded. Then I looked more closely at his face; the swarthy skin was bruised and abraded, and one eye was swollen. "Did you have an accident?"

"No, no." Filipo grimaced ruefully. He noticed Aaron watching from the workroom doorway, and turned his back slightly before muttering, "Was Alonzo. He thinks the joke is not funny."

"More gifts?" asked Aaron. "Honestly, Stretch, I can't keep up with this guy. I'd better get going."

"Wait a minute, would you? We're not done. Filipo, are you in trouble with Joe? You really shouldn't have taken this stuff, but as long as it's all here—"

"Joe says I am fired, then says I am not." He shrugged.

"We have big party tonight. He needs me. If Carnegie forgives, Joe forgives."

"You're forgiven, then." I had my own place back; I could afford to be generous. "Just stop harassing Alonzo. And tell him he can have those roses in the white vase, for his girlfriend."

I waved as Filipo descended the stairs, then shut the door and turned to see Aaron giving me a speculative look.

"So, we're not done?"

"I meant with the disk! We should turn it in to the police."

"And tell them what, Stretch?" He crossed the room to me, putting on his coat. "That it came from Li Ping and contained a blackmail note that has now disappeared? What does that accomplish, besides getting her in trouble and getting us laughed at?"

"But maybe they could decrypt the video."

"Oh, no," said Aaron, and clenched his jaw in a way that I recognized. "I'm not doing the blackmailers' job for them."

"The police would keep it private. Wouldn't they?"

He laughed grimly. "Mike Graham might. But you know how often evidence goes missing, even in a well-run cop shop? And a sex film that gets passed around for various technicians to work on, how private would that be? Kraye's victim might be the murderer, but he might not. No, I know someone who might be able to crack this, someone I trust. I'll try him first."

I conceded that point, but I had another one to make. "About what happened earlier . . ."

"Yes?" He moved closer.

I took a deep breath and told myself, *I have principles.* "Don't ever do that again."

"Only by request, Slim." Aaron grinned, and opened the door to leave. "Only by request."

To call the rest of my day "disjointed" would be a considerable understatement. Unpacking all my stuff, while trying to think about party arrangements, while trying *not* to think about Aaron's arms around me, while pondering mysterious blackmail schemes, while anticipating an evening with Kevin—it was all too much. When I found myself putting my hair dryer in the refrigerator, I stopped cold and sat down at the kitchen table for some methodical deep breathing.

That's when I got the final good-news phone call: Qwik-Kleen had found my jade silk dress. Now there's comfort and joy for you. So what if I didn't know the identity of Jason Kraye's victim, or whether I should listen to Aaron's explanations, or if tonight's party would further my romance with Kevin Bauer.

At least I knew what I was going to wear.

Chapter Twenty-Five

THIS TIME I ARRIVED EARLY, LIKE A GOOD LITTLE EVENT PLAN-
ner, and spent a busy but straightforward two hours in the
Habitat warehouse, directing the placement of tables and
decorations, testing microphones for the carolers and the
speeches, and showing the DJ where to set up his sound system and portable dance floor. Kevin's "cookies, punch, and
a boom box" staff party had evolved into quite a festive affair. Habitat had put on a children's party at the local community center that afternoon, with games and a Santa,
which meant that tonight's bash didn't even have to be kid-
proof. Kids are great, but adult parties are easier.

Fiona was on hand to help me out, along with a couple of
warehouse workers, three waiters from Solveto's, and the
panini chef Joe had found for me. He was a long, lanky, gray-
ponytail type named Rudy, and to my delight, he and Fiona
hit it off right away.

They bantered as they ran in a power cord for the sandwich grill, and joked as they arranged the trays piled with
provolone, prosciutto, roasted peppers, and other delights. Then Rudy got down to the serious business of testing his grill, and Fiona joined me for the final decorative
touches.

"Do you mind MFC forcing its way in on your plans?" I

asked her as we set a centerpiece of candy canes and roses on each white-clothed table.

"I did at first," she admitted. Fiona's braids were gone tonight, her hair swept back in a soft chignon, a perfect style for her long vintage dress of deep brown velvet. "But then I thought, if we're going to change ownership, why not do it in style? Besides, Kevin says that MFC has promised no lay-offs. It's time to party!"

As we worked, our few voices echoed strangely in the dim, cavernous space all around us. The toylike forklifts were parked and silent in a far corner, and the tiers of coffee sacks rose high into the shadows. I looked around, with the last centerpiece in my hands, and had the same thought I always did in a new venue: that the warehouse was like an empty theater. At seven P.M. the lights and music would come up, the cast would appear, and the stage would spring into vibrant, glittering life.

And there's the leading man now. Kevin Bauer made an undramatic entrance—did he always wear that same sweater?—but when he spotted me, his eyes lit up. I set down the roses and he gave me a quick, decorous hug.

"Carnegie, you've done wonders! Who'd have guessed the place could look so nice?" He frowned a little at the waiters, one unwrapping platters of Christmas cookies, another lining up wineglasses at the bar, while the third set out hot plates for the mulled wine and spiced cider. "You're sure they understand, no food or drink outside this area? And those glasses had better be—"

"Plastic," I assured him. "We may get a few spills, but there won't be any broken glass in the coffee beans, I promise. Shall we go welcome the Tylers?"

Ivy had the character actress role tonight: devoted wife,

proud businesswoman, indulgent mother of the difficult but undeniably lovely ingénue. MFC's chief executive wore a chic jacket and skirt in Yuletide-red silk, with starry diamonds at her throat and wrist.

But Sally's long pale hair and short black dress made her mother look almost dowdy—a contrast that Sally no doubt enjoyed. Charles Tyler wore a dark suit and a gay red vest, but he looked gaunt and worn. Frank, affable as ever, went off to fetch their drinks, while Charles sank into a chair and smiled fondly at both his "girls."

He didn't smile at me. Last night's flirtatious courtliness was gone, replaced by a chill, formal courtesy. It chilled even further as the doors were propped open, and Lou Schulman lumbered eagerly across the room toward me. When Charles saw that, he turned away, his face stern, and concentrated on the Habitat people that Kevin was introducing to him. Most of them seemed quite impressed; even after years in seclusion, Charles Tyler was a celebrity.

"I was kinda hoping you'd wear that same dress," said Lou.

"Sorry to disappoint you." *What's your role in this production,* I wondered. *Minor villain, or just comic relief?*

"That one's OK, too." He glanced around. "Nice party. Hey, have they got any beer?"

"Yes, there's beer," I assured my gallant swain. "You know, I was hoping to talk to you some more. About your investments, remember?"

A complacent smile spread across his features. "Sure. Let's go somewhere private, though. How 'bout up in my office?"

"Well, I shouldn't leave the party for very long. . . ." I thought fast. Lou's office, the elevated computer center where I'd cut my hand, was off in the roasting area, a little too remote for comfort. And the more I thought about it, the more Lou seemed to be a likely candidate for Jason's partner in blackmail. *But surely an unlikely murderer?*

"Come on, just for a few minutes," he said. "I got lots to tell you."

"Well . . ." At least the office had glass walls. If I opened the venetian blinds, what could happen there in plain sight, either villainous or amorous? Lou was our best lead.

"OK, but I've really got to do my job first." I checked my watch. Seven-fifteen. "I'll meet you there at nine o'clock?"

"You got it."

Lou went off in search of his brew, and I was free to watch my event unfold. The traffic pattern I'd envisioned was flowing nicely. People poured in through the side door from the gravel parking lot—I had a fellow out there directing cars—passed the corridor to the rest rooms, and stopped at the coatracks I'd rented. Then, just inside the door by the main bar, they were met by Kevin, Ivy, or one of their lieutenants, who offered personal greetings, introductions, and name tags.

Simon Weeks was in his element: shaking hands, slapping shoulders, and keeping a close eye on Ivy. If she faltered for a name, he provided it, and when she looked around for her drink, he was there to place it in her hand. He was her go-to guy, all right, and I couldn't help wondering if he was something more as well.

Another greeter was Madison Jaffee, the picture of sophistication in a sapphire-blue sheath and silver jewelry. Or was it platinum? She waved at me across the tables, then went back to work, smiling at each Habitat employee that

Fiona introduced to her. MFC and Habitat were presenting a graciously united front tonight.

On a low stage in the center of the party space, the carolers led off with "Winter Wonderland," and continued with a spirited medley of holiday songs. By seven-thirty there were laughing throngs at the bar and the panini station, happy chatter was rising all around, and the combined body heat of the revelers was taking the chill off the air. I could smell cider and warm wine, Rudy's sizzling sandwiches, and beneath it all, the dark perfume of coffee.

Even with mysteries on my mind, I do love a good party.

The media people were easy to spot; Madison was providing each one with a sample pack of coffees and a press release in a glossy MFC folder. I made sure the TV fellow with the shoulder cam had enough light to work with, and that the reporters got seats by the stage and a good supply of food and drink. Free food may not influence the press directly, I had found, but it sure didn't hurt.

Then MFC's marketing contingent arrived, and a new player took the stage: Darwin James, tall and handsome and stiff with self-consciousness. His dark suit and tie stood out among his casually-dressed coworkers as much as his handsome ebony face stood out among their white ones.

I stared, and I wasn't the only one. A buzz of curious whispering began, as the people who followed local news informed the people who didn't, that the black guy over there had been a "person of interest" to the police in a murder case.

I was curious myself, but on another count. *What is Ivy thinking? Or does she even know—*

Ivy knew perfectly well. She shook Darwin's hand, then brought him to meet Kevin and Fiona. As a vote of confidence in her employee, it couldn't have been more public, or more unmistakable. Ivy Tyler was announcing to the world her belief that Darwin James had been falsely accused.

Aaron, the cynic, might say that she was also scoring political correctness points for having a black man at her photo op. Or would he? Like so many biographers, Aaron seemed to have become infatuated with his subject.

But never mind Aaron. I shared Ivy's confidence in Darwin, so I went over to greet him myself, with a cup of hot cider for each of us.

"Hey, Carnegie." He took the cider. "Not spiked, is it?"

"Not even a little." Only Lily's brother could joke at a time like this. "Darwin, it was brave of you to come tonight."

"Well, Frank talked me into it, and Lily, too, when I told her I was invited." He ventured a smile. "She says for you to have fun tonight, and for me to report back on this Kevin person. Is that him up there?"

"That's him. Listen, I want you to know how sorry I am—"

"I do know," he said gently. "Shush now, the man's talking."

Kevin had stepped onto the stage, prompt to the eight P.M. time noted on our agenda. He thanked the carolers, and promised the crowd more music soon. Then he tugged nervously at the cuffs of his sweater, frowned at the floor, and launched into a lengthy speech about the history of Habitat, the virtues of shade-grown coffee, the merits of his employees, the advantages of teaming up with a major player like MFC, and . . .

And I couldn't tell you what else, because I was stupefied. First with dismay at his mumbling monotone, and then with boredom. Kevin Bauer was handsome and considerate and a straight-arrow guy, but as a public speaker he was an absolute and total snore. I noticed the *Times* reporter fidgeting, and the woman from the *Journal-American* examining her manicure with intense absorption.

Even the TV cameraman panned around the warehouse just for something to do, and I panned my gaze around as well. Over near the coats, out of earshot, Ivy was in quiet conversation with Simon Weeks. It was business, apparently; he had his cell phone out, and was alternating speaking into it and consulting with her. Then he ended the call, gave her a quick hug and a not-so-businesslike kiss on the cheek, and strode toward the exit.

Ivy returned to her seat; she had plenty of time, as the speech droned on—and on. The Habitat employees, sitting at the decorated tables or standing in groups with their plates of party food, simply rolled their eyes and smiled in a "That's our Kevin" sort of way. The Meet for Coffee people, mindful of their CEO's eye on them, sat quiet and polite and drained their drinks.

Eventually, finally, at long last, Kevin finished, to a minor ripple of applause and quite a few sighs of relief. Then Ivy took the stage and woke everybody up.

Chapter Twenty-Six

"CHANGE IS NEVER, NEVER EASY," IVY DECLARED IN A RINGING voice, and let the words hang in the air. The crowd fell silent. "Change is damn hard. You have a great little company here, a good team, a terrific boss, and then some bigger company marches in and takes over. So you're wondering, What the hell is the new year going to bring for me? I'll tell you what . . ."

And she told them, in her own bold, blunt, and mercifully brief way, that MFC was going to take Habitat's shade-grown coffee and serve it all over the country, and that the country was going to love it, and that everybody who worked hard to make that happen was going to earn a barge-load of money. Then she strode off the stage in her chic red suit, and there was nothing dowdy about her.

How often do you see a standing ovation at a corporate function? The reporters crowded around, the TV camera closed in, and Ivy and Kevin posed for picture after picture, clasping hands with every appearance of good will to all. Ivy stole a moment to kiss her husband on his haggard cheek, but then had to return to her interviewers.

Meanwhile, Ivy's new and old employees mixed and mingled with a pretty good will of their own. The DJ cranked up the dance music, couples flocked to the floor, and soon the overall noise level had risen to an uproarious clamor. The professional side of me could relax; my event was a rousing success.

"Isn't Ivy phenomenal?"

Madison was at my shoulder, and Darwin had moved away. I caught a tantalizing hint of musky scent, and recognized her perfume as one of those brands where a quarter-ounce costs more than a car payment. We both hesitated; it seemed that we were tacitly agreeing not to discuss Jason's murder tonight. Not when we were both working, and socializing as well.

" 'Phenomenal' is the word," I replied. We chatted a little about the speeches, then I asked, "How is Charles doing? This must be a strain for him."

"Oh, he'll be OK," said Madison, with the cruel indifference of the young and strong. "His wheelchair's in the car. Ivy fusses about him too much."

"I doubt if Charles thinks so," I said sharply, resenting her cavalier tone. I noted the cool gray luster of her pendant and bracelet; that was platinum, all right. Silver has a much warmer quality. *Must be nice.*

Madison seemed to sense my disapproval, because she changed the subject—to one that reminded me I was in her debt for all the marketing advice. Definitely an alpha female.

"I saw that good-looking Frenchman of yours in the paper, Carnegie, the one who put you down on television?"

"Beau Paliere." I finished my cider. "What's he up to now?"

"Just doing the usual sort of interview, but he worked in that 'beauty and perfection' line a couple of times. So you see what I mean about summing up your message and then repeating it . . . Hi, Frank."

"Hey, Madison." The bridegroom was looking a bit furtive. "Uh, Carnegie, you didn't happen to bring my stuff from the bachelor party?"

"Shoot, it's the one thing I forgot. I'm sorry, Frank."

"No problem, I just didn't want Sally to, uh . . ."

"The box is safe in my office," I reassured him. "Why don't I keep it there until you pick it up?"

"That would be great." He nodded vigorously, then gazed around with ponderous nonchalance. "It's really interesting, seeing these guys' operation. Hey, is that Aaron?"

Madison craned to look. "Yes, but he's late. I hope he caught the speech."

It took Aaron a few minutes to reach us through the crowd, which gave me time to compose myself. *Of course he's here, for his book. No big deal.*

Aaron wore another oxford cloth shirt, blue this time, with a burgundy tie and a salt-and-pepper herringbone jacket, along with his special accessory—a wide, teasing grin.

"Hi, Frank. Maddie, my dear, your boss should run for office. I'd vote for her twice." He gave her a hug—warmer than necessary, in my opinion—and gave me a raised eyebrow and a smirk. "Hiya, Slim. Quite a bash. Who wants to dance?"

"I'm pretty busy—" I began.

"Love to!" said Madison, her green eyes bright.

She smiled and moved toward the dance floor, while Frank left me in search of Sally. Aaron turned back and spoke quickly in my ear.

"Talked to Schulman yet?"

"Nine o'clock."

"I'll catch you later, then. I've got some news."

"Good or bad?"

"Not good. Be careful, Stretch."

Then he had Madison Jaffee in his arms, swaying slowly, their dark-haired heads close, her blue dress brilliant against his gray jacket. They danced well together. I watched for a moment with a queer feeling in my stomach. *I must be hungry,* I told myself. *That must be it.* I turned away and collided with a sour-faced, tipsy-looking woman who seemed vaguely familiar.

"I'm sorry, uh ..." Why don't people wear their damn name tags? She stared at me, not helping, as I tried to connect the dots. *The marketing department ... the wicked witch ...* "I'm sorry, Nora. Merry Christmas!" Then, flustered, I blurted out what was uppermost in my mind. "Madison's very pretty, isn't she?"

The secretary made a sarcastic noise in the back of her throat. "She *buys* pretty things. Like all that jewelry she's been wearing lately."

"I suppose Madison's quite successful in her work," I said demurely. "The company must pay her well."

"Better'n they pay me, that's for sure. You should see the car she just bought, like James Bonds. James Bondses' car. Who does she think she is?"

Not tipsy. Drunk. Good thing Fiona had reserved some taxis for this event. My view of Aaron was blocked as more dancers joined in, Sally and Frank among them. I was pleased to see they were behaving themselves, as ordered. But not at all pleased with Nora's company.

"Ivy's speech was wonderful, don't you think?" I said, looking for a harmless topic.

"Hunh. Simon Weeks probably wrote it for her." Nora

leaned toward me and leered. Not a pretty sight. "He does everything else for her, if you know what I mean."

Of course I feigned not to know what she meant, but inwardly I was fascinated. *So, I'm not the only one speculating about Ivy and Simon being lovers. Looks like Sally was right, after all.*

I didn't reply except for a bland smile, meanwhile telling myself sternly to quit speculating. While it might be Sally's business if her mother was having an affair, it was certainly none of mine. I wished Nora a Happy New Year—*fat chance*—and went off to look for Kevin.

I found him deep in conversation with Rudy at the panini bar. The topic was Charles Tyler, but the chef looked less than enthralled.

"And I saw his last performance, at the Kennedy Center," Kevin was saying. "It was heartbreaking. . . . Hi, Carnegie. It's going really well, don't you think?"

"Couldn't be better." Behind us, the DJ put on a fast song with an irresistible backbeat. Tapping my foot to it, I said, "The acoustics are great in here."

"Yes, I suppose they are. You see, Rudy, Charles wasn't just a conductor. His compositions are so innovative, but still so—"

Rudy had a customer at that point, and I couldn't restrain myself any longer. "Hey Kevin, come dance with me."

"Oh, I don't dance."

"But it's a party—"

His lips tightened in annoyance. "I said, I don't dance."

"Sorry!"

He smiled and took my hand. "No, I'm the one who's sorry. Let's go sit somewhere and talk, all right? Maybe we could leave a little early—"

"Kevin Bauer, that's dereliction of duty!" Embarrassment made me extra-cheery, and the contrite look on his handsome face made me think, *Dancing isn't everything, after all.* "We're both here until the bitter end. In fact, right now I'd better get back on my rounds. See you later."

"All right, but first tell me, are you free for a concert Tuesday night?"

"Yes, I think so. Some kind of Christmas event?"

He smiled almost shyly. "Much better than that. The Next Music Consort is coming down from Vancouver B.C. to play a program of Charles Tyler's work. It's at a private home in Seattle, and Ivy's invited us. Charles might even be there!"

"Oh. That sounds . . . wonderful." *Except that your hero despises me at the moment, and Joe says his music is a chore to sit through.* "Let's talk more about it later, OK? I really should get to work."

No kidding; it was eight-forty already. What was I doing, thinking about dancing when I had a party to run, and a rendezvous to keep? And why did I make the rendezvous so late? The wait was nerve-racking.

I checked in with the waiters, and cued the carolers for their final set. Eight-forty-five. Picked up another cup of cider and set it down again. Did the same with a glass of wine. Ten to nine.

I didn't see Lou anywhere; he must have slipped away already, though it was hard to tell for sure in the constantly shifting crowd. The buffet looked good, but I couldn't bring myself to eat anything.

Finally, at five minutes before the hour, I left the confines of the party and headed toward the roasting floor. Along the way I decided on a quick detour to the ladies' room, to redo my lipstick; might as well play my own role properly. As I detoured, I saw Frank Sanjek coming around the corner from the coatracks and gave him a big encouraging smile.

Just keep behaving yourself, I thought, *and keep a lid on Sally tonight.* Then, walking down the corridor to the rest rooms, I passed Madison coming the other way. She nodded to me, her platinum earrings swaying, but didn't speak, and I wondered sourly if she was hurrying back to Aaron.

The corridor was dim and utilitarian, its flooring bare cement that was soiled now by all the guests coming in from the parking lot. There was a puddle on the floor, too, some thin dark liquid, coffee or wine, spreading out from under the closed door of the men's room. *Well, I told Kevin there'd be spills, but I don't have time to deal with it now . . .*

Then I got closer, and caught the reflection of the overhead light in the surface of the puddle. The dark liquid was opaque, not clear, and the reflection's gleam was ruby-red.

Not coffee. Not cider, or mulled wine.

Blood.

Chapter Twenty-Seven

I NEVER HEARD ALL THE DETAILS—I NEVER WANTED TO—BUT I did hear that the cause of this second death was similar to the first: massive blood loss. Only this time, the killer's blade severed the carotid artery of the throat. No murder weapon was found, only a pair of bloody rubber gloves, lying in the sink where the weapon was apparently rinsed off.

The setting was similar as well. The murderer struck at the site of a lively party, leading to confused recollections about which individuals were at which location, at what time and in whose company. There was one important difference, though, at least to me; I didn't have to identify the body.

Because everyone at Habitat knew Lou Schulman.

The reporters had a field day, of course, although your basic business writer lacks the gut instinct for a crime scene. The TV camera wasn't a live feed, but the minute the police let them go, the television people raced back to their studio and ran some footage on the late-late news. Kevin and I had seen them roaring out of the Habitat parking lot, when he'd excused himself from the police and walked me out to Vanna. It was hardly the romantic end to the evening that we'd envisioned.

They were running the footage again now, on Sunday

morning. It was only eight A.M., but I'd given up on sleep hours ago. Bundled in sweats and slippers, I was hunched in a kitchen chair, staring dully at the portable TV I keep on the counter. *At least I'm home again. I needed to be home.*

"An extraordinary scene last night at a coffee-roasting plant in Snohomish County," said the lacquered brunette on the little screen. "A man was murdered during the company Christmas party at Habitat Coffee. While scores of people were celebrating nearby, the victim, whose name has not yet been released, apparently bled to death from—"

She hit the word "bled" with a nice mix of gravity and excitement. *Isn't this terrible? Isn't this thrilling?* I turned off the sound and watched the silent images. A pan of the party, and then the corridor, crowded with milling figures. No puddle of blood, but there was the men's-room door swinging open, and stunned faces emerging. Then the film cut to the Habitat visitor center and a tense gentleman from the Snohomish County Sheriff's Office.

The sheriff made a brief statement, declined to answer questions, walked away past the microphones and the antique coffee equipment. Standing gravely in the background were Kevin Bauer and Ivy Tyler, both of them pale and numb with shock. My joke about staying to the bitter end was no joke. Charles Tyler had departed in a wheelchair, with Sally at his side, but Ivy and Kevin had remained in place like captains going down with the ship.

I wasn't on camera at all, which suited me fine. I had been sequestered in an office with a sleepy young deputy, making photocopies of the guest list and confirming the names of people I had seen in the course of the evening. In offices throughout the building, guests had been questioned, lists cross-referenced, and massive amounts of notes taken down. It all took a very long time.

Searching the site for a murder weapon would take even longer, of course, with all that machinery... *all those sacks of coffee beans... debris in the coffee beans...* I nodded off and then awoke, startled and disoriented, to the sound of a knock on the kitchen door. Kevin? I ran a hand through my hair and pulled the door open.

"The light was on, Stretch, so I figured you were up."

Aaron looked awful, his face almost as pale as his long white scarf.

"I was, sort of. Come in, I'll make more coffee."

I had already brewed and consumed a pot full, using the Habitat beans Kevin gave me just a few days ago. So long ago. *Was it only Tuesday that I toured the roaster?* I mused, waiting for the kettle to boil. *This is Sunday. Two weddings in the next two weeks, and Christmas in there somewhere. I've got to get organized.*

But I wasn't disorganized; I was simply in shock. And the shock was yielding to caffeine at a pretty good clip. The thought of Christmas brought Lily and the boys to mind, and with them, Darwin. Would he be suspected of this murder, too?

No doubt about it: Aaron and I would have to turn over Jason's CD now, even if we got in trouble for withholding it in the first place. It was evidence that the murderer was a blackmail victim. *Unless...* I had a hunch, but it was still shaping itself in my mind, like a Polaroid image slowly emerging from its gray void.

I carried two mugs to the table and put one in front of Aaron. We hadn't spoken to each other in all the confusion at the warehouse, but now I recalled our earlier conversation near the dance floor.

"You had some news, you said. Bad news."

"Yeah." He rubbed the back of his neck as if it hurt. "Remember I had someone who might be able to decrypt the video? Guy from the *Sentinel*. It wasn't his fault."

"Oh, no."

"Oh, yes. The file almost opened, but then it self-destructed, just like the READ ME document. So now we've got nothing but an unlikely story. And both the blackmailers are dead."

"Not necessarily," I said slowly.

Aaron frowned. "You don't think Lou and Jason were working together?"

"No, I *do* think that. I just wonder if there was a third blackmailer."

"Such as who?"

I tapped my coffee cup with a fingernail. Over Aaron's shoulder, I could see the lake turning silver as the morning brightened into another fine winter day. Not silver, though. More like platinum.

"Such as Madison Jaffee."

"*What?*"

"Well, look at it, Aaron! She was Jason Kraye's girlfriend, she could easily have been in on the scheme. You said yourself you wondered what she saw in him. Maybe she saw money. She was wearing expensive new jewelry last night, and apparently she just bought some kind of sports car."

"That's not much to go on."

"But there's more." The mental image sharpened. "When I met with her last Wednesday, she said she'd just come in from Tokyo the day before. I've been trying to remember something she said at the party last night, and it just came to me. She talked about Beau Paliere, this wedding planner who one-upped me on television."

"So what?" Aaron began stirring sugar into his coffee.

I tapped faster. "So, the TV spot was on the air Monday morning. *How did Madison see it if she was in Tokyo?*"

He stopped stirring for a moment, and then shrugged. "Maybe she didn't, maybe someone told her about it. Or maybe you misunderstood about Tokyo."

"Or maybe she set herself up with an alibi for Jason's murder! And that's why she wanted to know everything we were finding out, in case we suspected her."

"Why would Madison kill her own partner, who was also her boyfriend? It's absurd."

"*Because* he was her boyfriend, and he was cheating on her with Li Ping."

"Hell hath no fury?" He teetered back in his chair, and even smiled a little. "I don't think so."

"Well, I do! I think she killed Jason, and then once she'd gone that far, she killed Lou because she wanted the profits for herself. I saw her there in the corridor, remember. Maybe because she was the brains of the outfit, and he was such a dope that he was a danger to her. It's possible."

"Possible, but nowhere near probable." Aaron tipped forward again, thumping his elbows on the table, and turned his palms up. "Maddie's female, remember? Maybe she could have hidden in the men's room, to ambush Lou, but crashing a bachelor party? That's not too brainy."

"She wouldn't have to go inside the Hot Spot, just out back where the body was found."

"But the streets were deserted that night except for the

guys at the party. She would have stuck out a mile, coming or going. Any woman would."

Aaron was right, of course. But he was so ready with his arguments that I had a sudden and uncomfortable insight. He must have suspected Madison, too, and then talked himself out of it. *Why? Because she's such a beautiful, sophisticated female?*

He was looking at me quizzically. "Why do you dislike her so much, Slim?"

"I don't dislike her! I just thought she was a possibility. Have you got a better one?"

"Maybe I do." He took a gulp of coffee and rapped the cup back on the table. "I'm following a couple of leads."

"So tell me about them."

"Not yet," he said flatly. My conjectures about Madison had definitely touched a nerve. "I'm still checking them out. I'll tell you when I'm ready."

"What am I, Della Street? Tell me now."

He glared at me. "No."

"First you want me to listen," I snapped, "and then you won't talk. You should make up your mind."

"And *you* should grow up!" Aaron's fuse was even shorter than mine this morning. "You think this is a game? I've been trying to explain something really serious—"

"If being married was so serious, why didn't you tell me about it before? Being made a fool of didn't feel like a game to me."

"That's because you don't know the whole story, and you won't let me tell you! You're being completely unreasonable!"

If Aaron hadn't shouted at me, I might have confessed the truth. I might have said that refusing to hear him out was giving me some juvenile sense of having the upper hand. Of getting payback for being duped. I might have told him I was only hanging on to an unreasonable position out of obstinacy and wounded pride, and that I was almost ready to stop hanging on. But I *hate* being shouted at.

"I'll be unreasonable if I want to!" I shouted back. "And I want you out of my house!"

"Fine!"

Aaron came out of his chair so fast that it toppled over with a shocking clatter. He picked it up and slammed it back in place with white-knuckled hands, and as he did, the trailing edge of his heavy pea coat caught my cup. Coffee sloshed across the table in a dark, spreading pool. The cup spun around, skidded to the edge of the table, and plunged to the floor between us.

I shrieked. I couldn't help it. The sight of the dark liquid, the visceral memory of Lou's shattered mug slashing my hand, the strain of all this anger in my home ... I shrieked, and then I started to sob.

"Carnegie, don't cry. I didn't mean to—"

"Just go away!"

He reached down for the cup—it hadn't even broken— saying, "Let me help you with this. Got some paper towels?"

"Aaron, leave it *alone*. Leave me alone."

"Are you sure?" He stood, the cup dangling from one hand, and looked at me. His face was stone.

"Yes. Go."

So he did. Aaron set the cup on the table, buttoned his coat, and walked out the door. I heard his footsteps on the dock outside, distinct in the Sunday morning hush. Then even the footsteps disappeared.

Alone. Exactly what I didn't want to be at the moment. I

mopped up the coffee, drawing long, ragged breaths, then went into the bathroom to mop at my face. My self-appointed task for the day was to move Made in Heaven's operation out of Joe's offices and back into my own office upstairs. But I couldn't face it yet. First I needed some TLC.

My mother was off on her trip, but this was far too complicated a situation to discuss with her anyway. So I called Lily, grateful to be back in her good graces, and hoping to be invited over. The company of loved ones is always better than a voice on the phone.

I was surprised when a man answered.

"Mike? It's Carnegie. What's going on?"

I heard him moving to another room, and a door closing behind him. "Darwin's been rearrested. The Snohomish County people found a knife in his car."

"No! No, I don't believe it."

"It's just a utility knife." Mike sounded very tired. "It was in with some gear for his artwork."

"So there's no blood on it."

"No. But the theory is that he rinsed it off, there in the men's room. Anyway, even if they can't prove it was the murder weapon, Darwin sure as hell can't prove that it wasn't. Not unless someone finds the real one."

"What about fingerprints or DNA or something, inside the rubber gloves you found? I'm sorry, I'm telling you your job."

"That's OK. As far as we can tell, the killer wore a second pair of gloves, inside the first, and took those with him along with his weapon."

"Oh. Mike, I was going to come over. Would that be OK, do you think?"

He covered the phone with his hand. I heard muffled voices, then he came back on.

"Lily says, yes, please."

It was full daylight by the time I got there, sunny and chill, with pale patches of frost lingering on roofs and lawns, anywhere the tree shadows fell across them. Lily's windows were covered with crooked paper snowflakes in rudimentary shapes; she'd been keeping the boys busy.

Mike answered the door. "They're taking cookies to the neighbor. Be back in a few minutes."

I followed him into the warm, fragrant kitchen. The table bore a cheerful jumble of eggshells, sticky bowls, and spilled sugar. On the counter, half a dozen red paper plates were piled with decorated snowman cookies. Mike handed me one, and munched the top hat off another.

"You must not be on duty," I said. "You have flour in your hair."

"Do I?" He smiled ruefully and leaned against the sink. "My boss replaced me on the Kraye case, and strongly suggested I take a few days off. He's a good guy. Lily needs someone around."

Not just someone, I thought, chewing slowly on my snowman. *She needs you. A solid, reliable man she can trust.* Either the cookie was dry, or my mouth was, because I was finding it difficult to swallow.

"Before they get back," Mike was saying, "I need you to do something for me, if you would."

He was a courteous man in a coarse world, and I loved him for it, for Lily's sake. "Anything."

"OK, tell me again what you saw at the Hot Spot, minute by minute, everything you can remember. There's some small detail that's sticking in the back of my mind, but I can't shake it loose."

So I ran through the story again. The memory was like a grim little movie that I'd seen too many times: the dark Ship Canal, the slope of bushes, the scuffling figures, the nearly deserted street. But at the end of my account, Mike shook his head in frustration.

"There's something there, Carnegie. I can feel it, but I can't nail it down. I'll have to let it percolate for a while. Speaking of which, want some coffee?"

"I'm over my limit already, thanks." I opened the fridge and helped myself to a glass of milk, and then to another cookie.

I was stalling. Should I tell Mike my idea about Madison Jaffee? I had such a strong instinct that she was hiding something, but instinct isn't evidence. This was no eyewitness account like the one I'd rendered about Darwin's fight with Jason. And look at all the grief I had caused by doing that. Anyway, Aaron was right. The killer must have been a man, a man who'd attended both parties. But which one? And was he a blackmailer, or a victim of blackmail?

"Aunt Carrie!"

A stampede of small boys, both of them, surged into the kitchen with Lily bringing up the rear. Little Ethan raised his arms for a hug, while big brother, Marcus, who was all of six, regaled me with the day's adventures.

"I used the rolling pin 'cause Ethan's too little, and he dropped a egg—"

"*An* egg." Lily and I said it simultaneously, and laughed, but her eyes were anguished. I put Ethan down and opened my arms to her.

"He dropped an egg and Mike said a bad word and Mrs. Hill says they're the best cookies ever and . . ."

Marcus continued, a keyed-up little bird piping in the background, while Mike gently herded him and Ethan away from us into the living room. Lily and I stayed in the kitchen so the boys wouldn't see her cry.

"Darwin will be home soon," I whispered as I hugged her. "I swear, he'll be home soon."

Chapter Twenty-Eight

MONDAY WAS JAMMED. BONNIE BUCKMEISTER'S WEDDING WAS coming up fast, on Thursday night, so tying off the loose threads of her Yuletide tapestry would have been plenty in itself—especially given the disarray of my desk and my files. Added to that was the possible postponement of Tyler/Sanjek, after this second death in the wedding party.

Postponement was still only a possibility, because I had so far failed to reach any of the principals by phone. I suspected that Sally would want to press on, but Frank or Ivy might have other ideas, and if that was the case, I had to be ready. Rescheduling a wedding, especially at the eleventh hour, is an unholy hassle.

On top of all this, I needed to do some hard thinking about Madison Jaffee. But my angry parting from Aaron left a shadow over that whole question. Were my suspicions about her really as far-fetched as Aaron thought they were, or was his own instinct for the truth being clouded by emotion? Or were my own emotions being clouded by misguided instincts?

An uncomfortable dilemma, any way you looked at it, so I decided to concentrate on wedding work first. As Eddie would say, I had too much corn poppin'.

Eddie himself was still incommunicado, which made for another loose thread. If he didn't call in before returning in person, he wouldn't know we were back in business at the houseboat. Well, that was his problem. I left a message on his home number, and double-checked that Made in Heaven's phone was still forwarding to Solveto's.

Kelli had agreed to keep fielding calls for me until Eddie got back. Solveto's was busy every day and night of the holidays, so she'd be working overtime till New Year's Day. The forwarding had worked so well, and I used my cell phone so much anyway, that most of my callers never even knew about my temporary change of location. But I didn't want to take any chances, especially with my new bride Andrea still out there somewhere.

Even with too much to do, it was a pleasure to be back at my battered old desk, gazing out of my newly reinforced windows. Amazingly, the weather was still fine and frosty, with a high bright sky of the palest blue and the snowy peaks of the Olympic Mountains making a jagged edge along the western horizon. A few hardy souls had their sailboats out on the glittering lake, and a few even hardier souls were kayaking, stroking past the houseboats like waterborne joggers, moving fast to keep warm. Straight down below me, a little convoy of Canada geese paddled among the pilings. In the spring there would be goslings . . .

After a few minutes of daydreaming about simpler, warmer days ahead, I tore my attention away from the water. Admiring the view wasn't getting me anywhere. I put on a baroque Christmas album, made some fresh coffee, and buckled down to work, starting with another attempt to reach Ivy. Once again, her assistant Jenna answered, but this time she had news.

"I was just about to contact you," said Jenna. She was an efficient older woman, rather formal, who seemed to put in endless hours at MFC. "Ms. Tyler called in to say she's spending the day at home with her husband. She'd prefer not to be disturbed."

"I understand. Is Charles all right?" Jenna and I had a good working relationship, even though I used first names and she didn't.

She lowered her voice. "I'm not sure, Ms. Kincaid. They were both quite upset. Ms. Tyler had me call her daughter and ask her to come up to Snohomish."

"Oh, dear. Well, if you hear from either of them, I need to know right away if they're thinking about a change in wedding plans. Keep in touch, OK?"

I worked steadily all afternoon, absorbed in my paperwork, and jumped when someone knocked on the office door. I opened it to a thin, pale, diffident-looking individual, blinking in the sunshine as if he'd just stepped out of a cave. Everything about him was thin and pale, from his long nose to his lank locks to the droopy raincoat he wore, surely not much help in this winter weather.

"Can I help you?"

"Well, I'm—"

"Surprise!" A familiar face peeked around his shoulder: Bonnie Buckmeister, her round cheeks rosier than ever. "Brian's here, isn't he wonderful? Daddy's parking the car, but he said to go on up. Carnegie, we were so excited for you to meet Brian that we said let's just go see her! Let's just go right now! And then that nice Kelli told us you weren't in Fremont anymore, you were back in your houseboat, so we drove over here!" She nudged her fiancé playfully. "Brian, isn't Carnegie wonderful?"

"Well, I—"

"There you are, Mother, the happy couple and the woman who's gonna make it all happen!" The senior Buckmeisters were mounting the stairs. "Aren't they just the handsomest couple, Carnegie?"

Buck reached the landing and stamped his feet, and I swear my floating home rocked a little on the water. "Boy *howdy,* it is cold out here."

"Come on inside," I said helplessly. "Brian, it's good to finally meet you."

"You, too," he said. Even his voice was thin. "I'm sorry, I'm a little—"

"The boy's jet-lagged all to pieces," said Betty, patting him on the arm. Then she looked around Made in Heaven's good room, rubbing her chilled hands together, and sighed contentedly. "You must be pleased as punch to be back in your own sweet little houseboat again. I was telling Brian, Carnegie lives in the sweetest little houseboat. How is your friend Alan, dear?"

"Aaron." Joe Solveto cohabited with a devilishly handsome man named Alan, but the Killer B's had never met him. "Aaron's fine. He's just fine."

"Nice fella," rumbled Buck. "Real nice. In the newspaper business. You'd like him, Brian. Now that you're gonna live in Seattle, we'll have to hook you up with Alan sometime."

"I'm sure he'd like that very much," I answered absently, with a longing look at the pile of work still on my desk. "He's kind of new in town himself. Well, now that we've met, I expect Brian would like to rest up before we talk about the wedding. Maybe tomorrow? . . ."

But no, all three Buckmeisters assured me, Brian was

just bursting with curiosity about every jolly detail of Christmas Eve eve. This seemed doubtful to me, but we settled ourselves in the wicker chairs and went through the entire event point by point. I reviewed each decision we'd made, from the fragrant cinnamon sticks nestled in the cedar wreaths, to the gentlemen's mistletoe boutonnieres, to the decorated tree that would serve as a gift table.

"That's where Joe Solveto's model trains will be, in a big loop around the bottom of the tree. He's got a locomotive that puffs steam, and boxcars that say 'Happy Holidays,' and all kinds of stuff; it'll be great. Now, Bonnie's first dance with her father will be to 'Silver Bells' . . ."

Through it all, Brian just sat and nodded and blinked—was he even awake?—until I got to the guest book. "Your guests will sign in at a small table just inside the entrance of the Arctic Club. We've picked out a crimson leather book with gold—"

"No." Brian held up a pale, narrow hand.

"Pardon me?" I stopped short, and even the Killer B's were silenced.

The bridegroom gnawed a thoughtful lip and said slowly, "Instead of a guest book, why don't we have everyone sign a big fancy white Christmas tree skirt? Then every year when Bonnie and I put up our tree, and put the skirt underneath, we'll remember our Christmas wedding."

Instantly, Betty, Bonnie, and Buck went into happy raptures.

"Brian, that's perfect!"

"Isn't he wonderful?"

"The boy's a genius!"

"What a clever idea," I chimed in myself. I wasn't sure which surprised me more: Brian out-Yuleing his in-laws, or

Brian completing a sentence. "I'll find a tree skirt today, and some fabric pens."

"I always said Brian was Mr. Right," said Bonnie, clasping his narrow hand in her plump one.

Betty tittered. "I used to say that exact same thing about your daddy—"

"Now, Mother," warned Buck fondly.

"—'cept I'd say that his first name was Always!"

I joined in the merriment that followed, then stood up with a decent show of regret. "Folks, I really have to get back to my desk."

" 'Course you do!" Buck rose and patted me heartily on the shoulder. I tried to stay upright. "You get some rest, too. You're lookin' a little peaky."

I felt peaky, too, if that meant worn-out and hungry for sleep. Monday night I crashed early, and Tuesday morning I awoke with a bit more energy, and the determination to pin down the plans for Tyler/Sanjek, so I could clear my mind and give some serious thought to Madison Jaffee. Maybe I should swallow my pride and consult Aaron again, this time minus the shouting.

First things first, though. Did I have two weddings coming up, or just one? Sally and Ivy still weren't answering their cell phones, so I tried Jenna again.

"Ms. Tyler's not coming in today, either," she told me. "Madison Jaffee is taking all the press calls about the merger." Her voice grew more animated than I'd ever heard it. "MFC stock is up five and half just this morning!"

Wall Street, it seemed, was not interested in the death of Lou Schulman. But if the doyenne of child-friendly caffeine was going to serve politically correct brew, well, that was news.

"OK, I won't bother Ivy at home," I said reluctantly. "But I really do need to know about the wedding. So if she calls—"

"Won't you see her tonight at the concert?" asked Jenna. "She said you'd be there, with Mr. Bauer."

Oh, hell. Did I agree to go to this thing?

"The concert, right," I temporized. "Is Sally going, do you know?"

"The whole family is attending, and Mr. Tyler has prepared some remarks."

"Well, of course, I'll be there, too. No question." I badly wanted to redeem myself with Charles, and maybe I could nail things down with Sally, too. And come to think of it, I did tell Kevin I'd go with him.

Sure enough, Kevin called me at mid-morning to confirm. As far as he was concerned, we had a date.

"I'm sorry I didn't call till now, but it's been a madhouse up here, with the police searching the warehouse and the reporters underfoot. Are you all right? After a shock like that—"

"I'm fine, really. I'm home in my houseboat! You'll get a chance to see it tonight. That is, unless you want to meet at the concert?"

"Of course not." He sounded mildly shocked. "Just give me directions, and I'll pick you up at seven."

An old-fashioned date, then. Sweet. I e-mailed him a map to my dock, and went back to work with a right good will. In fact, I got so much done that I knocked off a little early, to allow for sipping a glass of wine while I got dressed at my leisure. *My dark red dress for tonight,* I thought. *I'm tired of the jade silk.*

But when I got downstairs to my bedroom, I discovered

that leisure wasn't in the cards. In my haste to leave Ivy's apartment, I'd left behind a good pair of shoes, some earrings, and who knew what else. The earrings I could do without, but those black suede pumps with Cuban heels would look so good with the swirling skirt of the red dress . . . and I still had Ivy's key.

Half an hour later I was letting myself into the apartment in the Market. I'd meant to go back anyway, just to neaten things up, although with Ivy sequestered at home, it hadn't really mattered. Fortunately, a quick look around showed the kitchen tidy, and all my toiletries out of the bathroom. Then I entered the guest bedroom and flipped on the light switch. With a little *whump*, the three-lamp track lighting above the head of the bed sparked and died.

"Damn!"

I tried feeling around the floor of the dark closet for my shoes, but came up empty. *I should be a good guest, anyway. It won't take long.* The broom closet in the kitchen yielded a pack of light bulbs, and soon I was standing on the bed in my stocking feet, keeping my wobbly balance while I unscrewed one lamp at a time, trying to figure out if a single bulb was dead, or all three.

Then something odd happened. The middle bulb, when I got to it, fell into my hand like a ripe pear, far heavier than its companions. Puzzled, I stepped down from the bed and took it into the kitchen. What I saw by the kitchen light made me sick to my stomach.

The object in my hands wasn't a lightbulb at all. It was a spy camera.

Chapter Twenty-Nine

MY FIRST THOUGHT WAS THAT IVY HAD BEEN SPYING ON ME, me personally, but that was crazy. And the notion that she secretly filmed all her houseguests was even crazier. I know people aren't always what they seem, but my friend and mentor Ivy as a high-tech voyeur just didn't make sense.

What *did* make sense was Ivy Tyler, CEO of family-friendly Meet for Coffee, the woman who lived in a fishbowl, as a blackmail target.

I entered Ivy's room and looked up at the ceiling. Sure enough, the track lighting over her bed had been roughly removed; I could see dark marks on the white ceiling where it used to attach, and a small gaping hole for the wiring. Ivy must have discovered the camera and torn it out, but she hadn't checked the guest bedroom. Who could think straight when their most intimate territory had been violated?

My next thought was to call Aaron. He could hardly be pleased to hear from me after being banished from my home, but this wasn't about us. It was about murder.

At the sound of my voice, Aaron was wary, but once I explained my discovery, he was all business.

"So you think the blackmail note was about Ivy?"

"I'd bet on it. Jason would have heard the rumors about

Ivy and Simon Weeks, and he could have gotten Lou into the apartment. Lou was the one with the technical know-how. So what do you think we should do now?"

A long pause. "Nothing."

"Nothing? But this proves our theory!"

"Does it really? Or does it prove that you were snooping around a private residence, and that a prominent business-woman likes to make kinky home movies? Or that she just likes to keep tabs on her houseguests?"

"You don't believe that, Aaron."

"Of course I don't, but the police might. Ordinary people do use these cameras."

"Oh."

Aaron's train of thought was steaming elsewhere. "The guy who knocked you down in her hallway. Could that have been Lou Schulman?"

The thought made me shudder. It was full dark now out-side the apartment windows, and the sound of cars and voices from the Market below seemed far away. "It could have been. In fact, it must have been, don't you think?"

"Makes sense. Lou's partner is killed, so he panics. He wants to get those cameras out of there before they're traced to him. Ivy and I were at the apartment all Tuesday evening, so he has to wait for Wednesday. He made a lousy burglar, but then Lou wasn't all that bright outside his own com-puter expertise."

Another pause, while we both thought about the life and death of Lou Schulman. Then Aaron said, "Listen, put everything back the way it was, OK? It's not doing any harm now, and I don't think you want to confront Ivy with it. We need to get together and consider this some more."

"How's tomorrow morning?"

"No, Maddie's coming to my place, to talk about the book."

"You do interviews at your apartment?"

"She suggested it," said Aaron blandly. "I gave up my office at the *Sentinel,* and she gets interrupted too much at MFC. Could you meet me somewhere tonight?"

"No." I glanced at the kitchen clock, one of those artsy types with no numbers, and decided to be specific about the reason. "Kevin's picking me up soon."

The temperature plummeted. "Ah. Well, let's not interfere with your social life."

"It's a concert of Charles's music," I said severely. "I need to be there. And anyway, my social life is none of your business."

"Absolutely not," said Aaron. "I'll let you go. Oh, by the way, Lily called to tell me about the dot-com where Lou and Jason worked. Guess what their biggest account was, for those pop-up ads?"

"Spy cameras?"

"Good guess, Nancy Drew. Enjoy your concert."

Getting dressed back on the houseboat, I could see that the Cuban heels looked terrific with the red dress, but I hardly cared. The thought of Ivy Tyler's most private moments being secretly recorded, only to be thrown back in her face with a threat to broadcast them to the world . . . it was horrible. I could almost understand killing the men who did that to her.

No, I can't. I paused in front of the bathroom mirror, hairbrush in hand, and looked intently into my own eyes. *No, murder isn't understandable, or excusable, ever. No.*

Kevin was late picking me up, so I met him at the front door in my coat.

"How about a nightcap and a look at houseboat living, after the concert?"

"Sounds good."

He gave me a kiss on the cheek, and opened his car door for me like a gentleman. Kevin drove a black SUV, one of the smaller ones, and judging by the mud spatters, it got some actual use on rough roads. Behind the wheel he was quiet and preoccupied, and I was quiet myself as I spread a street map on my lap, helping him find our destination by the glow of the dome light. I had a lot to think about.

Braemere Heights was a gated neighborhood overlooking Elliott Bay, with houses set far back from the twisting road, behind masses of rhododendrons and sculpted evergreens. We found the right number on a gate post that loomed out of the darkness, and parked before a huge brick-and-stucco home with a slate roof and a row of tall leaded-glass windows. Bright lamplight spilled onto the lawn, along with the muffled sound of voices and laughter.

As we walked up a flagstone pathway to the front door, we could see perhaps twenty or thirty people standing about the living room, chatting. In a farther room, beyond rows of empty folding chairs, a quartet of two men and two women in formal black were tuning their string instruments.

"We made it," said Kevin with relief, and I realized that his preoccupation was with being late, not with the investigation going on at Habitat. "I can hardly believe we get to do this! The Next Music Consort is world-famous."

Not to me, of course, but I didn't mention that.

The door was opened by a large woman in a loud caftan, who proved to be Mary Ellen, our hostess for the evening. She welcomed us in and led us down a wide hallway lined with brass planters on marble columns, and adorned with various antiques. We passed a display of Japanese vases, and an artful arrangement of Louis Vuitton steamer trunks from the 1930's. Why collect stamps when you can go for the big stuff?

Mary Ellen pointed out the elegant little red-and-gilt powder room, then led us across the hall from it into a coatroom crowded with skis, tennis rackets, a croquet set, soccer balls, camping gear, and boots and shoes for every possible sport.

"It's the boys' junk," she laughed. "I'm always telling them we could open our own branch of REI! Leave your coats and come on, there's still time for a quick drink. Kevin, you've met Mr. Tyler already, haven't you? I'm so *thrilled* to have him here."

So was everyone else, apparently. We entered the living room to see Charles seated on a damask love seat, surrounded by a crowd of well-dressed people who were hanging on the great man's every word. His snow-white brows were drawn together, but in thoughtfulness, not distress, and I was glad to see that his hands were hardly trembling.

"The piece reflects my commitment to the acoustic realm," he was saying. "I have no interest in the electronic milieu."

Ivy, looking sharp in diamonds and a white silk pantsuit, stood at the edge of the crowd, watching Charles solicitously. Simon Weeks was there, too, his broad shoulders and thick gray hair adding a distinguished note to the crowd. His fond and watchful eyes were always on Ivy, I noticed, just as they had been at the Habitat party, as if he were enjoying the occasion on her account rather than his own. I was glad that Simon had left the party early, while Lou was still alive; I didn't want to suspect him.

When Ivy saw me and Kevin, she turned to give us each a warm smile and a hug. I bet most CEOs don't hug the owners of the company they just bought.

"Is Sally here?" I asked her.

She shook her head, and answered my unspoken question about the wedding.

"They're out to dinner somewhere, talking things over. Frank's thinking about delaying the date again, but Sally wants to go ahead. Charles and I told them they have to decide for themselves this time. I'll let you know soon."

"Soon would be good," I said, thinking, *Now would be good,* and she turned back to listen to her husband.

"You're right, young man," Charles was saying. "I make use of a polyrhythmic conversation between the violins and lower strings, striving toward a basic connectivity..."

Kevin pressed forward to hear, but I peeled off and made for the sideboard, where Mary Ellen was dispensing drinks. I had the feeling I was going to need one. I wanted to get back in Charles's good graces, but it wasn't going to be through my grasp of polyrhythmic conversations. Or tonight's human conversations, either. The ones I overheard on my way to the bar might as well have been the cries of jungle birds.

"...mindful of atonality, but ultimately outside considerations of tonal center..."

"...more visceral than his early works. Legato is out the window..."

"...long, declamatory jabs of the bow..."

No, I'd just let Charles see my smiling face in the audience, and keep my mouth shut.

Mary Ellen was a generous bartender. With about a pint of Chardonnay in hand, I turned to survey the room—and found myself face-to-face with Charles.

"My condolences on your friend Mr. Schulman," he said coldly. "You must be devastated."

"I wasn't . . . I mean, I didn't . . ."

But Charles was already walking away. I was debating going after him—*to say what, though?*—when I was suddenly greeted by the last person on the planet I would have expected to see: Juice Nugent, wearing a man's tuxedo jacket with her leather pants, and holding hands with an attractive brunette.

"Hey, Kincaid," she said, "I didn't know you were into new music."

"I'm doing some work for Ivy Tyler," I said vaguely.

"Cool. This is Rita."

Rita, the girlfriend I'd heard so much about, smiled and nodded at me. She was more conventionally dressed, in a skirt and bright sweater, but she, too, had a slashed haircut and multiple earrings.

"Mary Ellen is Rita's cousin," continued Juice, "so we got in with the in-crowd. Some house, huh?"

As I agreed with her, Kevin joined our little circle. He was smiling at me as he came, but when he saw Juice, his smile stiffened.

"We should take our seats," he began.

"In a sec," I replied, slugging my wine. "Kevin Bauer, this is Juice Nugent, a fabulous cake baker, and this is Rita? . . ."

"Morales. Are you a musician, Kevin, or just a listener like me?"

"Yes," he said. "Yes, nice to meet you. Carnegie, shall we go in?"

"That was a little rude, wasn't it?" I whispered as we entered the music room. So few houseboats these days have a really decent music room.

Kevin raised his eyebrows at me. "I was surprised, that's all. What's someone like that doing here?"

"The same thing we are, I suppose. Juice is—"

"Shh," said an impatient voice behind us. Mary Ellen began to introduce her honored guest, a man whose work had been a revelation to us all for years, a man who inspired so many young composers, a man who . . .

It was a nice introduction, but long. My gaze drifted over to Ivy, listening intently to this praise of the man who sat beside her, her husband and benefactor. Eddie was right, she was a fine-looking woman.

Simon Weeks had taken the seat on Ivy's other side. When Mary Ellen concluded by asking Charles to stand, and leading a round of applause, Simon whispered something in Ivy's ear. Still applauding, she turned toward him and laughed in private understanding.

Suddenly I felt a hot, uneasy blush welling up from my throat. "Naked and crazy," the blackmail note had read. I hadn't even seen the damn video, and now I couldn't look at Ivy and Simon without thinking about it. Was their affair a playful one, or heartfelt, long-term or one-time? Whichever, it had become a poisonous threat to Ivy's standing as a darling of the business world, and her role as a famous man's loving wife.

Because Ivy *did* love Charles, you could tell. But love takes many forms. Ivy Tyler was in the prime of life; her husband was ill and frail. Simon Weeks, strong and vital, had been at her side throughout the adventure of creating MFC. It wasn't hard to understand. So many people have secrets, and not all of them can be condemned.

Charles's remarks, and the performance that followed, were equally wasted on me. Any other time, even if I hadn't cared for the music, I would have been enthralled by the sight of the string quartet playing, their intense concentration and the intricate choreography of sound. But tonight, Charles Tyler's harsh, discordant creations were just a backdrop to my dark musings.

I was glad when the intermission came, and I could slip away to the powder room. When I emerged I saw Kevin across the hall, getting something from his coat pocket.

"Isn't this amazing?" He was even more animated than he'd been at Etta's. "Mary Ellen said she'd put me on her mailing list for private concerts. I want to give her my business card before I forget."

I joined him and glanced around. We were alone. I'd intended to avoid the subject of murder tonight; it seemed a shame to spoil Kevin's enthusiasm, and somehow rude to Mary Ellen, as if doing so would bring a sinister shadow into her home. But now I couldn't help it. Whoever the killer was, the thought of him going free while Darwin stood trial, at risk of his freedom or even his life, was too much.

"Tell me, Kevin, did the police find anything useful at Habitat? The murder weapon, or anything else?"

"Nothing." He changed gears easily; the subject wasn't as far from his mind as I had thought. He dropped the business card case in his shirt pocket, frowning, and set his fists on his hips. "You know, I'm not sure they even looked all that hard. I mean, they went over the men's room for hours, but there are so many places on the roasting floor where you could stash a knife, and the search out there went pretty quickly."

"They're done already?"

He nodded. "They told me they might be back, though I

doubt it. But we close for Christmas week anyway, so if they need to—"

"If no one's going to be around," I said eagerly, "maybe you could search some more yourself. Or could we both? If we found the knife, we wouldn't touch it, we could just call the police back in. There's an innocent man in jail, and I'm going to find the guilty one, no matter what it takes."

Kevin smiled, and pulled me to him for a kiss on the forehead. "You're quite a public defender, aren't you? Tell you what, I'll do it myself, and call you if I find anything. I've got time on my hands this week, except for driving to Portland for a few days to see family. And *you* were telling me how busy you are right now."

"I am, actually. In fact I should— What's that?"

I'd heard a sound from the hallway, and went to look. Charles Tyler, apparently on his way to the powder room, was braced against the wall, his right arm in spasm, a wild look in his eyes. Mary Ellen had just entered the hallway behind him, and we both rushed forward to help.

But not quickly enough. Charles reached one twitching, clawlike hand across the air between us, and slid slowly to the floor.

Chapter Thirty

"Are you sure he's all right, Jenna?"

"Ms. Tyler says he just needs rest. He was pushing himself, going to the concert so soon after that terrible business at Habitat."

It was Wednesday morning, the day before Buckmeister/Frost. With Bonnie's arrangements under control, I was once again on the phone with Ivy's secretary, trying to find out what was happening in the Tyler household. Ivy disliked being called at home at any time, but I especially didn't want to intrude on her today.

"That's a relief," I said. "He looked like death for a minute there."

After a short, frightening silence, Charles had insisted that he wanted only his wife, not a doctor or an ambulance. Mary Ellen, distressed but capable, had taken charge of the situation the way I would have at one of my weddings, dispatching me to the music room to fetch Ivy, and sending Kevin to bring the Tyler car around. Then, with Charles on his way home, she'd made a discreet announcement to the audience, and directed the quartet to finish their performance. I couldn't have done it better myself.

I asked Jenna to keep me posted, and got back to work.

But I was soon interrupted by a call from a happily agitated Kelli.

"Carnegie, guess who was just here, in *person* this time? Beau Paliere! He had more flowers for you and everything. I told him how to get to your houseboat. Isn't he cute?"

"You told him . . . Kelli, remember how I asked you just to take messages for me?"

"Oh, that's right. But he was so disappointed when you weren't here." Big giggle. "And he's so cute, I just couldn't say no!"

You and a lot of other women, I thought. But all I said was, "I understand. Be sure and let me know if Eddie calls in, would you, Kelli?"

"Sure. I bet you're lost without him!"

"You can't imagine."

In his own way, Beautiful Beau was as much a force of nature as the Buckmeisters. He stepped into the good room a few minutes later with a gust of wintry air, a dazzling smile, and a fine cluster of royal-blue irises whimsically arranged in a cocktail shaker. He was dressed, as before, entirely in black.

"Vintage silver," he announced, setting the shaker on the table with a flourish, "and here is the top for it, so that we can share a cocktail next time I am in Seattle. But now, let us be off!"

"Off where?"

He blinked his bedroom eyes. "To Mariella's trunk show, of course. Ten o'clock, I said in my message. Come, come, or we shall be late."

"I didn't get any . . . oh." The light dawned; Kelli said "in person this time" because Beau had called earlier. She'd just neglected the little detail of informing me about it. *How does Joe put up with her?*

"Beau, I wasn't invited to Mariella Ponti's show."

"But I was, and you will be with me." His quiet laugh was liquid, debonair. Then he lowered his voice, and stroked his fingertips lightly along my cheek. "I think you will enjoy being with me."

Personally, I don't enjoy having my face poked at in the middle of a conversation. I know women in the movies love it, but they're so often idiots, aren't they? I took a quick step away and considered this sudden dilemma.

On the one hand, Beau was insufferable. On the other hand, the one that paid Made in Heaven's bills, the Ponti trunk show would be Rich Bride Central. And even better, Rich Mother.

"Let me grab some business cards and tell Kelli where I'm going."

And make sure the little twit hasn't forgotten a call from Andrea as well. But no, Kelli swore that my mystery bride had not been heard from, so we took off. Beau's limo—black, of course, and longer than my houseboat—conveyed us downtown to Le Boutique, an exclusive bridal shop across from the Olympic Hotel. From the shop's second-floor display window, a row of white-gowned mannequins gazed disdainfully down on the mere mortals below. Once they were upstairs, customers could see the detailing on the back of each gown—exactly what wedding guests see a lot of during the ceremony.

Le Boutique's owner was an entirely un-French woman named Hazel Cohen. Her selection of gowns was always up to the minute, and she was ever so well-connected to the top designers. Hazel could get you that Basque-waisted dress in pink Duchess satin that your client just saw in a magazine, and she could get it for you in two months instead of five— *if* you were on her good side. Cross Hazel Cohen, and you could just wait your turn.

So far, the grande dame and I were on nodding terms only. But that was about to change.

Hazel stood at a delicate gilt reception desk, complacently surveying the flock of ladies and girls who cooed and twittered around the shop. Barely five feet tall, she was dwarfed by the towering flower arrangement on the desk. But there was nothing delicate about Hazel Cohen; she looked like a very short linebacker in a Chanel suit.

"Beau! Always a pleasure. And I see you brought your friend." As Beau made the introductions, Hazel peered up at me. "Carnegie, huh? That's a funny name."

"Well, my father—"

"Whatever." She waved a maroon-taloned hand at the sheer white curtain that billowed behind her, dividing the shop in half. Beyond the gauze, I could see an abbreviated runway surrounded by rows of gilt chairs, all empty so far. "Mariella's still tweaking her models. Get yourselves some champagne, look around. Go, circulate."

So we did, though it was more like holding court. Beau was not only famous and gorgeous, he was the only spear carrier in the room. Matrons who might have brushed me off at a bridal show were only too eager to meet me, just to get close to my masculine companion. One daughter, starry-eyed but clever, even asked for my card and then dropped it right where Beau would reach down and retrieve it for her. Every woman in the place, except me and Hazel, was suddenly in love. The man was a master.

And he knew his wedding gowns, I had to give him that.

If last night's musical argot was beyond me, today's talk of cowl backs and mermaid skirts, Juliet caps and Watteau trains, was right up my alley. But also his. Without usurping Mariella's authority as the designer du jour, Beau managed to convey his intimate knowledge of styles and fabrics, as he assessed the face and figure of each bride in turn and offered suggestions for her to consider. Flattering suggestions, of course.

"I see you in strapless," he said to one porcelain-skinned debutante, "with a chiffon bolero, to draw the eye to those exquisite shoulders." And then, to a wisp of a Japanese-American girl, "A poem! In gossamer tulle, very soft and flowing, you would be a poem. Ask Mariella what she's done in tulle this season."

I was agreeing with him—and admiring his technique—when I caught a glimpse of a familiar figure through the gauzy curtain. Was that Andrea crossing behind the runway from one dressing room to another? I was about to find out, because Mariella Ponti herself, tall and formidable, was stalking up on the other side of the gauze.

She threw the curtain open with a grand gesture. "Ladies! Welcome to my new creations."

Just as she spoke, heavy footsteps came pounding up the stairs by the reception desk. Then a second spear carrier entered the harem: Mike Graham, out of breath and way out of his element. He glanced around at the buzzing women, spotted the one he wanted, and made a beeline for me, speaking intently as came.

"Carnegie, when you saw the stripper through your binoculars, how did you know it was her?"

I felt myself go scarlet. Unhappily for Mike, and even more so for me, silence had fallen the moment he appeared, so that every word of his question rang clear across this shrine of femininity. A whispering, tittering tide of reaction arose, as the detective lieutenant went red-faced himself, and I hustled him back down the stairs and out to the sidewalk.

"Sorry!" I'd never seen him blush before. As Kelli would say, 'Cute.' "I'm really sorry. That receptionist just said you were at some kind of store, and if it was important I could go find you. I thought . . . never mind. This is important. I was going over what you told me at Lily's. You said you saw the stripper walking away from the Hot Spot that night. But could you see her face clearly enough to be absolutely sure it was her? Because a woman could have slashed Kraye, it wouldn't take much strength—"

"I didn't see her face at all," I said, sorry to puncture his new hypothesis. "But I didn't need to. She was wearing her Santa Claus costume."

"What? You never said anything about Santa Claus. You just said you saw the stripper leaving the area on foot."

"But I did see her! She was wearing a Santa outfit. I saw her when she arrived and I saw her leave again." I clamped my fists in my armpits and shivered. "Mike, I'm freezing out here—"

He tore off his own overcoat and wrapped it around me, but with an entirely impersonal expression on his face. It echoed the way he'd looked at the Bayou, when he realized I knew something about Jason's murder.

"Carnegie, listen to me. Strippers don't put their costumes *back on* after a performance! They just slip on a coat and leave. And that's what this one did. Valoree Wells, we tracked her down and she told us. She wasn't sure of the exact time, but she put on a tan raincoat and carried her costume with her in a tote bag. Walked two blocks west from the Hot Spot, drove away in a Honda Civic, met a friend for a drink. No connection to Jason Kraye, no motive. We didn't question her again."

"But I saw her . . . No, I saw *somebody* dressed as Santa Claus, walking up the street away from the café. Walking east. Mike, did I see the murderer?"

Shoppers and office workers—the midday crowd— brushed past us on the sidewalk. Mike ignored them, his eyes focused on me like lasers.

"I'd bet money on it."

I recalled the red-suited figure I had seen that night. He—she?—had been striding along, with the look of a job well done. I shivered again. Madison Jaffee? If I told Mike my theory, I'd have to tell him about the blackmail, and expose Ivy by explaining about the spy camera and—

"Oh, my God!" Now I recalled something else: Aaron's voice on the phone, as I stood in Ivy's kitchen yesterday with the spy camera. *I'm meeting with Maddie tomorrow,* he had said. *I'll feel her out about this Tokyo business.* If she was really the killer, if she thought Aaron suspected her . . .

"What?" Mike asked. "Is there something else? I should get back to the office and get on this."

"Nothing," I said slowly, and slipped off his coat. "I have to make a phone call, that's all."

I skulked back up to Le Boutique, where I endured a few more titters, and waved a vague "got to go" sort of gesture at Beau. He looked irked, and Hazel Cohen looked curious, but a model in a one-shouldered Greek-column gown was gliding down the runway, and they couldn't speak to me without stopping the show. I snatched my coat and bag and took off, tapping in Aaron's number while I was still descending the stairs.

No answer, just his recorded message. *Probably at lunch.* Out on the sidewalk, I tried to remember where I'd parked. But of course, I'd come in Beau's limo. I tried the number again with clumsy fingers, remembering that hideous pool of blood. *I'm probably wrong anyway.* Got a wrong number this time. Tried again, got the recording again. *But if I'm right . . .*

I looked up and down Seneca Street, as if the answer could be found there. And I found it: the taxi rank in front of the Olympic. I jaywalked—ran—across two lanes of traffic, got myself yelled at, and slid into a cab just ahead of a matron who would have fit right in at Le Boutique, except for her regrettable tendency to nasty language.

I didn't know the exact address of the Lakeshore, but I gave the cabbie—a huge fellow in a turban—the general idea and a fifty dollar bill. I was out of twenties. "Fast as you can, please. It's an emergency."

"You will pay any tickets?" he inquired happily, in an Indian singsong.

"Sure. Just—whoa!" I was flung sideways as he hooked right on Fourth, then I was slammed back against the seat as we went screaming up Westlake. We tore out Fairview Avenue along Lake Union, with blaring horns and shrieking brakes fading away behind us, and renewing again at every intersection.

"Up there on the left," I gasped, an amazingly short time later.

The cab bucketed to a halt in the Lakeshore's parking lot. I got out, wondering whether to ask the cabbie to come with me. But I guess he was afraid I'd ask for change; he tore off again with a screech of wheels and a foul-smelling burp of exhaust. I barely noticed, because I was running past a line of parked cars, then around a corner of the building toward—

Toward Aaron and Madison, strolling away from me. Aaron, in shirtsleeves, had a folder of papers in his hand; Madison wore her long wine-colored coat. He escorted her to a fancy little red sports car in a farther section of the parking lot, held the door as she entered, shut it, and waved as she drove away. *What a gentleman. What a goddamn gentleman.* I waited, feeling nine kinds of foolish, until he returned.

"What's up, Stretch, you miss me?"

I told him what was up. Standing there in the parking lot, I told him about Mike's brainstorm, and my woeful ignorance of the ways of strippers. I just didn't tell him I'd been afraid for his life. "So you see, Madison *could* have been at the Hot Spot that night!"

"But so could anyone else," he said slowly, shocked out of his sarcasm. "Even Ivy, or . . . Come inside, OK?"

Aaron still hadn't personalized his furnished apartment, unless you counted the welter of books and papers that covered every surface of the living room. He swept clear a space on the couch, but I was too excited to sit down. I still didn't believe Ivy was the killer, and I'd thought of a way to make sure.

With Aaron watching me, I called Ivy's office again.

"Jenna, I meant to ask you before, where was it that Ivy stayed when she was in San Francisco? She recommended it to me, but I forgot the name."

Efficient as ever, Jenna provided both the name and the phone number. I hung up and then called it.

"Golden Gate Inn, may I help you?" said a cheery woman's voice.

"I'm calling from the accounting department at Meet for Coffee in Seattle," I said, trying to sound like an utterly bored office worker. I used to be one, actually; that's why I took up wedding planning. "I just need to verify an expense report for Ms. Ivy Tyler, for the night of Sunday, December twelfth. Or was that two nights?"

"Let's see . . . no, just the one. Did Ms. Tyler receive the bracelet all right?"

"Bracelet?"

"Yes, she was so worried about it she had the taxi come back. I was afraid she'd miss her plane! We found it later Monday morning, and mailed it to her."

"Oh, right, the bracelet," I said. "It got here just fine. Thank you so much."

I put away my phone, and related the conversation to Aaron. He threw himself onto the couch and looked at the ceiling.

"So Ivy didn't leave San Francisco until Monday morning," he said, "which means she couldn't have killed Jason on Sunday night. But eliminating Ivy doesn't point the finger at Madison."

"It narrows the field of suspects, and Madison's one of them! Did you ask her how she saw me on TV if she was in Tokyo Monday morning?"

"Yeah, I did. Somebody at the office knew that you were doing Sally's wedding, so they taped the show."

"Who?"

He shrugged. "She didn't say."

"And you didn't press the point? Aaron, you're not acting like a reporter anymore. What's going on?"

"Nothing!" He stood up and started pacing. "Look, I'll find out who taped the show, and if I have to, I'll call Tokyo to verify Maddie's alibi. Will that satisfy you?"

"That and one other thing," I said. "Promise me you won't be alone with Madison until this is all settled."

Aaron cocked his head at me and chuckled. "Stretch, are you worried about my safety, or about her feminine wiles?"

"Shut up," I explained. "I've got enough on my mind, getting Bonnie Buckmeister married tomorrow. So just shut up and promise."

Chapter Thirty-One

BONNIE BUCKMEISTER, SOMEWHAT TO MY SURPRISE, MADE A fairy-tale bride. Not the elongated, enervated, white-sugar sort of Disney princess, but something far more womanly, vivid, and vital. A folktale bride, from a mythic medieval winter of regal panoply and firelit feasts and snowy forests full of wolves and woodcutters. She might have been daughter to Good King Wenceslas.

Royal and voluptuous and clad in velvet the color of rubies, Bonnie came down the aisle of St. Mark's with a dignified bearing and a secret smile. A hooded cape was thrown back on her shoulders, and a circlet of holly leaves and berries, entwined with gold cord, nestled on her dark curls. Waiting wide-eyed at the altar, Brian Frost reflected all of her joy and even some of her splendor, the young prince in his formal black tailcoat with white tie and vest. The choir swelled, the guests sighed, and I dabbed at a tear, with murder and mayhem forgotten, at least for tonight.

An hour or so later, under the sparkling chandelier that hangs from the dome of the Arctic Club's ballroom, I was surprised again: Buck Buckmeister asked me to dance. The band I'd hired included the usual guitar, keyboard, and horns, but also four unusually talented vocalists, male and female, now nearing the end of their pre-dinner set. They had just segued from a whimsical "Baby, It's Cold Outside," to the languid harmonies of "I'm Dreaming of a White Christmas," when Buck marched up, bowed, and began to sweep me skillfully around the circular parquet floor. Who'd have thought such a big Texan would be so light on his feet?

"You did a fine job for my little girl," he told me, his usual roar moderated to a contented rumble. "Her mother and I will never forget that."

"I'll never forget this wedding," I said, quite sincerely. "Bonnie's an angel."

Two hours after that, the angel's crown of holly was dangling from the chandelier. Bonnie had flung it there during the after-dinner dancing, which grew more vigorous and more uproarious with every song. Awed by the ceremony, enchanted by the Yuletide decorations, and wined and dined into a state of sated bliss by Joe Solveto, the Buckmeisters' nearest and dearest were now getting seriously down. Soon Juice Nugent's gift cakes would be served, and boost their energies even further.

As I circulated through the party, tending to details, I felt the flood of relief and triumph that comes when one of my weddings, especially a big one, plays out perfectly. Some people get high climbing mountains. To me, Buckmeister/Frost was the summit of Mount Rainier.

"Kharrnegie, Merry Christmas!"

Boris wore a decorous black suit, but his tie was a garish affair featuring St. Nick on a skateboard. No fervent hand-kissing this time, just the rib-crushing hug he bestowed on everyone he didn't actually hate. When Boris took your breath away, he did it for real.

"Same to you!" I had to speak up to be heard above the din. "Isn't this glorious?"

"*Da!* I have suppressed myself!"

"Surpassed. I meant the whole wedding, but your flowers are glorious, too. How was dinner?" As usual, I'd been too busy to eat.

"Very fine," said Boris judiciously. "But some confusion at the tables."

I sighed. "Buck kept asking extra people, so we had to squeeze in more place settings. In fact, I see an extra over there I need to talk to. Excuse me."

Aaron was chatting with the waiter at the coffee and hot chocolate table. His tie had little menorahs all over it.

"*Gut Yontiff*, Stretch," he said as I approached. "That's happy holiday, to those in the know."

"Don't tell me, let me guess. Buck invited you at the last minute."

"Yeah, he said because I'm new in town, I should come meet some friendly folks. Who do you suppose told him I was new in town?"

"I can't imagine. But since you hate Christmas, I'm surprised you came." I requested some cocoa, hold the rum, and sipped at it gratefully. As far as I'm concerned, whipped cream is one of the four major food groups. "So, what did you find out about Madison? Was she really in Tokyo that night?"

"Won't know till tomorrow. She was booked at the Hotel Narita, but I have to talk to a different manager to get a direct confirmation. Anyone can book a room." Aaron gazed around the Arctic Room, with its wreaths and trees and high-spirited faces glowing in the light of many candles. "I don't hate *this* stuff, Stretch. Good cheer in the middle of winter and all that. It's the manufactured sentimentalism that turns my stomach, and the pressure to buy a lot of crap that nobody needs."

"Well, I don't like that part of Christmas myself. I just don't let it bother me."

"Easy for you to say." Aaron wasn't drunk, but he hadn't passed up the rum, either. "You didn't get dragged to the principal's office when you were eight because you wouldn't write to Santa."

"That's awful! Where'd you go to school?"

"South Boston. Southie did not exactly celebrate diversity." He set down his cocoa mug and wiped his mouth with a holly-patterned napkin. He didn't meet my eyes. "Boring subject, anyway. I came here to meet new people, right? I'd better get to it."

And with that, he walked off toward a gaggle of bridesmaids and asked the prettiest one to dance.

Well. You think you know someone, then you get an unsettling glimpse like that. Not that I'd been encouraging confidences from Aaron, of course, especially lately. But even before his bombshell about being married, we had skated lightly over the surface of our histories. He seemed to prefer it that way, and I had gone along. It occurred to me that Lily and Mike probably knew all about each other's school days, and more besides.

Half-lost in such thoughts, I circulated some more. Then, to get myself refocused, I decided to run through my private checklist one last time. So I made my way to the locked side room where I'd stashed my envelopes of tips for the staff, along with the bride's cape, the wedding certificate, various vendor contracts, and the outfits that the happy couple would change into for their getaway.

Buck had lobbied for a grand horse-and-carriage ride around town; I think he was secretly hoping that he and Betty could ride along, just to hold on to their little girl a little longer. But Brian had calmly put his foot down. He was driving his bride to an undisclosed hotel—he knew Buck better than I thought—and then to the airport in the morning for their flight to Kauai. "From Christmas trees to palm trees," he kept saying, and since Bonnie thought that was the cleverest thing she'd ever heard in her entire life, Buck had to concur.

I straightened the velvet cape on its hanger, and was checking my list when a tap came at the door. A seedy-looking fellow with a crooked bow tie and a fancy camera poked his head in: Mitch Morrow, the local stringer for several celebrity rags. He could have worked full-time for any one of them if he'd been willing to live in L.A., but Mitch actually liked the rain.

"Hey, Carnegie, can I catch a couple of you with Paliere? He's over by the gift table. I mean, the gift tree."

"Sure, why not." I was happy to cooperate. Mitch had been careful not to crowd Bonnie's own wedding photographer, and Beautiful Beau had been unexpectedly gracious about my abrupt departure from Le Boutique. Besides, to be crass about it, a celebrity photo wouldn't hurt my business, either. And Joe might get to see his precious Lionels in print.

As I trailed Mitch across the room, I plucked a glass of champagne from one of the bars. A glass of kir, actually, the *crème de cassis* giving the champagne a festive tinge of pink. We skirted the dance floor and arrived at the stately giant of a Noble fir tree, strung with white lights and hung with tiny toys, which presided over a colorful heap of wedding gifts. Beneath the branches, Joe's model trains chugged in a wide loop through the boxes and baskets, to charming effect.

Beau waved to me over the shoulder of a slender blonde in a little black dress. *Very* little. Then she turned her wide-eyed face in my direction, and I forgot all about the fashion critique. Andrea! What was my mystery bride doing here? Come to think of it, what had she been doing at Le Boutique yesterday?

"Hello there," I said brightly. "How nice to see you again."

Then I waited for an explanation of her recent rude behavior, but I didn't get it. Not from her.

"Run along, *ma chère,*" said the fabulous Frenchman. Andrea flapped her eyelashes and took her breasts elsewhere, and Beau raised his glass to me. The crystal sparked in the flash of Mitch's camera, and so did the glossy waves of all that photogenic blue-black hair. "Carnegie, I salute you. A wonderful event. *Merveilleux!*"

"Thanks." I held my peace for a few more pictures, but the minute Mitch wandered off, I demanded, "What's the deal with Andrea?"

"Ah, straight to business." He gave me an incandescent smile. "I like that. Andrea is . . . a dear friend of mine. A model. If I had known she was to be in Mariella's show, I would have explained earlier."

"Explained what, exactly? So she's a model who's getting married soon. What else?" The light began to dawn. "Oh, wait a minute, are *you* the fiancé? Is that what all the mystery is about?"

Beau laughed aloud. "No, no, no! There is no fiancé. I sent Andrea to interview you. Or shall we say, to audition you."

"You *sent* Andrea?" I couldn't quite take it in. My wealthy new client, my first and only lavish wedding for next year, was a hoax? "Audition for what?"

He stepped closer, and did the fingertips-along-her-cheek routine.

"To be one of my girls," he breathed. "I want you to bring the Paliere touch to Seattle."

Then he dropped his hand, and brought the Paliere touch slithering down my rib cage to my left hip. But he didn't get any farther than that, because I went ballistic.

"You bastard!" I kept my voice down, but the effort it took made me even more furious. "Who do you think you are, jerking me around and, and...I ought to touch you with *this*!"

I lifted my glass as if to fling the rosy contents right in his face. I wouldn't have done it, of course; only people in soap operas throw drinks in public places. But then, other people in soap operas always stand still to have drinks thrown at them.

Beau didn't stand still, preferring instead to leap backward with balletic grace. Alas, the leap collapsed when his perfectly shod feet became entangled in the piles of wedding presents. He landed underneath the Christmas tree like a gaffed salmon.

The tree swayed, boxes crunched and skidded, ribbons and bows were mashed, and a glossy black clump of... *something* detached itself from Beau's head and sailed onto the chugging line of train cars, just in time to snag on the passing caboose.

Mitch Morrow hadn't wandered far, so he got it all on film: the tree, the gifts, the sprawled, bald figure and—trailing merrily along the train tracks—Beau Paliere's toupee.

Chapter Thirty-Two

THE REMAINDER OF BUCKMEISTER/FROST IS A LITTLE VAGUE IN my memory, but I know that my overriding goal was to keep the evening running smoothly without breaking into hysterical whoops of laughter—or into tears of anxiety about causing a scene at a client's wedding.

Not a big scene, surely? I could tell by the contented murmur of voices that most of the guests were settling down to their Christmas feast in happy ignorance of the entire incident. Not many people had seen Beau fall, or watched him bolting for the nearest men's room.

But they'll all see Mitch's photos in the tabloids soon enough, I fretted. That was the big question: Would it be a front-page story, prompting Beautiful Beau to take some hideous revenge on me, or a minor item that he would laugh off once he was safely back in Paris?

As I prayed for the latter, I rearranged the wedding gifts, aided by two of Joe's waiters and then by Joe himself. Most of the boxes were undamaged, and Betty could do triage on the rest when she took them home to hold for Bonnie and Brian's return.

"How on earth did Paliere fall?" Joe asked, kneeling down to tenderly examine his little locomotive. Then, satisfied with its condition, he thought to inquire after Beau's. "He wasn't hurt, was he?"

"Only his pride."

A snicker escaped me, anxiety or not, but I cut it decently short as I rose to look over at the dining area. Bonnie and Brian stood smiling at their special duet cake, while the guests *ooh*ed and *aah*ed over the rest of Juice's confections now being delivered to their tables.

"I've got to go cue the toasts and the cake-cutting," I told Joe. "Um, when Beau comes back, I wouldn't fuss over him. I think he'd rather forget that this happened."

I wasn't planning to fuss myself, but I was planning to apologize. Only Beau never came back; he just sent a waiter to summon Andrea, and disappeared. I took the liberty of conveying his regrets and good wishes to the father of the bride, and then got back to work, still snickering and still fretting.

The toasts were a nice distraction from my faux pas. They ranged from ribald to romantic—Brian, uninterrupted, was quite eloquent in his tribute to Bonnie—and the rest of the evening flew by in a joyful and delicious blur. Suddenly, it seemed, the cakes were eaten, the candles extinguished, and the Arctic Room was empty save for me, Joe, and the cleaning crew. Joe brought me a flute of champagne, as he often did, and we happily surveyed the wreckage.

"Your best yet," he said, touching his glass to mine, and then stifled a yawn. "Do me a favor, darling, and stash that cake top in the cooler at my place? I'll wrap it for freezing tomorrow, but I've got to be up in a few hours for a brunch and I want to get my trains home."

"No problem," I told him. It was a bit out of my way, but the holidays are crazy for caterers and I was happy to help. "I've still got the keys."

I made my first trip down the block to Vanna with the cake box balanced carefully in both arms, shivering in the icy night and glad of the heavy coat I wore over my jade silk. The chocolate Yule log was long and lavishly decorated, not heavy, but unwieldy. Not too long ago, I'd watched an entire cake disintegrate inside the original Vanna, so I carried this one like a baby. Someone else's baby.

Parked right behind me, yellow in the yellow glow of the streetlights, was Aaron's banana-mobile. He was trying to start it, and by the sound of things, he'd been trying for a while.

"Good timing, Stretch!" He climbed out, rubbing his gloved hands together. He wore a formal topcoat, a bit like Eddie's, and his usual long white scarf. "You can give me a ride home."

"You could call a tow truck," I pointed out, settling the box on the backseat.

"I left my cell at home. Besides, I don't want to deal with the damn car tonight. Piece of junk, anyway. Come on, be a sport."

"OK," I said, "but you'll have to work for your ride and help me carry stuff. I'm stopping in Fremont first."

As we stowed the paperwork, garment bags, and other odds and ends in the back of the van, I realized I still had Frank Sanjek's box of gifts. The reminder of the bachelor party brought back the memory of Jason's lifeless face, and the thought of Darwin in a jail cell. The evening's exhilaration melted away, leaving doubt and depression behind.

"Aaron, don't you think we should talk to Mike?" I said as I stopped at an intersection. It was late, and the dark, frost-slick streets were nearly deserted. "Just tell him everything we know or suspect? About what Li Ping told me, and the CD, and—"

"And your idea that Madison is the killer?"

"Well, yes."

A long pause. In profile, in the half-dark, I couldn't read his expression. He finally spoke just as the light changed.

"Give me a little more time, Stretch. Let me hear back from the hotel in Tokyo, and make some other calls, and then we'll talk it over. One more day, OK?"

"I don't think we should—"

"Just a *day,* for God's sakes."

"All right, all right! Don't yell at me."

"I wasn't yelling," he said sullenly. "I was making a point."

"Well, you made it. Now be quiet and let me drive."

We were heading north on Westlake Avenue, toward the Fremont Bridge, and hitting patches of black ice on the roadway. I leaned forward at the wheel, anxiously feeling each loose little slip of Vanna's tires. At the next red light I sat back, and glanced over at Aaron again. He had a cigarette pack in his hands, tapping one loose.

"Hey, don't smoke in here! If you're going to mooch rides, the least you can do is show some—"

"So I forgot!" He jammed the pack back in his pocket. "Can't you ever give me a break?"

We drove the rest of the way in silence. But when I parked at Joe's building and reached into the van's side door for the cake box, Aaron got out as well.

"You want help with that?"

"No. Yes." I pulled Joe's spare keys from my tote bag, and tossed the bag back in the van. "Just open doors for me."

As we rounded the corner to the building's back entrance, I tried not to look down through the skeletal trees at the cold black surface of the Ship Canal. No lighted window tonight, across the water in the Hot Spot. No tipsy young men. *No knife in the darkness.* Aaron, ahead of me, didn't seem to feel my unease. He flipped on the lights and surveyed the tasting room.

"It's like a little bistro in here." His tone was carefully neutral. "Nice."

"Joe designed it himself. Unlock the cooler door, would you? The smallest key on the ring." The cooler was about eight by ten, with rows of shelves and an overhead light on a timer. Inside, I looked for a clear space to set down my burden among all the wine bottles and food containers. "Could you come move this champagne for me? There's a doorstop by your foot."

Aaron propped open the door and followed me in, and I stepped farther into the narrow space, to make room. Suddenly, a gust of air swirled through the small, cold chamber, carrying a faint but definite whiff of perfume. Familiar perfume . . . The door of the cooler slammed shut.

Shocked speechless for an instant, we heard the lock snap into place, and a clatter of quick, retreating footsteps. Aaron attacked the bare metal door, I added my weight to his, and we both shouted in anger and dismay. But after a few long minutes of unavailing effort, we fell silent again and listened.

More footsteps and then, barely audible, the tasting room's door to the street, banging closed. After that came only our own breathing, and the tiny ticking of the timer overhead.

The light went out.

Chapter Thirty-Three

AND HERE I THOUGHT I COULD SWEAR. AARON'S VOICE MADE A strange metallic echo as he cursed the door, the person who shut it, the person who built it, and life in general, all in terms that would have made my father blink in admiration.

"Feel better?"

"Not really." In our close, utterly dark confinement, his words seemed both loud and far away, and when he pounded the door one last time, I jumped. Then I heard him draw a deep breath. "I'm done now. Sorry."

"Don't mention it. What are you doing?"

"Looking for the emergency latch." I heard brushing, slithering sounds, as he ran both hands around his end of the compartment. "Where the hell . . . Aw, don't tell me there isn't one. That's illegal!"

"It's an old cooler. Joe bought out a restaurant that was closing."

"Too bad the old temperature control works so well. I don't suppose you have your cell phone on you."

"In my tote bag."

"Which is—?"

"In the van."

"Good place for it, Stretch."

More soft sounds, cloth on cloth, as we each drew our

coats tighter around us. *Tomorrow's Christmas Eve*, I was thinking. Surely Kelli and the cooks would arrive early in the morning. But how early?

"At least it's not a freezer," I ventured.

"Thank you, Pollyanna." Aaron shifted; I could hear his shoes rasp on the cement floor. "So what do you think, a burglar? Does Joe keep a lot of cash around, or valuables?"

"Just those serving pieces up in the storeroom, and then his equipment. But it wasn't a burglar, Aaron, it was Madison Jaffee. I'm pretty sure I recognized her perfume. I told you she's the killer!"

"Then why didn't she kill us? And why follow us in here in the first place?"

"I don't know, but I bet it was her."

"And I bet it wasn't."

Silence. Chilly silence.

"OK," said Aaron at last. "I agree, it's too much of a coincidence that Ivy had a burglar and then Joe did, too. Whoever locked the door on us is involved in the murders somehow. So let's be ready in case they come back. There must be something in here I could use. . . . Ah, champagne, just the ticket!"

Straining to see didn't help; the lack of light was absolute. So I strained my ears instead, and heard Aaron's hand closing around the foil-wrapped neck of a bottle.

"I'll set it here at the base of the door. If I have to swing it, stand back. I don't want to clobber you."

I heard the *clink* of glass on cement. We waited. And waited some more.

"Might as well get comfortable, Stretch." The shelving at my shoulder vibrated as he leaned a hand against it. "I'm going to sit down and—ow!"

"What happened?"

"Damn!"

A confusion of sounds, and a muted *thud* as something hit—first Aaron, then the floor. Then a pause, while he apparently retrieved it. The soft *whump* of a plastic lid coming unsealed. The sound of munching, and a familiar savory aroma.

"Some kind of cheese things," Aaron said. "Want one?"

"They're parmesan sticks with black sesame seeds, and no, I don't. How can you eat at a time like this?"

"I think better when I eat." More munching. "Seems to me, you don't lock people in a cooler if you're going to kill them. You do it so you have time to get away."

"So you think we're not in danger?"

"Only of catching cold. Whether that was Madison or not, looks like we're going to be here a while. As I was saying, I'm going to sit." His next words came from floor level. "Care to join me?"

"Well . . ."

The air was chill but not painful, not yet. I could always run in place to get my blood going, but right now I was very tired. Too tired to theorize about Madison, and too tired to spend the next several hours on my feet. I settled gingerly down next to him, with my back against some kind of crate, and tucked my hair into my upturned collar like a scarf.

Minutes passed. Aaron ate another parmesan stick. I closed my eyes and opened them again. No difference.

"You warm enough, Stretch?"

"I'm OK."

His hip and shoulder bumped against mine. "Snuggle up, we'll both be warmer. Come on, I'll behave."

He did, too. He just pulled me to him so he could wrap

his arms around my shoulders, and slid his knees under mine, to keep my legs off the cold floor.

"So what do you do at Christmastime, Stretch?"

"Usually I visit my mother." It felt very odd, making small talk in the dark. "This year she's in Cannon Beach with friends, so I'll be at Lily's. How about you? I'm sorry, that's a dumb question."

He chuckled. "Actually, I have my very own Christmas tradition. I fly to Miami and visit my grandfather. Most of his nursing-home cronies go home for the holidays, so I drive him around and play chess with him."

"I didn't know you played chess."

"Like I said the other day, there's a lot you don't know about me."

Silence again, but companionable silence. My head felt heavy, and I dropped it to Aaron's shoulder. More time passed. Half an hour? Hard to tell, but long enough for me to do some serious thinking. Sometimes things get clearer in the dark.

"Aaron?" I said into the thick soft wool of his coat.

"Right here."

"Would you please tell me about your marriage?"

The arms around me tightened, just for a moment, and he sighed softly.

"It was like this . . ."

Aaron's story was not an unusual one, not the first part. A college romance, an early wedding. A certain distance creeping in as Aaron worked long hours at his newspaper job, while Barbara—that was her name, Barbara—began to travel for her own employer, a major credit card firm.

"In college we talked about having kids, but then somehow we never talked about it again. We were always so busy. We bought this condo in Charlestown, but we were hardly ever there. Then after a while, she didn't like that I made less money than she did. Kept offering to find me something at her company. I didn't *want* a corporate job. And I didn't want to travel with her, just tagging along as the spouse. Maybe that was my mistake."

"Oh?" My neck was cricking, and I sat up.

"She called me one night from London. She'd met someone, they couldn't help themselves, same old same old."

Aaron leaned away from me suddenly. Then came a sequence of small sounds that I recognized from countless weddings: the crackling of foil, the tiny rattle of wire, the thin repeated *squeak* of a cork turning in glass. Then a hollow *pop* and a hissing *fizz*, and a spattering like raindrops.

"Ladies first?"

"Why not."

I pulled off a glove and stretched out my hand, feeling smooth cold glass pressed into my palm. Even swigged from the bottle, the champagne was damn good. *Joe's best stuff, I bet.* I felt down Aaron's arm to his hand and gave it back. A long gulping, and another sigh. He clinked the bottle down and picked up something else.

"Sure you don't want a cheese thing?"

"I'm sure. Aaron, if you don't want to say any more—"

"Oh, we're just getting to the good part now. You don't want to miss this." More munching, and another gulp. "See, she came back home and said she was sorry, she didn't mean it to happen, let's start over. So we did. I did, anyway. Tried to be home more and all that. But she kept taking more trips, and it turned out they weren't all for business. The London guy actually worked in her department. I'll spare you the details. Bottom line, after a few months I got the paperwork to file for divorce, but Barb beat me to it. She hired a lawyer, a real shark, and when things got nasty, he got her a 209A."

"A what?"

"A restraining order, because she feared for her safety."

"But you didn't—?"

"No, I didn't. I never touched her. But I yelled at her, and the neighbors corroborated that, and once she got the order, the name Aaron Gold went on a registry of batterers and stayed there. See, the 209A's an important legal tool, to protect women from domestic violence. I understand that. But a few women started using it as a weapon in the divorce wars, and my darling wife was one of them. I was barred from entering my own goddamn home until I could make my case at a hearing. But that was going to take time, and meanwhile, I *had* to get back in, to get some notes for a story I was writing."

His voice was unsteady. He gulped more champagne, and took a series of deliberate breaths.

"I thought she was out of town. But she was there, with her new man, and while he and I were shouting at each other like a couple of adolescents, Barb went into the bedroom and called the police. They handcuffed me, Stretch. I went to jail."

"Oh, *Aaron*. That must have been horrible!"

I felt him shrug.

"Just for the weekend. Could have been worse. But you don't forget it. I made things worse, actually, after that. I was drinking a lot by then, and I screwed up at work, more than once. The *Globe* offered me medical leave and counseling, but I was too self-righteous to take it. Too humiliated. So I lost the divorce wars, and I lost my job. I came to Seattle to hole up and lick my wounds, and smoke too much instead of drinking too much. And then I met you."

His hand found mine and held it.

"Tell me, Carnegie, did you really want to hear all this on our first date?"

"No, of course not. But..." It felt cruel to probe, after such a confession, yet I had to ask. I had to know. "You went back to Boston at Thanksgiving. Why?"

A huge, cathartic sigh this time, but when he spoke again he sounded almost matter-of-fact.

"Barb found a lump in her breast, and she was scared about the biopsy. Terrified. And her new man was no longer around. So yeah, I went back. Turned out it wasn't cancer, but she really appreciated my being there. We had a couple of drinks and a long painful talk, and that was that."

His arm came around my shoulders again, and shook me gently.

"So that's my sordid story, Stretch. I know I should have told you sooner, but... I didn't. I was wrong, you were right. So you can go on being right, or you can get over it and give us another chance. What's the verdict?"

The verdict was rendered silently, to the satisfaction of both parties, and probably set a world record for longest kiss in a refrigerated space.

"Aaron," I gasped, when we broke for air. "I hate to be unromantic, but I can't feel my feet. I've got to get up."

"Good idea. But wouldn't you rather get out?"

He withdrew one hand, and I heard a *click* and a small scraping sound. Then a flame blossomed in the darkness, painfully bright to my dilated eyes, and threw a globe of light around us. The crowded shelves of the cooler sprang into view, and with them, Aaron's cocky grin.

"You had your lighter all along?"

"Well, I forgot about it at first." He scrambled to his feet and helped me up, as our shadows jumped and wavered around the tiny golden flare. Then he began to paw through the shelves, one-handed at first. "Hold the light for me, Stretch? Thanks. Here we go . . ."

He'd found a stack of plate-sized paper doilies, and began rolling one into a loose twist. *To burn for smoke?*

"Aaron, there's no smoke alarm in here."

His eyes flashed as he glanced at me. "You're quick, aren't you? Took me twenty minutes to think of this. There's a crack along the bottom of the door, where the gasket's worn away. I felt it when I put the bottle down. If we can snake some paper through and light it, I bet there's a smoke alarm out there."

"I'm sure there is. We can crumple all the paper in here and shove it— Wait a minute!" A thought struck me, so hard that my hand jerked and flipped the lighter closed, plunging us back into darkness. "*Twenty minutes?* We've been here a lot longer than that. Did you keep me here in the dark when you had a way to get us out? You rat!"

Aaron's voice was jubilant. "All in a good cause, Stretch. Besides, it was tougher on me."

"How so?"

I flicked the lighter into flame, and dissolved the darkness once again. His grin grew wider.

"I'm a Jew of Eastern European descent. You know how hard it is not to talk with my hands?"

I was not amused. Well, maybe a little.

But the firemen were definitely not amused. They came charging into Joe's building looking for flames, but discovered instead a minor smoke cloud, a mess of scorched doilies, and an illegal cooler containing a man, a woman, and an empty champagne bottle. It all looked like a lark gone wrong, and the mildest comment we heard, from one of the big guys in their bulky black coats, was "Don't you people have a bed?"

Mike Graham wasn't too charmed, either, when I rousted him out of his bed with a phone call at five in the morning. Aaron wanted to wait—he thought the bed suggestion had a lot of merit—but I insisted; for the sake of my conscience, I had to tell all. Groggy at first, Mike woke up fast as I stumbled through my story.

"Jason Kraye was a blackmailer? Is there evidence?"

"Not as such," I admitted. "There was a message on a CD, but it kind of erased itself. Aaron and I both read it, though."

"And Gold's with you now?"

"We're at the houseboat."

"Stay put, I'll be right over."

I spent the time leaving phone messages: a bon voyage for Bonnie and Brian, a few details for the Arctic Club, and a regretful and rather complicated explanation for Joe, who was in for a serious fine about that safety latch. Meanwhile Aaron ran over to the Lakeshore to fetch the CD from his apartment.

When Aaron returned and Mike appeared, I had Jason's ski jacket and a pot of coffee waiting. My time in the cooler left me craving warmth, inside and out.

By the time the pot was empty, the detective was furious.

"Do you realize what you've done?" Mike sat facing me at the kitchen table, in jeans and rain parka, more visibly upset than I'd ever seen him. "You've delayed the investigation,

you've interfered with the chain of evidence, you've...
Dammit, I should charge you both!"

"Never mind us," I protested, wincing under the on-
slaught. "What are you going to do about Madison Jaffee?"

Aaron, leaning against the counter with his arms folded,
gave a skeptical snort. "What can he do?"

"Exactly," said Mike. No, not Mike anymore. Detective
Lieutenant Michael Graham, official and stern. "We were interested in Jaffee from the beginning, of course, because you
saw her coming out of the corridor just before Schulman's
body was found. And then again, because the person in the
Santa Claus clothes at the Hot Spot could have been a
woman. But perfume? Please."

"What about the blackmail, then? What about the spy
camera?"

"That's not evidence, Carnegie. That's hearsay about a
perfectly legal piece of electronics. Which you found, I
might add, during an unauthorized search of a private
home."

I faltered, then rallied. "You can't ignore all this."

"I don't intend to. It's not my case now, but I'll turn it
all over to Bates." Mike rose, closing his notebook and letting slip a trace of a smile. "I don't envy him, interviewing Ivy Tyler about her domestic arrangements. But he'll
do it."

Then he leaned his fists on the table, to glare fiercely at
me, and turned his head to glare at Aaron.

"Bates will do everything that needs to be done, and you
two amateurs will do nothing further. No interviewing, no
searching, no *thinking*. Is that understood?"

We nodded meekly.

"All right, then. Get some sleep. You look like you need it."

As the saying goes, alone at last. I closed the kitchen door and flipped the dead bolt. Aaron, right behind me, slipped his hands around my waist.

"You need sleep, Stretch?" he murmured into the back of my neck. His warm breath stirred along my skin, and sent a tingle right down to my toes. All of them.

"Not really," I said. His hands began to roam. "In fact, I'm wide *a-ah!* Aaron, stop that ... No, don't stop that ..."

My bedroom is twenty, maybe twenty-five feet away from the kitchen.

We made it to the couch.

Chapter Thirty-Four

I'LL NEVER LOOK AT MY LIVING ROOM COUCH THE SAME WAY again. Aaron had a teasing, tender way about him that made me think about taking up permanent residence there. And judging from his final groan and his blissed-out stare at the ceiling, he was pretty pleased with my own ways, too.

"Move over," I whispered, as I pulled a woolen throw from the back of the couch to spread across us.

"I'm already over."

"We could move to the bedroom."

"Too far," he said drowsily.

"You're right . . ."

We laid there, dozing and waking and dozing again, for a delightful hour or two, but eventually we migrated to my bed and made love again, slowly this time, lingering as long as we could. Then we fell fully asleep at last beneath my down comforter, slick with sweat and pretzeled together, in a much cozier darkness than the one in Joe's tasting room.

The bedside phone, when it rang, was shockingly loud, and the cloudy winter light outside seemed unpleasantly bright.

"Don't answer."

"I wasn't planning to."

Just to make sure, Aaron propped himself on one elbow and pinned me to the bed with a kiss. The kissing went on for a while, but so did the ringing, until I snaked a hand out from under the covers.

"I really should get this. Poor Joe."

But it wasn't Joe. It was Bridezilla, bawling her eyes out.

"Carnegie, you have to talk to Frank! We had it all settled about New Year's Eve, and now he says"—Sally paused for a hiccupping sob—"now he says maybe we should *reconsider*!"

"Shhh, don't cry." I smiled ruefully at Aaron. His hair was sticking up in all directions, and he badly needed a shave. Then he rolled to the other side of the bed and stood up; he looked really fine from the back, too.

I turned away to try and focus, glancing at the clock as I did so. *Noon? Good Lord.*

"Um, does Frank want to reconsider the date, or"—I hated to say it—"or the wedding?"

"I don't know! What am I going to do?"

"First of all, take a deep breath. One more . . . there you go. Now, where are you calling from?"

"S-Snohomish. We came up here for Christmas Eve, and to talk about the details of the wedding, but, but—"

As if a dead best man was a detail. Exasperated, I said, "Isn't your mother there?"

"She's no help!" Sally wailed. "She's just being mean. Frank went out for a walk, but he didn't want me to come, and I don't know what to *do*. I need you here."

I try to go above and beyond for my brides, but right now I didn't care to go beyond the reach of Aaron Gold's hands. "Sally, I can't drive all the way up to Snohomish just to— Hold on."

Aaron, having retrieved his trousers from somewhere down the hall, was back in the bedroom and signaling to me. I covered the phone with my hand.

"What is it?"

"Go ahead with your day, Slim. I've got a plane to catch."

"A plane?"

"Miami, remember? Though I suppose I could cancel . . ."

We looked yearningly at each other, sharing a vision of the glorious horizontal days before us. Then we sighed, and even laughed a little. We both knew he wouldn't cancel. Romeo and Juliet would have killed themselves, I suppose, at the prospect of spending this week apart. But Aaron and I were adults, and we recognized the needs of other people— especially grandfathers—in our newly established Republic of Two.

I blew him a kiss and got back on the phone. I had no other plans for today, and I needed to nail down this decision ASAP. Calling off a wedding on short notice, besides being traumatic for the principals, is hard on the vendors. Made in Heaven would get most of the payment for Tyler/Sanjek anyway, but we really needed all of it—and my reputation didn't need the loss of a big holiday event.

"All right, tell Ivy I can be there by three o'clock."

"Oh, thank you! Are you sure you can't come earlier?"

"Quite sure," I said firmly. "I have to take someone to the airport first. Someone important."

Imagine Sally Tyler saying "Thank you," I mused, driving north on I-5 a couple of hours later. The weather had turned Seattle-normal: a low leaden sky, a fine drizzle, and a layer of wet haze rising from the road surface, kicked up by a thousand hissing tires. At the moment, Miami sounded pretty appealing.

Aaron had just barely caught his plane. Part of the delay was arranging a tow truck for his Volkswagen, but most of it had to do with fondling me. At the houseboat while we dressed, at his apartment while he packed, inside Vanna at the Sea–Tac parking garage, inside the terminal while he waited to check in . . . It was going to be a long week. Well, I had Christmas morning at Lily's tomorrow, and plenty on my plate today with the resolution—I hoped—of Tyler/Sanjek.

But still, all these days apart from Aaron, not to mention all these nights . . . Memories of last night, or rather this morning, kept me dreamily preoccupied almost the whole way to the Tylers'. Then as I swung Vanna into the private gravel road, the drizzle became a downpour, and I had to concentrate on my driving.

Vanna splashed through the dim tunnel of fir trees with her wipers on high and the rain drumming on her roof. I switched on the headlights, and just as I did, another set of lights appeared, swerving around a bend and plunging through a broad rain puddle on its way past me. A small scarlet car . . .

Ivy Tyler, driving like a bat out of hell. A wave of dirty water slapped heavily across my windshield, making me flinch, but I caught a glimpse of Ivy's face, pale and forbidding, as she sped away.

What's sent her out into the rain, I wondered as I parked at the house. *A rash decision to run off with Simon Weeks? Or a further blackmail threat from Madison, now that her partners in crime are dead?*

"No thinking," Mike had said, but I couldn't help it. Hard to imagine what was going on in Ivy's mind right now, but clearly it wasn't her daughter's nuptials. I dashed resentfully through the deluge to the front door, shielding my folder of paperwork under my coat. This better not be a wasted trip.

"Is Ivy coming back?" I asked Sally as she let me in. "Because if we're arranging a postponement, she needs to be here."

"I don't *know*." My bride was festively dressed, in narrow black velvet trousers and an ice-blue shantung blouse with pearl buttons. But her face was swollen with weeping, and her voice sounded like a little girl's. "She got a phone call and just took off. Nobody's making any sense today. Do you want some wine? I'm going to have some wine."

"Maybe later." I followed her to the kitchen by way of the dining room, where a rosewood table bore the remains of an elaborate lunch for four. "Is Frank still on his walk? He'll be soaked."

"Serves him right," she said with unconvincing bravado. "He shouldn't have gone out like that."

"And where's your stepfather?"

"Lying down. He spends most afternoons in his room, but I think he just wanted to get away from us."

Sally reached into a built-in wine cooler and pulled out a bottle, seemingly at random. The cork remover she reached for next looked like a surgical instrument, but she wielded it with ease, hardly glancing down as she opened the bottle and poured herself a hefty glassful of something red.

She took a slurp, then gave me a long, plaintive look. "Charles said I was being heartless. Carnegie, I'm not heartless, am I?"

What an opening. I'm a poor liar anyway, and the temptation to let her have it between the eyes was severe. But she was still my bride.

"Let's sit down a minute." We settled on either side of the island where Andy had prepared his sushi. "Do you want an honest answer?"

The familiar pout began to form on Sally's pale, pretty features, but then it gave way to a wobbly smile. "Am I that bad? All I want is my wedding date. It's not like Lou was Frank's brother or anything."

"That's not really the point, is it? The point is that Frank has reservations about the timing of the wedding. There are two people getting married here, not one. Did you give him a chance to talk about how he feels?"

She jutted a lip and toyed with the stem of her wineglass. "I guess not."

"Don't you think you should? You know, the fun of having your reception on New Year's Eve will be temporary, but starting your marriage with a sense of respect for each other could last the rest of your life."

"Oh. *Oh.*" Sally's eyes grew wide and shining, as if the truth had set her free.

Chapter Thirty-Five

I THOUGHT, I REALLY THOUGHT, THAT I'D FINALLY GOTTEN through to Sally Tyler. But unfortunately for my self-image as a fount of wisdom, she wasn't even looking at me. She was gazing over my shoulder at the kitchen doorway where Frank Sanjek, dripping with rain, was gazing back at her. His clothes were sodden, and his curly hair was pasted flat above his mild, troubled brown eyes. It was the perfect moment for Sally to apologize.

"Frankie!" She flew to him. "I was so worried about you out there in the rain. How could you do that to me? I was frantic! How *could* you?"

This little embellishment had precisely the desired effect. Sally knew her man.

"I'm so sorry, baby," said Frank, holding her close. The ice-blue shantung soaked through in seconds. "I didn't mean to scare you. I just had to think, you know? I'm sorry."

"I forgive you," said Sally, and wriggled even closer. "I *love* you, Frankie. So, can we get married on New Year's Eve just like we always wanted?"

"Sure we can, baby. Anything you want."

So much for respect. I reached for Sally's wineglass and took a slug. Not bad.

"Ms. Kincaid?" Eleanor, the maid, had followed Frank in. "There's a phone call for you."

I glanced over at the kitchen phone. "I didn't even hear it ring."

"We turn the ringers off when Mr. Tyler is resting," she explained. "Except for my cordless."

"I see." Sally had begun to peel Frank out of his wet clothes. My work here was through. "Why don't I take it in the living room?"

Eleanor directed me to the wing chair by the fireplace, and a telephone with an actual rotary dial. Something told me the phone was Charles's preference, not Ivy's. What was it Joe had called him? An old-fashioned gentleman.

"This is Carnegie."

"Hi, it's Kelli. Gee, I hope it's OK for me to call you there, because you didn't answer your cell phone even though I tried and tried."

I blushed at that. The phone was still in my tote bag, but the bag was lying somewhere in the houseboat, drifted over by my jade silk dress and some hastily removed lingerie.

"So anyway, I said I'd try calling around for you because he said it was really important—"

"Slow down, Kelli. Who said what was important?"

"Kevin Bayer. Bauer? Kevin Bauer. Were you really locked in the cooler like you said in your message?"

"That's why I left the message."

"Wow. Joe isn't coming in today, he's got three different events, but I told him all about it."

"I bet you did. Kelli, when did Kevin call, and what did he say?"

"Oh, just a few minutes ago. It was kind of weird. He said he found what you were looking for at the Habitat warehouse, but he wouldn't tell me what it was. He wants you to go there and see it, and he said the authorities are on their way. Does that make sense? I wasn't sure what he meant by authorities."

"Yes." *The murder weapon.* My heart began to thud, hard and fast. "Yes, it makes perfect sense. Thanks."

Ten minutes later I was steering Vanna back down the gravel road, trying to calculate the fastest route to Habitat. My thoughts were racing. Kevin must have gotten back from Portland, and searched the warehouse as he promised me he would. If he'd found the murder weapon, then Darwin's utility knife would be shown for what it was—an innocent art tool. And if the real weapon had fingerprints, or could be traced somehow, maybe Lily would get her brother home for Christmas...

It wasn't until I pulled into the Habitat parking lot that I spared a different kind of thought for Kevin Bauer. *Oh, hell.* Sally wasn't the only heartless one; I had to tell Kevin that I wouldn't be going out with him again. Christmas Eve was an unfortunate time to let someone down, especially when the someone has just done you a huge favor. But what else could I do?

Vanna was the only car in the lot; Kevin and the police must have parked on the other side of the building. Or maybe the police hadn't arrived yet. I decided to be sensible, and wait until they'd come and gone before I gave Kevin the bad news. But meanwhile, I was eager to see what he'd found, and where he'd found it. I remembered the half-dream I'd had, about a knife among the coffee beans. A premonition?

Evening was closing in. A narrow band of light showed me that the side door of the warehouse was propped slightly ajar. The rain had let up a bit, so I didn't get too wet as I crunched across the gravel.

"Kevin? It's me!"

My voice echoed in the high, open space. The party paraphernalia was gone, of course, and the warehouse was back to looking like an empty stage set, with safety lights here and there barely piercing the gloom. The toylike forklifts were still, some of them still bearing their loads, and the lofty tiers of coffee bags were dark and silent.

At the far end of the warehouse, I could see a desk lamp shining dimly through the blinds of the glassed-in computer room that overlooked the roasting floor. I hurried toward it, refining my strategy as I went.

I'll be friendly with Kevin, I was thinking, *but I won't let him kiss me, because he'll be embarrassed about it later.* I began to climb the open steel staircase to the office door. *I just hope he won't be angry—*

Then I pushed open the door, and rational thought fled as the figure inside turned toward me. Charles Tyler, with a mad light in his onyx eyes and an old-fashioned straight razor in his upraised hand.

He lunged. I screamed and leapt away. And then I heard my scream echo as I fell backward down the clanging stairs.

Chapter Thirty-Six

I HAULED MYSELF UPRIGHT AT THE FOOT OF THE STAIRS, AND clung to the steel handrail for the space of one shocked, gasping breath. I was winded but unhurt—until I put weight on my left foot, and cried out at the pain that stabbed through my knee. Could I even walk on it? No time to wonder. Charles came clanging down the stairs behind me, and I fled.

Charles? I thought in bewilderment, hobbling desperately away. I could hardly take in what I'd seen. *The razor... Could he be the one who killed Jason and Lou? But why?*

I didn't get far, just to the big tank of the main roaster. Charles must have seen the direction I took, but I had some confused hope that if I dodged and hid for long enough, he'd relinquish the hunt and leave the building. So I crouched behind the tank, keeping the weight off my knee, and listened.

Footsteps, first ringing on the metal stairs, then striking the concrete floor. Not the hesitant gait of an old man, but a purposeful, relentless stride. Had Charles been faking all this time, exaggerating the severity of his illness? Or was it just adrenaline driving him on? I held my breath. The steps came closer, the only sound in the vast, dim, unpeopled silence. The entire building was empty save for the two of us—and Kevin Bauer.

Kevin. My thoughts seemed to sharpen, even as they gathered speed. How soon after Kevin's phone call to Kelli had Charles come upon him? Faced by the nightmare apparition at the head of the stairs, I hadn't looked into the office beyond. If I had, would I have seen Kevin lying there in a pool of his own blood?

I tried to swallow down the horror that rose, choking, in the back of my throat. The police had been summoned, after all. Surely they'd arrive any minute now. *But they're not here yet, and I can't afford to wait. It only takes minutes to bleed to death.*

Part of me, the cowardly part, said that Kevin was almost certainly dead already, and that I could only save myself. But another part remembered Kevin holding my injured hand while Fiona drove us to the clinic, and the warmth of passion in his voice when he talked about founding Habitat. I knew then that I wouldn't abandon him. Not while there was still a chance.

The footsteps reached the roaster. I stood up.

Charles Tyler and I stared at each other over the top of the tank, perhaps a dozen feet apart, but separated by a maze of pipes and ductwork that crisscrossed the air between us. In the dim light his eyes were black stones, and when he spoke his voice was weirdly serene and very, very cold.

"There's no point running away, you know."

"Charles," I said urgently, "don't you recognize me? Carnegie Kincaid. You don't want to hurt me."

He took a step to his right and I mirrored the movement, keeping the full width of the machinery between us.

"Hurt you, my dear? After what you did, don't you think I have reason to hurt you?"

"But I haven't done anything."

If we kept circling like this, Charles would move farther from the staircase while I got closer to it. My plan—if you could call it that—was to rush back up the stairs and lock the office door against him. I'd do what I could to help Kevin, call an ambulance, and wait for the police.

Another step. Two. I had to keep him distracted.

"Tell me, what is it you think I've done?"

"Don't play the innocent!" His lips drew back from his teeth. "You disgust me, fawning over that lout Schulman, helping him and Kraye in their loathsome scheme. Taking secret pictures, trying to destroy my wife."

"You *knew* they were blackmailing Ivy? You knew about the affair?"

Slowly, slyly, horribly, Charles smiled.

"Of course I knew. I know everything about my girls. I listen to their telephone calls, and I watch them come and go." Charles made these bizarre statements in a perfectly conversational tone. "Ivy believes that she has protected me all these years, and I suppose she has. But I keep watch over her, as well. She's found a partner for life now, who'll be with her after I'm gone. I won't permit her happiness to be ruined."

"I understand."

Of course I didn't understand, not in the least. Was this more *noblesse oblige,* protecting his family from scandal while his wife made love to another man? Had Charles Tyler accepted his own physical decline that philosophically, and subdued his masculine pride that far?

It didn't matter. I had to keep him talking, keep his gaze locked onto mine.

"Did Ivy know about . . . about what happened to Jason?"

I had almost reached the broad tube where, on my tour

with Kevin, I'd seen the coffee beans flying upward like bees. *I'll run when I get to that point,* I decided. *Just a little farther. I can do this.*

"Of course not!" Charles seemed offended by the idea. "I chose a time when she would be away."

The thought of that night at the Hot Spot recalled something Ivy had mentioned once, on our way into Solveto's. I took another sidestep. "So you used the Santa costume from Ivy's holiday party as a disguise."

"Exactly. It was all quite simple. Schulman was more difficult, however. He was pressing her. I had to act quickly." Charles stopped where he was. His voice grew louder, the snow-white eyebrows lowering above the onyx eyes. "They were despicable men, both of them. I watched from the library doorway the night they came to threaten my wife. The insolence! Invading my home, defying my authority, demanding more and more money from her. Bleeding her dry."

Authority? The word snagged in my mind, but the thought eluded me. Charles reared back his head and his eyes caught the light. Not onyx now, but obsidian, glittering and razor-sharp.

"In the end," he said, "they were the ones to bleed."

I took a breath and tensed my muscles to dash for the staircase. But as he spoke these last words, Charles took another sidestep, and through a gap between the ductwork I saw the razor in his hand once again.

The clean, gleaming razor.

No blood. I released my breath, as the facts shifted into place like colored glass shifting in a kaleidoscope, to make a new and terrifying pattern. *If he'd slashed at Kevin, wouldn't there be blood on the razor? Because Kevin called from the office . . . Kelli said he had called "the authorities" . . . Why would Kevin use a British term?*

He wouldn't.

Charles hadn't slashed at Kevin, after all. Because Kevin wasn't here. It was Charles who placed the call to Solveto's office, and the police hadn't arrived, because they were never called in the first place.

There was no one in the roasting plant for me to rescue, and no one was coming to rescue me.

"Charles, listen. I wasn't helping Lou and Jason, honestly I wasn't."

I hardly knew what I was saying, as I tried to decide what to do next. Could I use Charles's deception to my advantage? *Worth a try.*

I took a pleading tone. "Kevin wasn't involved, either, don't you see that? Please, tell me, did you hurt Kevin? Won't you let me go back upstairs to the office and help him? Then we can talk about this, and I can explain everything. Please?"

"Back upstairs . . ." I could see the calculation on Charles's face, as he realized my error. Why hunt me through the building, if I was willing to go docilely to my doom? "Yes, that's right, Kevin is upstairs. We'll go up to the office now, my dear, and we'll talk. I won't hurt you."

This time we each stepped in the same direction, decreasing the distance between us.

"Charles, wait! I'll go up first, all right?"

I had to get a head start somehow. Despite his age and whatever his condition, my wrenched knee would put us on equal terms in any race. Not even equal. He had a weapon; I had nothing.

Or did I? Just off to my right, a handle protruded from the

side of the tank. The tryer. I remembered Kevin pulling it out and showing me the coffee beans nestled inside. The tryer was a heavy steel cylinder, not an ideal weapon, but better than nothing. I edged toward it, and kept on pleading.

"I just want you to stay back from me a little, because you're scaring me. Just a little, I mean, I know you wouldn't really hurt me . . ."

I was babbling now, as I frantically tried to recall the layout of the building. There must be another exit somewhere. Why couldn't I remember where it was? I'd had a tour. . . . Of course, the tour ended when I cut myself on Lou's coffee mug. That settled it; I'd have to run back the way I came. The warehouse door might be farther away, but at least I knew where it was, and that Vanna was there waiting for me.

Charles shifted impatiently. "Very well, you go on. I'll stay back. Here, do you see?"

So sure of himself was he, in his madness, that he actually took a few steps away from the roaster, and away from me. On the instant I turned and ran, grabbing the tryer handle and pushing myself away from the roaster tank like a swimmer pushing off from the side of the pool. It took Charles a precious extra moment to realize that I was running for the warehouse, not the office stairs, and then he followed.

My knee was agony at first, but soon the pain blurred into the fear, and my awareness narrowed to simply reaching the tiers of shelves. I ducked down one of the narrow aisles, acting on instinct like fleeing prey, but the instinct served me well, and by the time I reached the shadowy end of the passage I had another plan.

I slipped into the narrow gap where the end of the shelving met the warehouse wall, pulling the tryer after me, and

slipped out again in the next aisle over. Then I waited, hoping to make Charles commit himself to coming down the
passage after me. Or at least to make him stop and think it
over while I caught my breath.

Luck was with me. Seconds later, Charles arrived at the
mouth of the first aisle I'd taken, just too late to see where
I'd gone. I froze, and listened to his labored breathing as he
hesitated. I could almost read his mind: Did he have the
wrong aisle? Should he follow it down to the end, and take a
chance that I'd spring out at him from hiding?

Perhaps I should have tried that. Perhaps I should have
taken a stand and swung the tryer at Charles, on the chance
that I could force the razor out of his possession. But my left
hand still ached from the gash I'd gotten, and my memory
still held the image of Lou's blood pooling on the corridor
floor, and I just couldn't bring myself to do it. The thought
of that dreadful blade slicing toward my face was more than
I could bear.

Charles made his choice. He plunged down the first aisle
after me, toward the warehouse wall. I ran the opposite way,
toward the mouth of the second aisle, praying that he
wouldn't double back and cut me off. He didn't. I heard his
faltering steps reach the end of the first aisle, and the scrab-
bling sound as he, too, slipped through the gap. I was out in
the open central area by then, and loping for the door.

Without the injured knee, I would have made it. But my
lead narrowed fast, and I could hear Charles panting, getting
closer. His breath was ragged, though; maybe another dash
down an aisle would wear him out just enough to save me. I
ducked into yet another narrow passageway, walled solid
with coffee sacks, and stumbled my way to the far end.

To the dead end.

There was no gap here, not on either side. The shelving was bolted tight to the warehouse wall, and I was bottled in like a moth in a jar. I had a crazy thought about shifting some of the coffee sacks, to clear myself a tunnel. I set down the tryer—my fingers ached from clenching it—and yanked at the corner of one sack. They were jammed tight. *And besides, what did Kevin say they weighed? A hundred pounds apiece? Two?*

"Waiting for me, my dear?"

At the mouth of the aisle, Charles stood in silhouette against the muted glow of the safety lights beyond. His left hand was twitching, but his right, the one holding the razor, was as steady as death. Sobbing with rage, I picked up the tryer again, two-handed this time, and hefted it like a baseball bat.

"I'm not falling down drunk like Jason Kraye, Charles!" I shouted. "I don't have my back turned like Lou Schulman!"

He stood silent for a moment and then, without a word, he stepped away from the narrow slot of light and disappeared. I held my stance for one minute, then another, my knee trembling under me. I was desperate to sit down and rest. The tryer was getting heavy. I began to lower it, but I heard noises from somewhere beyond my line of sight, and lifted it again. Was he trying to lure me out there?

It won't work, I thought grimly. *I'll outwait him, if it takes all night.*

More odd noises, a grunting and whining, somehow familiar. Then something blocked the light at the mouth of the aisle: a forklift. It rolled slowly but inexorably toward me, bearing a pile of coffee sacks on a wooden pallet. A pile taller than me, which would pin me to the wall so that Charles could take his insane revenge.

I couldn't see Charles behind the sacks, I couldn't hear my own sobs above the whining motor, I couldn't think anything except: *This is so unfair, Aaron and I have just found each other and I'm going to die before I see him again* . . . But I didn't wait to be crushed, or slashed. I staggered forward, and in blind defiance threw the steel tryer under the wheels of the forklift.

What happened next was like a monster dying. The machine whined and screamed and slewed sideways, but there was nowhere for it to go. The pile of heavy sacks struck the shelves on one side, then the other, swaying and tottering.

Then the forklift and its load—and its operator—toppled over to the floor away from me in a slithering, deafening crash. Charles must have gripped the razor to the last, because at least one sack was slit from end to end.

As I stood watching, aghast, the sack disgorged its contents in a hissing, clicking stream of coffee beans that poured across his broken body like a hundred pounds of small, dark pebbles, and spread out on the floor around him like a pool of blood.

Chapter Thirty-Seven

I SPENT CHRISTMAS MORNING LYING FLAT ON A COUCH—BUT instead of Aaron's amorous attentions, I had to make do with ice packs on my swollen knee.

The company was wonderful, though, even with Aaron far away in Florida. Mike Graham had raced up to Snohomish when he got the call about the situation at Habitat, and although he himself needed to remain on the scene, he'd had one of his men drive me and Vanna back to Seattle, to Lily's house. Apparently, if you're a witness and a victim both, they take care of you first and question you later. As I curled up under Lily's quilts, late at night on Christmas Eve, I decided it was a fine, fine policy.

On Christmas morning, Lily brought me a giant croissant and a mug of cocoa doctored with rum, and sat with me to watch Marcus and Ethan open their presents. I slid into a contented, half-asleep haze of warmth and safety, occasionally rousing myself to admire a new treasure displayed by one of my honorary nephews.

"Need anything else?" Lily asked, over the boy's excited chattering.

"Just hand me my cell phone, thanks. I want to try Aaron's motel again."

But once again the Miami number rang and rang, and

then switched to a voice-mail system. This time I left a message, though I couldn't say much with the boys in the room.

"Aaron, it's me. Um, Merry Christmas. Sorry, I can't remember that happy holiday phrase you told me about. Doesn't matter. Oh, God, I miss you! Listen, you might hear something on the news, about Charles Tyler's death. It's a long story, but I'm safe, and I miss you. Call me, OK? Bye."

I set the phone down and nestled back into the cushions with a disconsolate sigh.

"Still not there?" said Lily sympathetically.

"No. It's a three-hour time difference, so I guess he's out somewhere with his grandfather."

"Have you called your mother? They're not saying your name on the news, but if she knows that you're working for the Tylers, she might wonder."

"I left a message at the house in Boise. She's still in Cannon Beach with her friends, but I don't have a number for the cottage they rented."

The doorbell sounded then and Marcus scampered to answer it, brandishing his new cowboy hat.

"It's Uncle Dar!" he shrieked, dropping the hat to the floor and wrapping his pajama-clad arms and legs around the new arrival.

Little Ethan joined him, bouncing up and down like a wind-up toy, and chanting, "Unkadar! Unkadar! Unkadar!"

Above the shouting, giggling children, Darwin stood tall, gazing at his sister like a man who's come home from a long and fearsome journey. Lily rushed to embrace him, and the four of them blurred in my vision through the happy tears.

I wiped my eyes on the cuff of my borrowed nightgown,

and saw Mike Graham standing over by the Christmas tree, surveying the reunion with a quiet smile.

"Carnegie, how are you doing?" Mike sat down beside me. "Is your leg—"

I cut him off, with a hug and a grateful kiss. "How'd you get Darwin out so fast?"

"It's Christmas," he said simply. "I called in some favors to have things expedited. Hey, there!"

Lily had plumped herself down on Mike's lap, and now she laid a kiss on him, just as grateful as mine, but far more vigorous.

"You staying for Christmas dinner?" she asked. "We're having a picnic in the living room, so Carnegie doesn't have to get up."

"Can't." He kissed her once more, and they stood up regretfully. "We'll be piecing this case together for quite a while yet. Carnegie, you'll be getting a call from Bill Bates, about taking your statement. You sure your leg's OK?"

"I'll be staggering around any minute now," I told him. "In fact, I'm going back to the houseboat tonight."

Lily laughed. "She's been in exile so long, she's spurning my hospitality! I told you, stay as long as you like."

But I was anxious to be home, and after our midday picnic and another nap, Darwin helped me load Vanna with some leftovers and my own presents—a luscious shawl from Lily and a bottle of lemony hand lotion from the boys. Then he gave me a gift of his own.

"Lily told me what happened," he said. His eyes, so like Lily's, were shining. "I'm grateful."

"The police would have figured it out," I told him.

"Mike's being nice about it, but I think mostly I got in the way."

Darwin smiled, and gathered me in his arms for a hug to rival one of Boris Nevsky's.

"I feel like I've got two sisters now. Merry Christmas."

Good thing I'd hurt my left knee and not my right, and that Vanna Two was an automatic, and that I drive pretty well while I'm crying.

I parked as close to the dock as I could, and hobbled stiffly through the drizzle to my door, taking special care on the ramp that spanned the brief gap of dark water between the dock and my deck. Inside, the early dusk made a chilly near-night, so I turned up the heat and switched on all the lights. Aaron still hadn't called back on my cell, so I checked for messages on my personal line and also Made in Heaven's. Nothing.

Not from Aaron, anyway. I did have a call from Eddie, saying he'd be back at work on Monday, and another from Joe Solveto, saying he was furious about the cooler, delighted that I was safe, and curious as hell about Charles Tyler.

I didn't have the energy to call him back. I didn't have much energy at all, in fact, so for the rest of the evening I laid on my own couch, dozing and pondering. Some things about the last few days I understood, like the Santa Claus costume, and Charles Tyler's phony call to Joe's office. Kelli had never spoken to the real Kevin Bauer, so how was she to know?

What I couldn't figure out was Madison Jaffee's role in all this. Charles hadn't even mentioned her, so if she was involved in the blackmail scheme as I thought, he hadn't discovered it. But Madison must have been involved, or why else would she have locked me and Aaron in the cooler? Unless it was someone else wearing the same perfume . . . a perfumed burglar . . .

With this improbable thought I fell asleep, so deeply that I was slow to recognize the chirp of my cell phone and dig it out of my coat pocket.

"Hey there, Stretch."

"Aaron? Is that you?"

"The one and only. I'm sorry, were you asleep?"

"Yes, but never mind. I'm just so glad to hear from you."

"Same here." There were voices in the background; he was out in public somewhere. "So what's going on? Tyler *died*?"

"Yes. I thought you might have heard about it."

"Why would I? He's not that big a celebrity."

I yawned and shook myself awake. "It's a really long story. Tell me first, do you miss me?"

"Of course," said Aaron, but there was something odd in his tone. "The truth is, Slim, I've mostly been thinking about Izzy. That's my grandfather, Isaac. He had a stroke yesterday, while I was flying down. That's why I wasn't around to get your call. I'm at the hospital now."

"I'm so sorry! Is he, I mean . . ."

"He's going to live. In fact, they now think it was fairly minor. But I'm sticking close."

"Of course."

So much for asking Aaron to fly back early. I couldn't be that selfish. And after all, I had work to do. Even if Tyler/Sanjek was postponed—which seemed a certainty—there was still the wrap-up on Buckmeister/Frost.

"I'm glad you're there for him," I said with my best imitation of sincerity.

"Me too. So tell me, what's all this about you being safe?"

The long story got even longer, at first because Aaron had so many reporter-type questions. And then, before I got anywhere near the end of the story, Aaron's emotional relief at my escape somehow turned to thoughts of a more corporeal nature, and I happily set aside the subject of murder for the rest of the conversation. I'd never understood the appeal of phone sex before, but by the time we hung up, I was beginning to get the idea.

I spent Sunday working out the stiffness in my knee, and indulging in domestic pleasures—opening Christmas cards, restocking the kitchen, and generally settling back into my floating home. But not reading the paper or watching the news. I wanted to forget about Charles Tyler for a little while, until the nightmare memories had faded.

Not that I had much success. Reporters kept calling me, and I kept hanging up, but I left the phone on in case my mother called. She did, finally, and we had a long conversation, reassuring for her, but rather a strain for me. Even Eddie, when he checked in to say he'd be back in the morning, demanded a complete explanation of "what the hell happened at that coffee place." Maybe it was better this way; telling the story over and over began to put the nightmare at a distance.

Sunday night was better. I had another fervent and purely personal talk with Aaron, during which we agreed not to talk about anything murderous until we could do so in person. That was followed by a long, uninterrupted sleep. Heaven—but a lonely heaven. Suddenly the bed was too big.

Monday morning found me bright-eyed at my desk, determined to keep myself busy till Aaron's return. I had just pulled out the bulging Tyler/Sanjek folder when Eddie came in, shaking the drizzle off his jacket like a fastidious cat.

"I see the cold spell's over," he said gruffly. "Don't know which is worse, that or the rain."

"Nice to see you, too, Eddie. Merry Christmas."

"Oh, right. Brought you something. Merry Christmas."

He set a plastic bag in front of me and then busied himself at his own desk, shuffling papers and powering up his computer. Santa's little helper.

Inside the bag was a small driftwood sculpture, a leaping dolphin whose sleek contours were perfectly delineated by the silvery grain of the wood.

"Eddie, it's beautiful!"

I turned it over to look for the sculptor's name, and noticed an inconspicuous sticker with the name of the gallery: Cannon Beach Treasures.

"That's funny, my mother went to Cannon Beach for Christmas. I'm surprised you didn't run into her. . . ."

My partner kept his back turned. But even by the dim winter light from the window, I could see the blush rising up the back of his neck from his starched white collar and into his silky white hair.

"*Eddie?* Are *you* the friend Mom spent Christmas with? She never said a word on the phone!"

"Damn clerk was supposed to take the tag off," he grumbled. Then he swiveled his chair to face me, still blushing. "Louise said she didn't know how to tell you."

Louise was my mother, and Eddie's oldest friend. Or whatever.

"Tell me what, exactly?" Then I blushed myself. "No, I

don't mean exactly. I mean, OK, you took a trip to the Oregon coast together. That's nice."

"Yes, it was," said Eddie Breen, with a slightly defiant nod of his head. "It was damn nice. Might do it again."

We were interrupted, at this highly interesting juncture, by a knock on the office door. Eddie turned back to his desk, apparently considering the subject closed, and I crossed the good room to meet our visitor—who turned out to be Kevin Bauer. My heart sank. I'd completely forgotten about the uncomfortable conversation that lay ahead of us.

"Kevin, come in."

But he stayed out on the landing, and said in a subdued tone, "I'm sorry not to call first. I'm on my way to a meeting downtown, at MFC, but I couldn't decide whether to come by or . . . Could we talk downstairs?"

"Of course," I said, and added inanely, "I never showed you around after the concert, did I?"

"That's OK. I don't really have much time."

Kevin followed me down the stairs and into the first floor of the houseboat. I was braced to fend off a kiss, but he stayed near the door and kept his coat on. It was the chestnut-colored leather jacket I had admired on our dinner date, though it looked rather ordinary now.

"Carnegie, I know this is lousy timing." He shifted uncomfortably, and stared past me as if fascinated by the surface of my kitchen table. "But I thought it was best to be honest right away."

"Honest about what?"

Murder? I thought wildly, so closely did I associate Kevin with the roasting plant, and all the horrors that had happened there. *Or blackmail? Was it Kevin all along, and not Simon Weeks, who was Ivy's lover?*

"About us," said Kevin, neatly puncturing my melodramatic balloon. "I just don't think we're really compatible, do you?"

Chapter Thirty-Eight

I ALMOST LAUGHED IN RELIEF, BUT THEN I DIDN'T. GETTING dumped isn't really funny.

"Not compatible? Um, I guess we're not. Obviously we're not, if you don't think we are. I mean, it doesn't have to be unanimous, does it? It's not a vote or anything."

I was talking nonsense, but Kevin nodded eagerly. "I knew you'd understand. I was going to tell you the night of the concert at Mary Ellen's house, but then Charles fell . . ."

He continued to speak, but I just nodded mechanically, hardly listening, as another piece of the puzzle slotted home. I hadn't thought to wonder how Charles knew what to say in his phony message, but now I thought I knew.

Charles could easily have been eavesdropping on our conversation in the cloakroom, when I asked Kevin to search for the murder weapon. Then he either faked a seizure, or had a real one. We'd never know for sure, but it seemed to fit.

". . . so I promised Fiona I'd talk to you today."

"Fiona?"

Being a redhead, Kevin had a blush even redder than Eddie's. "Yes. We've been . . . She told me she's always felt . . ."

"Of course," I said hurriedly. "I'm sure you're compatible. Very compatible."

Poor Rudy, I was thinking. Though come to think of it, maybe I was way off base about Fiona and the panini chef, too. You'd think a wedding planner would be better at recognizing romance.

I saw Kevin out, both of us mumbling platitudes, and went back to work. Or at least tried to. I was so preoccupied that it barely registered when Eddie knocked off for the afternoon and left. I was alone, then, when the call came from Simon Weeks.

"Can I stop in at your office?" asked the harsh-toned voice. "Ivy asked me to discuss something with you."

He arrived soon after, and informed me that the "something" was Sally Tyler's wedding. It wasn't postponed. It was canceled.

"You understand why Ivy didn't come in person," said Simon. "She's devastated about Charles. And the girl's not talking to anyone. But Ivy didn't want to keep you hanging."

"I appreciate that."

Simon was standing by the office window, frowning out at the rain. Unlike Kevin's sweater and jacket, Simon wore a charcoal suit and a burgundy tie, but I wondered if they'd been at the same meeting. No doubt he'd be sitting in for Ivy at a lot of meetings now, and doing an excellent job of it.

How could I have imagined that Ivy would favor Kevin Bauer over a fellow executive like Simon Weeks? They were birds of a feather, energetic and ambitious. That would matter a lot to Ivy.

"Can you tell me what happened?" I asked it carefully, wondering how much Ivy's lover would know about Ivy's daughter. "Is Sally all right?"

Simon surprised me then, by breaking into a broad grin. "Nothing wrong with Sally Tyler that a good spanking wouldn't cure. You've worked with her all this time, you must know she's a spoiled brat."

I grinned just a little myself. "No comment. I am curious, though. Who called it off?"

"Frank did." Simon shook his handsome gray head, surprised but not at all disapproving. "She threw one last little hissy fit about her precious New Year's Eve party, and Frank just told her off and walked away. It was a sight to see."

"You were there?"

He nodded casually. "I'm helping Ivy with the press, and the funeral arrangements. We're very close, you know."

Not a word, not a look, revealed any sense of self-consciousness. Either Simon Weeks was unaware that I knew about him and Ivy, or he didn't care anymore. A decent mourning period, and then they could be together in public.

"Speaking of arrangements," he said, returning to the chair by my desk, "what does Ivy owe everybody, and what else needs to be done? She said you have all the contracts."

We went through the paperwork—Simon was quite efficient—and he wrote a number of checks on an MFC account. Including one to me personally, for quite a liberal amount.

"This isn't necessary," I protested. "We charge a commission—"

"I know. But Ivy thought you might have medical expenses, or . . . Well, she wanted to acknowledge what you went through."

"That's very generous of her."

I waited for a cryptic remark, a hint, an obliquely worded suggestion that the check was meant to buy my discretion. But it never came. So I folded the check and tucked it into a pocket, with some interesting thoughts about how to spend it.

"Well," I said, "I think that's everything. Except I still have a box of gifts from the bachelor party. It's been in my van all this time. But I'll call Frank directly about that."

"You might want to wait a while," said Simon. "Let him cool down. I think he went off on a ski trip, anyway. Maybe he'll meet a nice girl."

Once Simon left, I made a series of apologetic phone calls to Joe, Boris, and the other vendors for Tyler/Sanjek. Naturally, everyone assumed the cancellation was just a postponement, due to the death of the bride's stepfather. So I had to be the bearer of bad news, and tell them that a rescheduled date was not on the horizon.

With that unpleasant task out of the way, I went out to Vanna, to bring in Frank's box. I'd decided to throw out the gag stuff, figuring the ex-bridegroom wouldn't find them funny anymore, and just keep the valuables to give him later. I set the box on my kitchen table and opened up a black plastic garbage bag. No way was I going to let these particular items drift around loose in the Dumpster for the neighbors to see.

One by one, each tasteless item went into the bag, leaving only a bottle of Scotch, Aaron's box of mini-cigars, and a digital camera with a zoom lens. I'd noticed the camera before, without giving it a thought. But now, as it rested in my hand, something about it struck me as odd. The camera wasn't boxed, but even if Frank had unwrapped it, why would a gift item looked scuffed-up like this? No one from the party had spoken up about a lost camera...

But one person didn't have the chance to speak up: Jason Kraye. And if the camera was Jason's, then Lou Schulman would have been desperate to get his hands on it. He could have figured out that the camera was in with the gifts, and then tried to break into Ivy's apartment, where he knew I was staying, to steal it.

The more I thought about it, the more convinced I was. The burglary had failed, so Lou tried to get the box out of my van on the night of the sushi dinner at Ivy's house.

Secret pictures, Charles said. Maybe he meant the video-tapes, but maybe not...

I switched the camera on and turned it over, to where the screen on the back showed a menu of commands. I tapped my way through the menu to DISPLAY, and looked at the first photograph.

I never looked at the second.

Captured there on the tiny screen, crisp and bright, was the image of a pair of lovers standing just inside a window in a brick wall. The photograph must have been taken from hiding, from across the alley, because the lovers clearly believed themselves unobserved.

They were half-dressed, and twined in a passionate embrace. I recognized Ivy Tyler from the back, by her silver-blonde hair. And I recognized her lover's face, the jet-black hair tousled, the striking eyes closed in abandon. *A partner for life,* Charles had said. Madison Jaffee was very beautiful.

It took me a moment to find ERASE. When I'd deleted every image, I pulled out the memory card from inside the camera, and pulverized it on a cutting board with the back of a skillet. Then I took the fragments, and the camera, too, out to my front deck and threw them all into Elliott Bay.

Chapter Thirty-Nine

MIAMI BEACH WASN'T AT ALL WHAT I EXPECTED.

Sure I'd seen the pictures of high-piled hotels marching to the water's edge, and hundreds of tourists spread out on their towels like long pale fish being cured in the sun.

What I didn't realize was that if you stand knee-deep in the water, with your back to the hotels and the towels, all you see before you is the glittering turquoise Atlantic stretching eastward forever and ever under the cobalt sky.

That's a lot of ocean for a girl from Idaho, even if she did move to the edge of Puget Sound. The Sound is clouded gray half the time anyway, without a palm tree in sight, and even the Oregon coast is mostly rocks and cold water. Miami Beach has sand the color of sugar, and warm water so clear that it looks like blue Jell-O.

"Wow," I said to Aaron, who was standing at my side in shorts and a tropical shirt. "Wow, wow, wow."

"Nice, huh? Well, now you've seen it. Let's go back to the room."

"No way! I want a long walk with my feet in the water, and a seafood lunch, and some of that Cuban coffee you told me about. I want to visit the Art Deco district in South Beach, that I read about on the plane. I want to go dancing. I want to go *shopping*."

"Shopping!" Aaron's grin shone white as the sand. The man tanned in less than a week. Amazing. "Stretch, you disappoint me."

"Get used to it."

He tried to shove me in the water then, but I shoved back, and we ended in a happy tangle, sitting waist-deep in the blue Jell-O and laughing hilariously, just for the pleasure of laughing.

Ivy Tyler's check had nicely covered a last-minute flight to Miami, and I'd arrived late Thursday night, after wrapping up Buckmeister/Frost and turning my brain inside out for Detective Bates. He said I was free to go and I went, straight to the airport, and nine hours later Aaron and I had gone straight to bed.

Eventually, we even slept.

Once it was Friday morning though, the morning of New Year's Eve, I was ready to rock and roll. And even Aaron couldn't make love all day, much as he professed his willingness to try. So we walked the beach and had a fabulous fishy lunch and went sightseeing to my heart's content.

But by mid-afternoon, when my heart wanted to blow the last of Ivy's money on a really great dress, Aaron drew the line on keeping me company. He arranged to pay his grandfather yet another visit, and dropped me off on Lincoln Road, the shopping nirvana of South Beach. As I got out of the car, he handed me a business card for a restaurant named Spiga.

"Six o'clock sharp, Stretch. I had to call about twenty places to get reservations."

Well, sort of sharp. At six-twenty I was still hurrying down Collins Avenue, wearing the really great dress, and marveling at the change that came over the Art Deco hotels when the sun went down.

They were fabulous enough in the sunshine, sleek geometric blocks and curves and swoops of beautifully restored pastel-painted stucco from the 1920's, like big wonderful wedding cakes against the luminous blue sky.

But at night the neon came on, in electric pinks and greens and purples, and the music spilled out from the bistros across the crowded sidewalk tables and into the narrow street, and the palm fronds made soft clashings overhead in the breezy tropical night. I was in love with Aaron Gold, and in love with Miami Beach.

Mostly Aaron, though. I saw him before he saw me, sitting at a corner table on an open-air terrace, wearing a pale linen blazer and looking like a million bucks.

He was moving his hands on the tablecloth in an odd way, and as I came closer to look, I saw why: tired of waiting for me, he'd drawn ink dots on a pair of sugar cubes to make dice.

"You clown, what are you doing?"

"Playing left against right. Left is winning, but—oh, my God." He'd spoken without looking up, but now he was gazing straight at me. The dress was turquoise, like the ocean, and it moved when I did. "*Look* at you, Carnegie. You're always pretty, but tonight you're . . . I don't even know a good word. Forget dinner. We're going back to the hotel."

I slid into my seat, glowing. "Dinner and dancing. You promised."

"So I did." He tossed the sugar cubes aside, and waved to the waiter. Once my piña colada arrived, he grew serious. "You promised me the rest of the story about the Tylers. I heard on the grapevine that Ivy is retiring."

"I heard that, too." I took a sip and licked the sweet foam from my lips. "What does that do to your book contract?"

He shrugged. "I'll find out when I get back."

"I also heard," I said slowly, "that Madison Jaffee quit her job to move to San Francisco. You think Ivy will retire to San Francisco?"

"I wouldn't be surprised."

"You knew about them all along, didn't you?"

Aaron had a drink in front of him already, a nontropical Scotch on the rocks, and he ran one finger around the edge of the glass, around and around.

"I guessed. Just a vibe I got. I never asked anyone, working on the book, because I didn't want to start rumors. It was none of my business."

"It was none of anybody's business."

I told him about the camera then, and how I'd destroyed it. He lifted his eyes.

"Good for you, Stretch. Good for you."

In the little silence that followed, I thought of more questions, stray pieces of the puzzle, loose threads leading back into the central pattern of lovers and their secrets.

"So if you guessed about the two of them, then you must have guessed that Madison was lying about her relationship with Jason?"

Aaron nodded, and a lock of dark hair fell across his forehead. "At first I wondered, like you did, if she was the killer. But when she and I talked at my apartment that day, I just couldn't convince myself. I figured she had lied so she could get inside our investigation. She must have been searching for a camera, or at least for photographs, when she broke into Solveto's."

"So you stalled around in the cooler to let her get away."

He grinned. "Mostly to talk to you, but that, too."

I took another sip, for courage, before asking the real question.

"Aaron, why didn't you tell me about Ivy and Madison? Didn't you trust me to keep their secret? Maybe I seem flighty to you—"

He laughed aloud at that, and I relaxed a little.

"What a great word! I've got lots of words for you, Stretch, but 'flighty' isn't one of them. No, I didn't say anything because I didn't *know* anything. There was always a chance you were right, and Madison wasn't at all what I thought she was. And besides, it wasn't my secret to share. Blackmail's such a sickening thing, I just couldn't bring myself to speculate about Ivy's private life, not even to you. Does that make sense?"

"Yes. Yes, it does."

"Good, because I want to finish with Ivy and talk about us." He reached into his breast pocket. "I've got something for you. Kind of a late Christmas present. It's not wrapped or anything."

The ocean breeze stirred his hair, and the skirts of my dress, and the palm fronds overhead, as Aaron pulled out a small box covered in dark blue velvet and set it on the table.

The box was the wrong size for a ring. Or was it? I wasn't sure. I wasn't sure about anything.

I raised the velvet lid and looked inside.

About the Author

Deborah Donnelly is a sea captain's daughter who grew up in Panama, Cape Cod, and points in between. She's been an executive speechwriter, a university librarian, a science fiction writer, and a nanny. A longtime resident of Seattle, and a bloomingly healthy breast cancer survivor, Donnelly now lives physically in Boise, Idaho, and virtually at www.deborahdonnelly.org.

SARA PARETSKY

"Paretsky's name always makes the top of the list when people talk about the new female operatives." —*The New York Times Book Review*

	Title	Code	Price
___	Bitter Medicine	23476-X	$7.99/11.99
___	Blood Shot	20420-8	$7.99/11.99
___	Burn Marks	20845-9	$7.99/11.99
___	Indemnity Only	21069-0	$7.50/10.99
___	Guardian Angel	21399-1	$7.99/11.99
___	Hard Time	22470-5	$7.99/11.99
___	Killing Orders	21528-5	$7.99/11.99
___	Deadlock	21332-0	$6.99/8.99
___	Total Recall	22471-3	$7.99/11.99
___	Tunnel Vision	21752-0	$7.50/10.99
___	Windy City Blues	21873-X	$7.99/11.99
___	A Woman's Eye	21335-5	$6.99/8.99
___	Women on the Case	22325-3	$7.50/10.99

HARLAN COBEN

Winner of the Edgar, the Anthony, and the Shamus Awards

	Title	Code	Price
___	Deal Breaker	22044-0	$7.50/10.99
___	Dropshot	22049-5	$7.50/10.99
___	Fade Away	22268-0	$6.99/10.99
___	Back Spin	22270-2	$7.50/10.99
___	One False Move	22544-2	$7.50/10.99
___	The Final Detail	22545-0	$7.50/10.99
___	Darkest Fear	23539-1	$6.99/10.99
___	Tell No One	23670-3	$7.50/10.99
___	Gone for Good	23673-8	$6.99/10.99

RUTH RENDELL

Winner of the Grand Master Edgar Award from *Mystery Writers of America*

	Title	Code	Price
___	Road Rage	22602-3	$6.99
___	The Crocodile Bird	21865-9	$6.99
___	Simisola	22202-8	$6.99
___	Keys to the Street	22392-X	$6.99
___	A Sight for Sore Eyes	23544-8	$6.99

Ask for these titles wherever books are sold, or visit us online at *www.bantamdell.com* for ordering information.